THEIR Naughty OBSESSION

BREANNE BERGIE

Editing & Formatting: EJL Editing

Cover: Temptation Creations

Dedication

For all the good girls who wish for two unhinged, obsessed stalkers instead of one.

May they rail you and bring you to your knees once you turn the page.

"Good little slut."

Sin & Saint are waiting for you.

Playlist

The Tea Party - Temptation
Matchbox Twenty - Push
Lana Del Ray - Ultraviolence
Radiohead - Creep
Nickelback - Animals
The Civil Wars - Poison & Wine

Author's Note

This book ends on a cliffhanger. The contents are dark with triggering situations, please check the content warnings listed on my socials, website, or feel free to private message me directly. Your mental health matters.

One

Their Obsession

Liv

Heaven was his mouth on my pussy. His tongue licked, swirled, and lapped at the wetness between my thighs. Teeth bit—they pleased and teased. This was an escape from the man I hated. The hell I lived through with the devil himself.

My fiancé.

"Fuck. My little slut," he muttered from below as I rode against his face. "Your cunt tastes like fine wine."

My eyes rolled into the back of my head, and my hands buried themselves in his hair. The smooth locks of deep brown were a suitable length to grip, and I helped guide him to the rhythm I wanted. A complete stranger, but an attractive one with enough stubble to soothe the ache in my belly and ignite pleasure in my core.

"Oh, yes..." I moaned as his whiskers pressed against my clit and made me quake. "Make me come. Please, make me come."

Within the quiet depths of the hallway at my fiancé's party, my hips rolled, and I pushed deeper into the stranger's face, my legs spread to fit his head between them. My husband-to-be hosted his business entertainment while I wandered off and celebrated on my own with a handsome man. He only knew my name, just like the others.

They were all nameless; no personality except the determination to make me come. Again and again because I couldn't get enough. The need for release was a dark plague inside of me, and I sought the cure. An earth-shattering escape. Only for a small amount of time because bliss was better than the alternative: my husband-to-be and his cruel ways. No intimacy. I belonged to him. He owned me. We were only in this arrangement to please the public, but I was solely in this to save my family's future.

The man groaned into my sweet heat, and the sound vibrated into my spine. The quivering beat made my toes curl inside of my black Vera Wang high heels, and my head hit the wall as my back arched. A quiet sigh escaped my lips because I had to be discreet. No one could see, and I couldn't take any chance of my scandalous act getting back to my *dearly beloved.*

Secret bliss engulfed me. I was consumed by a skilled mouth with extremely fresh breath—I was glad I chose him. He took the bait from the lineup of men who couldn't take their eyes off me. Draped on my fiancé's arm with a twenty-five-million-dollar engagement ring on my finger, and I was a challenge any bachelor would love to conquer. I was a sinful sight any single man could indulge in, and this one ravished my taste. He was everything I needed. For tonight, at least.

"So fucking wet..." he breathed as he came up for air and kissed my neck. "Your pussy is taking my tongue like such a good girl."

I pulled his head from my neck and pushed him back down. "Less talking and more feasting."

He didn't argue.

He gave my clit a nip and dove his tongue back between my slit. The muscle thrashed inside me and caused me to bite my lower lip to contain a scream. A cry of pleasure built up inside of me, and I pressed my teeth in harder until I tasted blood in my mouth. The hairs on the back of my neck suddenly stood right up, and I was on high alert. An unwanted presence hid in the shadows, forcing me to open my eyes and peer around at an empty hallway. No one was there.

Relax.

"Oh, fuck..." I sighed with the next wave of passion.

But the touch of watchful eyes still lingered on my skin.

The heightened sense nagged at me as my climax climbed higher, and I imagined the observant stare rose in intensity too. The attentive gaze left the man who gave me oral pleasure and fixated on my busty breasts as they bounced with each passionate breath. It crawled higher up the nape of my exposed neck and assessed my lips. Intent eyes made me feel his kiss, and all the ways he could do better than this man trapped between my legs.

I clamped him tighter, my thighs compressing his head with the awareness of someone around making my adrenaline sour. The rush of another's existence I couldn't see was my undoing as I covered my mouth and screamed into it. My pussy drowned the man's face, and I rode out the release I ached for. Never envisioning my pleasure coming because of a watchful eye, I wasn't even sure was there. *But I knew he was.*

He had to be, or else I was on the verge of insanity. Thanks to all the sneaking around behind my unsuspecting fiancé's back.

Euphoria consumed me the way I had wanted. The ache was gone until the need came back with a yearning vengeance. Starved for more.

"Yes..." I moaned as the sound crawled up my throat, and the stranger groaned below me.

He pulled out his tongue, his hot breath fanned against my wet skin, and he gave the juncture of my skin one last lick. My clit throbbed for more, at a slow, painful beat, and then it was over. He withdrew his face from between my weak quivering legs, and my body relaxed against the wall.

"You're fucking amazing," he breathed with a grin and wiped the back of his hand across his soaked mouth. "I want more."

Just as his face moved in for a kiss, I had enough strength to stop him. My hand came between our lips, and I shook my head. "I told you the rules. Please me. No sex. Understood?"

His grin grew wider, and he kissed my hand. "Understood. But your resistance makes me want you even more. I'll call you when I want more?"

"Absolutely." I lied through my teeth, hoping to never see him again.

It was the same way with all the men who had fallen into my seductive trap. Let them please me. Not the other way around. I gave the order, and they followed my command. If they don't? I move on to the next.

I craved attention. My fiancé neglected me with no affection. What the hell did they expect of me?

All I needed was to feel desired. I was the only one to ensure I'd receive mind numbing orgasms. Especially when no one would ever love me.

There was no prince charming in my future. No devoted man for me. Only a selfish pig who viewed me as his trophy and a means to an end.

I added a fake number for a fast-food sushi bar I knew by heart into his cell phone contacts. He took the device back with a suave appearance on his face—this guy thought he was the total package. Little did he know, he wouldn't reach me anytime soon.

"See you in an hour," he said with a playful wink.

I'd be gone by then.

Deep breaths left my lips as I watched the handsome stranger depart, tucking in his erection. A small giggle erupted from me as I pulled up my panties from around my left ankle, and my other foot stepped inside. He'd have a firm dick to conceal for a while after I left him hanging.

Unpleased was the way I wanted them. I have felt this way every damn day since my parents forced me into this arranged engagement. Doomed for the rest of my life, or until my husband-to-be croaked. But my joy came to an abrupt end.

A low groan sounded from the same direction I had felt eyes on me. The stare that lingered up my body, watching and waiting—captured in my ecstasy.

The shadows hid him, but I knew he was there. To my unpleasant surprise, a black dress shoe stepped out. He was ready to make his presence known, and his creepy vibe pissed me off.

"Enjoy the show, asshole?" I snapped with displeasure.

I quickly pulled up my thong the rest of the way and fixed my dress. I flung my black hair with blonde highlights over my shoulder, communicating a *fuck off* vibe. I'd show him I was a bitter bitch he didn't want to mess with and crossed my arms.

"I loved every moment, Liv," he said from the darkened corner, and he moved half of his silhouette out before he revealed his creepy self.

Two
Their Obsession

Liv

How the hell does he know my name?

This fucker was getting on my last nerve when five minutes ago, I had let him help me climax. The thought of another person watching me made the temptation that much more inviting. And now I was giving him shit for it.

Why?

Because it's creepy as fuck.

And what does that make me?

A monster within his darkness.

"All right, the show is over. Why don't you come on out and show yourself?" I challenged. "Or are you too much of a chickenshit after you got your rocks off in your trousers watching me?"

"Who said I was watching?"

He had to be joking. But maybe he had just got there. *No, don't be an idiot.* The hallway only went one way; there was no way to cut any corners. This sick fuck was there the entire time.

I glanced around me with my hands up. "There's nobody else here?"

He laughed, and the sound of it crept into my ears. The sound of his amusement lingered and echoed, trapped to the point I wanted to cover my ears and scream for him to release me.

"I know," he answered as I watched his lips move and curl up into a half grin.

His right cheek bore an ugly scar that I should find scary. He wore a black tuxedo, and I could make out a bow tie. He was clearly here for the party and had wandered off.

Did he follow me?

He must have.

He pulled his hand out of his suit jacket pocket, distracting me before I could ponder further. His hand was large, and, from my standpoint, he appeared to be the same height as me. But I knew he had to be much taller because I was short at barely over five feet.

His voice oozed too much dominance—powerful for anyone in his vicinity. And I was. A clear bull's-eye for this crazed lunatic. A sure win in his books and a loss for me.

"Do you always do this in your spare time?" I asked.

"Do what?" he pressed with a tilt of his head.

"Lurk in the shadows like Michael Myers from those Halloween movies. He's always watching people get freaky," I answered and pointed toward him. "You wouldn't happen to have a knife hidden somewhere, would you?"

I grew nervous as I awaited his response. My body trembled, but I held my stance. Even if the guy made me anxious with his creepy vibes, I couldn't let him know. He probably got off on that shit.

"I always come armed," he replied with his laser beam eyes locked right on his prey. "But I don't lurk in the shadows for just anyone."

I had no idea why I was choosing to even speak to this asshole. I should hike up my dress and get out of here. But curiosity tempted me.

Maybe it was the way his voice rang through me. It could be the way the scar on his face lingered in my mind and made me question how he received it. Or maybe it was the darkness seeping from his pores.

"You..." I gulped and took a step back. "You don't?"

"No, I don't," he breathed as he took a step toward me with my one step back.

Shit. I had to get the hell out of here. But I should keep the crazy fucker talking.

Distraction was key in situations as dire as these, and a little personality helped too. Quick thinking was the trick to staying alive, but they don't have the brains in horror films. Those bitches die for the thrill. But I have watched it in documentaries about real life abductions.

"Why did you choose today to start?" I asked and stepped back once more.

He doesn't hesitate. "Because you caught my eye."

A chill ran up my backside when I realized he had targeted me. This man knew exactly why he had followed me. All the publicity from my upcoming marriage had put me in danger. I knew it was a possibility, but I never imagined it would happen so soon.

"Well, I'm getting married, fucker, and my fiancé has muscles the size of boulders," I said and held up my engagement ring to make my message clear. "I've got an excellent set of lungs on me, too."

"If you were going to scream, you would've done it by now." He gushed with confidence and stepped fully out of the shadows.

His hair was jet black and strands fell over his left eye. Dark eyes as black as molten lava rock swirled with a glint of mischief, and they pierced into me. His muscles pressed against his suit, making him appear huge, and with each slow step he took, I was surprised the fabric didn't tear. Each move left a tap from his expensive dress shoes, and my eyes grew wider with every sound. But I was no longer surprised by his presence.

Because I recognized him.

He was the extremely handsome man who had watched me over the rim of his drink at the party. His gaze roamed over me as I entered with my fiancé; I pretended to laugh at something he had said and looked over the crowd. A stern rule with every function my dearest hosted: always act presentable, poised, and engaged with the audience.

Sebastian gave a speech with me by his side. He spoke of fulfillment, his many achievements, and his dedication to everyone on his grand journey. But it was all a load of crap.

Sebastian was a bore.

When the yawn came, my eyes wandered. I'd search for fulfillment of my own. A man to please me, tease me, and make me forget who I was. One of those men had been this man. This lunatic. But goddamn, was he hot.

His eyes had followed me while my fiancé gave his speech, as if he'd eat me whole, with no regard to the man beside me, who wrapped his arm around my waist and introduced me to the crowd. This stranger had intrigued me, ravished me with his gaze, and made me wet between my thighs.

He was the one I was ready to choose—this phantom of a man within the darkness who had brought himself out into the light. But he had vanished.

So, I chose the next best choice, who seemed capable of releasing the ache in my belly. He was eager, willing, and not a crazed psychopath. The opposite of *him.*

God, I sure knew how to pick them.

He was delicious, with an intense edge from the old wound proceeding from his side burn down his left cheek. With him closer, I saw the scar was in the shape of a thunderbolt. I could tell someone had branded him for some unknown reason, and I wouldn't discover the truth soon.

"I can still scream," I added and glanced quickly behind me.

Fuck. The long stretch of hallway intimidated me, and with his long strides, I knew I couldn't outrun him. He was too powerful, too large, and far too tempting.

"And you think Sebastian will come running?" he huffed gruffly.

"He would," I lied as my breathing intensified, and I pointed at him. "And he'd beat the shit out of you if you even laid a finger on me."

He grinned. "Oh, I'd love to see him try."

And he took three rushed steps toward me.

I gasped in surprise, and he laughed. A cruel, harsh sound, chilling me right down to my bones. My being trembled; my heart thumped in my chest, and the sound pounded in my ears. I hated him, but I stood my ground, determined not to have him break me. We were at a public event, and the host accompanied me. People would notice my absence in less than ten minutes. The clock was ticking.

"My fiancé will wonder where I am any minute now. He'll start wandering the halls searching for me," I added and tried to keep my breathing steady. "And when I scream, which I'm going to, your ass will be behind bars."

He tilted his chin down, and his eyes grew cold. "Then I guess you'd better run, sweetheart."

One step backward, then two, until I turned, and my hair flung through the air. I knew with the low growl in his tone he enjoyed this. And I was a goner.

Three

Their Obsession

Liv

My legs pumped below me, but I only made it four little sprints before he caught me. His hand covered my mouth as I let out the scream I had promised him. He pressed himself up against me, muffling the sound with his hold, and I vibrated within his dangerous embrace.

"Oh, how you tempt me..." he whispered harshly in my ear and slowly licked up the side of my cheek. "I knew from the moment I saw you that you'd be feisty."

I pushed against his hold, but it was no use. He was too strong—too dominant and massive. He loomed over me and made my struggle appear pointless. The ghost had captured me and brought me into his nightmare. But he got one thing right: I was feisty. I didn't always play nice, and I had a good bite.

"Ah, fuck..." he muttered in pain.

My teeth drew a bit of blood. The taste was warm in my mouth, and I threw him off enough to elbow him in the stomach. He barely budged.

Fucker was stubborn, but I was too.

A scream came from me, but this time he gripped a hand around my throat. He took the air away from me and pushed me up against the wall. The back of my head hit with his iron grip and the force against my neck.

"Now, promise me you'll be a good girl and cut the fucking screaming," he demanded, his breath heaved into my face.

I gave a curt nod because I wanted to live. I didn't want to die, no matter how much I hated my life. My family needed me, and I couldn't let some psychopath kill me.

"Good girl," he whispered as he let go, but he didn't back away.

I gasped as air filled my lungs, tears spilled from my eyes, and my vision returned to normal. He still held me against the wall, and I couldn't escape him. But I wouldn't back down without a fight.

"What the fuck is wrong with you?" I coughed out and pushed at his chest.

"Me? You are the one wandering off to get your pussy licked." He sneered with amusement swirling in his dark gaze. "Just my type of girl."

"I'm not your type of girl. There is no one I belong to," I snapped back in anger.

I pushed at his chest again, and, to my surprise, he moved back. He gave me enough room to make another run for it, and I did exactly that. But he caught me by my wrist, holding me in place.

"And where do you think you're running off to?" He tsked with a raised eyebrow. "I haven't even formally introduced myself."

"Yeah, because you're too busy stalking me and trying to kill me!" I shouted in his face and jerked my arms. "Now let me go, fucker."

He chuckled. "Kill you? I'm not here to end your life, Liv. I'm here to enjoy you, taste you, and own you."

"Oh, yeah?" I huffed. "Taste this."

I spit at his face. The wetness landed directly on his lips, and he didn't move a muscle. Until his tongue slipped out of his mouth and licked up the mess I had made. He let out an all-consuming growl.

The sound vibrated through every fiber of my being. Although he had touched me in a repulsive manner, I couldn't help but feel drawn to the noise from such a disgusting man. The low husky rumble set a fire burning in the depths of my belly, and the ache I had soothed intensified all over again much too soon. To hell with this overbearing man.

"You've been a bad girl, Liv. You will pay for that," he breathed with flared nostrils as he licked his lips clean and pushed me back against the wall. "But don't you want to know the man who will give you a punishment?"

He had me right where he wanted and held me in a position where I had no choice. I had to play along. I had to talk his fucking ear off if I wanted to get out of this.

"And what would my punishment be, phantom?" I asked with a glint of strength in my eyes, even though my legs were weak.

"I appreciate the name you've picked out for me." He gave a curt laugh, and his eyes burned into mine. "But you'll find out soon, my little obsession."

"I'm your obsession?" I asked, my heart pounding in my ears.

"My addiction, Liv Valencia," he said with certainty. "And my real name is Sin Cruz. The very man who will haunt you in your dreams every time you close those beautiful eyes."

"I highly doubt that." I laughed right in his face.

Sin brought his lips toward me until they were inches from mine. "I'm betting on it."

The sure gleam in his eyes took my breath away. He had me captivated. Self-doubt lingered, and my body deceived me. My scent soaked my thong, and I bet he could smell it. My arousal made him even more dead set on me.

"Screw. You." I spat out each word.

Sin ran the back of his fingers down the side of my face. Electricity coursed through me, and the live-wire heat was overwhelming. He smelled of cedar wood and whiskey—the mixed scent set my world on fire.

"Does your husband-to-be appreciate your bratty attitude?" Sin questioned in a husky, low-toned whisper. "I'm not so sure my investor would like it, but I sure as hell do."

Sebastian? He was doing business with this creep?

"You're working with my fiancé?" I asked, shocked.

"Yes, Liv. Mr. Chamberlain has invested money in my nightclub."

My blood ran cold. Sin Cruz knew my fiancé professionally, and he knew my most intimate secret. He had watched me with another man feasting on my pussy. This man could ruin everything. I couldn't let that happen because too much was on the line, and I had to turn this all around in my favor. But I only had one advantage.

Mr. Sin Cruz wanted me. As crazy as the idea may be, I was about to flirt with fire before he burned me at the stake.

Four

Their Obsession

Liv

I gave into my pussy's urge. The bitch was wet again, and as much as I wanted to fight with every fiber of my being, I couldn't. Sin Cruz knew too much.

I questioned, "How much?"

My hands were no longer at my sides and crept up the collar of his suit jacket. Slowly, they climbed as my eyes met his and I saw the whip of flames blast inside his dark eyes. The sparks lashed at me and pulled me into him. Within the recesses of his darkened soul, the sole source of light was an open fire. A scorching, fiery blaze of desire. There was nowhere to run, nowhere to hide. I had to face the devil head-on.

"I'm not here to discuss business with you, Liv." He placed his hands over mine.

His touch ignited a heat of its own. One I didn't want, but I had no choice but to endure—to tolerate a gentle caress from him and enjoy it more than I wanted to.

"Why not? You seem to know a hell of a lot about me?" I asked, my patience growing thin, but I pressed on. "I want to get to know my phantom."

I roughly grabbed his collar and turned the tables on Sin before he could think twice. He was massive and strong, but he was no match for my seduction. He craved me and his obsession blinded his plan. I had him up against the wall in a matter of seconds. My breath fanned across his mouth as his face tilted down toward mine. His lips begged for a kiss, but I wouldn't give it to him yet. Not until I got exactly what I wanted.

Payback.

And for him to keep his damn mouth shut.

"What would my little obsession like to know?" Sin played along and his warm breath danced across my wet lips.

A shiver rippled through me at the brush of air that left his lips. The phantom had revealed himself and was ready to take off his mask for me. But Sin still had a wickedness to him.

I had to be careful.

"What makes Sin Cruz tick?" I asked as I brushed the hair away from his left eye and kept eye contact.

"You," he answered without hesitation.

Bullshit. This deranged man had never met me before today. But I had to indulge in his torment.

"Okay. Fine," I huffed, but gave him a flirtatious grin and continued. "What do you do in your spare time?"

"Follow you."

I blinked, stunned by his response, but I still had to remain on course. My other hand lingered over the scar on his right cheek and outlined the old wound. He was clean shaven—no stubble in sight—with the smell of aftershave coming from his skin. Cedarwood. That's where the scent came from, making my pussy melt for him.

I whispered curiously, "How did you get this scar?"

A strong guy like him with a crazy streak had to have a story. He was powerful and there was no way he'd give into this torture without a fight.

Something flashed in his eyes: a cold streak of petty emotion, or maybe there was none at all. A man as calculated as Sin Cruz seemed incapable of anything other than torment. Torture. The exact practice he had inflicted on me.

"Before I met you."

Well, obviously. Wise-ass with his brief answers, only involving me.

"Your world doesn't revolve around me."

"It does now," he admitted.

Fine. He wanted to be narrow-mindedly stubborn? I'd cut right to the chase.

"Okay. I'll make you an offer," I said as my hands ran down his neck and over a black necklace with a skull pendant. "You can do whatever you want with me. Whatever your dirty and depraved mind desires."

"Liv, Liv, Liv..." Sin tsked and caught my hands in his grasp. "I know exactly what you're trying to pull, and I dig it. I really do, but I'm not a desperate man, Liv."

Suddenly, Sin spun me around and pressed me roughly up against the wall. He put me back in my place, and my chest heaved with wisps of my hair getting sucked into my mouth. An angry fire built inside of me, consuming me with frustration. I was blinded by it and right back where I had started with this infuriating lunatic. He was on to me and rejected my seduction.

I huffed. "Then what are you?"

"I'm addicted. Patient," Sin breathed as he wiped the hair from my mouth and twirled a strand around his finger. "Biding my time until it's right."

"Right?" I asked with narrowed eyebrows. "Right for what?"

"For you."

"Me?" I asked nervously, my pulse racing. "I just gave you the opportunity to do whatever you want with me."

"And I am going to do that, Liv," Sin said and sucked in a deep breath, letting it out right against my cheek. "Whatever I want."

This fucking freak was confusing me. I gave him the option of sex, a blowjob, or jerking him off and he turned me down. What the hell was he really into? Did he want a finger up his ass?

"What the hell do you want, *Sin*?" I asked.

"Oh, fuck..." he groaned and sniffed my hair. "I love the way your sinful tongue says my name. Do it again and ask a question."

Whatever got this guy off. I'd yell his name from the rooftop if I had to. Anything to keep his creepy mouth shut.

I turned my head and purred into his ear, "*Sin*."

"Mm..." Sin moaned.

"What in the devil's name do you want?"

"I don't want to fuck you," he answered.

Fuck this. I was right—this creep wants a finger up his ass! Hell, he might want my whole fist.

"Then what the fuck do you want, asshole?" I snapped with anger and fought against his hold, but it was no use.

He pulled the hair wrapped around his finger, causing my head to jerk up. With my chin raised high, my gaze locked on his intense eyes as they seared into mine. The fight in me stopped. He had my full attention.

"I want to watch you get fucked."

Okay, so he's the freaky type. The rare kind of man who enjoyed watching. But this all made perfect sense, since he spent fifteen minutes hiding in the shadows while my juices leaked all over another man's face.

"No way, psycho. Now let me go."

Sin let go of my hair and he backed down, but didn't budge. He still had a wicked grin glued on his face. Sinful, but gorgeous as hell.

"What's so funny?" I snapped.

"Nothing. But you are damn defiant, and I like that about you," Sin answered with a corrupt gleam in his eyes. "I'm going to love watching you, Liv."

"Are you deaf?" I scoffed with annoyance. "I. Said. No."

Sin's face shot right up to mine, and he laughed wickedly when I jumped. My head smacked off the wall, a slight pain radiating from the impact. But he didn't lay a hand on me.

"I think I'll change your mind," he breathed against my trembling lips.

I pushed against his chest with all my strength, and he voluntarily took a step backward. He provided me with enough space to get away from him, and I stumbled awkwardly, wobbling from the intense stare boring into me and refusing to let me go. He might have physically freed me, but I knew deep down he wouldn't let me *ever* escape him.

"Fuck you!" I shouted as I turned and took off down the hallway.

No footsteps followed behind me. His evil taunt was over. But his amused laughter echoed down the hallway.

"I'd love to, but I owe you a punishment first," he answered, and his threat stuck with me.

Every damn word clung to me as I made my way back to the party and the entertainment I didn't want to be part of. I was stuck with a fiancé I never dreamed of having, with a phantom man etched into my head. Something about Sin Cruz got under my skin. He watched and waited in the deep abyss for me. Patiently, he'd buy his time until I was ready to play. But I'd never entertain his wicked games, and I never wanted to see him again.

Five

Her Phantom

Sin

Fuck. She was sexy as sin.

Wickedness in disguise as she walked into the room and captured the shadowy creature inside of me. She awakened a darkness I never knew I held until her. A phantom unconfined by his obsession.

All I could see was her. Bright, shining, and spellbinding. She illuminated my eyes until they went blurry.

Shit.

No.

That was the glitter from her damn dress hugging all her curves, and she was a goddamn goddess dressed in black. Perfect for me.

I watched with hungry eyes as my prey held onto Mr. Chamberlain's arm and flashed a fucking gorgeous smile toward everyone. Her eyes twinkled in the light and made the crowd the center of her world. She hexed every person with a heartbeat until the organ stopped beating. But I saw the fault in her smile.

A pain far too great—she had locked the truth inside, buried her suffering deep in her core and kept the sadness prisoner. Shackled away in her hollow soul, there was a brokenness I wanted to make whole.

There was a quick flash of panic when she peered up at her fiancé, and she held her breath while time seemed to stand still. Her busty chest wouldn't move, and I knew she wished in her blackened heart to be anywhere other than here. Her delicate neck was stiff without a throb as her pulse slowed down, and I wanted to make it speed up. I craved to see the little pebble palpitate in her throat beneath her skin from my touch. I would spark a light and set her world on fire. But I wouldn't burn her universe, leaving it dull and turning it to ash.

I was a man starved with a strained erection against my slacks when she finally took a breath. I imagined all the things I'd do to her, all the ways I'd make her mine. As she continued on, I instantly became obsessed. Attracted. Addicted. Whole-heartedly fucking consumed, and I had to have her.

Mr. Chamberlain introduced his fiancé and gave a speech, but I wasn't listening. My future was clear, and she was the apple of my eye. I'd sooner rot in the core of hell than let anyone else have her. Liv Valencia would be ours.

Six

Their Obsession

Liv

"Where did I put them?" I muttered under my breath.

I moved magazines aside, peeked inside of trinkets, and turned my condo apartment upside down. My set of keys weren't anywhere. The keys to my apartment and personal mailbox went missing last night.

I don't understand where they could've gone. I could've sworn I put them in my clutch before I left for the party. But they had disappeared. Gone in the blink of an eye.

Strange.

I had to get Sebastian to use his key to open the door late last night. I had created a scene in front of a group he was in the middle of business with and convinced the small crowd I wasn't feeling well. Despite Sebastian's insistence on staying, the older couple believed he should accompany me home. He agreed and escorted me out, but secretly cursed me for ruining his precious party. And I earned a harsh slap on the limousine ride home.

The resulting mark was more noticeable this morning, and I had to use concealer to cover up the bruise. A slap to the face was much better than Sebastian Chamberlain discovering the truth of my infidelity. Another one he didn't know about and a fresh one I had to conceal.

I gave up the search after leaving no inch of the condo unturned and cleaned everything up. I was frantic because I didn't need another reason for my fiancé to become angry. He'd take his rage out on me. I'd have to get another set of keys made immediately, before Sebastian found out. I'd order a backup set for my utter stupidity.

He had left for work at the usual time and wouldn't be back until late. I was happy when I woke up. The bed had long gone cold without his body heat, and I wished we never had to share one. But keeping me close was one of the many ways he controlled me.

My cell phone chimed with its normal sound, but it was far too early for a text from my cruel fiancé. I narrowed my eyebrows as I pondered who else would text me and placed the book I held back on the bookshelf. This place needed to be tidied up prior to Sebastian's arrival. He didn't agree with a cluttered home and as a stay-at-home bride-to-be, I needed to meet his standards. He provided for me, put food on the table, and gave me everything my heart could desire. Or at least he thought he did.

I picked up my cell and flipped it over to see the screen lit up with a text. It was an unknown contact; my heart stopped. Dread crept up inside of me as I read two words and knew nothing would ever be the same.

Unknown:

Miss me?

What the hell? Who was this? Why was this random freak texting me?

I shouldn't text back. I knew this to be true. But my fingers were far too tempted to type.

This message could be from some crazed maniac ready to kill me. Murder me in cold blood and I'd cease to exist while he did whatever he wanted to my dead corpse. Gross. Brutal image, I know. But I knew exactly who this unknown person was.

It was Sin Cruz. My phantom from last night, ready to interact with his obsession—unfortunately, me.

Sin had somehow got my number. *How?* I'd never know. But the answer didn't really matter because he was a stalker. A creep who lurked in the night and watched from the shadows. He haunted my dreams while I slept in a deep slumber and trapped me in his darkness. He was my pursuer, and he could be a serial killer ready to strike his next victim.

Me.

I was playing with fire, bound to get burned, but I was a stupid bitch. I'd play dumb and hope the cover fooled him enough to leave me alone.

Me:

Who is this?

The unknown number didn't hesitate and responded before I could swallow. I gulped the large lump in my throat, expecting to kill my nerves. But it was no use.

Unknown:

The man who enjoyed watching you while you got your sweet pussy licked.

Bingo.

It was Sin. I knew it! But I hated how my cunt clenched at his words.

The foul text Sin had sent caused my breathing to escalate, and I ran my tongue over my lips to relieve the dryness, but I was speechless. My shadow had caught me right in his evil trap.

A second text came through.

Unknown:

I bet your cunt remembers me.

I let out a gasp. Heat flushed up my body, and my cheeks turned bright crimson. I reached up to hide them but I was dumb for doing it because I was all alone. I hated the reaction he pulled from me. He wasn't even nearby, and it made me more flustered than ever before. And I only met him yesterday.

Damn him.

I still wondered what to type back. My stalker knew my dirty secret. He knew I met up with men I didn't know and let them please me. I let them tease me and leave me melting like putty in their hands while Sebastian wouldn't touch me. There was no intimacy between us. I only received sweet gestures from him for the press. He was only willing to entertain the public eye, and he loved to show off his bride-to-be as if we were a happy, engaged couple who couldn't wait to be husband and wife. But behind closed doors, the sweet image was far from the truth.

I hated Sebastian Chamberlain. I loathed his touch, despised the touch of his lips on my body, and the sound of his voice made me want to scream.

He hit me to keep me in line. Used harsh words against me and made me obey. He used his fortune as a pawn he held over my head.

Sebastian wanted to be dominant. He wanted to be powerful. And what better way than to control his future wife? But my stalker was no better.

Sin Cruz made me play his wicked game. He preyed on me and led me right into his trap. Because he knew I had to conform. He played the cards, and I had to play along. Just like my fucking fiancé.

Me:

What do you want, Sin? A quick hop in the sack? Would that get you to move on and leave me alone?

Unknown:

I already told you what I want, Liv. Slow down, sweetheart. We just met.

I could imagine Sin with a sly smirk on his face. His sinful way of toying with me as his corrupt personality came through. Which I was sure he thought was impressive, but I took no liking to his amusement. His enjoyment of my torment was astonishing and his face was gorgeous when it shouldn't be, since he was goddamn creepy.

I huffed as I typed, "You're an arrogant asshole."

Unknown:

I love it when you talk dirty, Liv. Which reminds me…

The silence grew thick while Sin left me hanging on his last words. He strung me along in his vile play. But I wanted nothing more than to reach through the phone and strangle him.

Unknown:

You've been a naughty little obsession, and you still require a punishment.

My eyes grew wide at his follow-up message, his reminder making my heart race. I had spit in his face. He had promised me discipline for my inappropriate behavior, but Sin Cruz wanted me all the same.

He wanted to watch me give into all my most intimate desires while someone else touched me, kissed me, feasted on me, and fucked me. The thought sent a shiver of temptation down my spine, and I hated myself for it. I'd never admit my body's attraction to him. He'd never see me give into him, and I'd fight him with all I had.

Me:

No. Punishment and watching me is not an option. Now, leave me alone before I call the police and file a report for harassment.

I waited. Bided my time, peering at my phone while my heart thumped in my ears. The steady drum of the muscle was the only sound I heard, with seconds turning into minutes. I paced on the spot as the minutes turned into an hour, and I bit my lower lip. My body raced with anxiety and my mind reeled with scenarios.

Did I scare Sin off? Or worse. Did I piss him off?

I couldn't be sure because a response never came through, and I placed my cell phone in the pocket of my brown Prada dress. I left the button flap open out of nervous anticipation of an incoming text. But nothing came.

"Calm down, Liv. Everything is going to be okay." I exhaled with a long, extended sigh.

My fingers fumbled with the gold belt on my dress, and I tried to distract myself, but it was no use. I went back to cleaning up the disaster I had created before Sin blew in at hurricane speed. He unleashed misery and caused utter chaos deep within the depths of my soul.

I was distraught. A mess. So fucking vulnerable.

I needed a drink.

Seven
Their Obsession

Liv

My black heels clicked across the kitchen tile as I headed toward the fridge for the ingredients I needed. A vodka tonic would help ease the tension and I'd unwind with the day. I created the easy to make alcoholic beverage in a tall crystal glass full of ice with a shot of vodka and a hint of lime juice. The tonic water adds a bitter, but refreshing taste.

Taking a sip, I was delighted that the drink coated my throat as I peered out of the floor to ceiling window and stared out at the city. My main floor condo apartment wasn't my choice, but my fiancé's. There were too many windows in this dang place for my liking. Too many ways for someone to see inside and know exactly what I was doing. But that was precisely why Sebastian had bought this condo for us.

He knew the openness of our home would encourage me to submit to him. The threat of anyone being able to peer inside would pressure me into being a good fiancée. And one day soon, a doting wife.

The sharp taste of my drink of choice snapped me out of the nightmare my phantom had plagued me in and back to reality. Back to the mess that needed my attention as I took another long swig of my drink and finished it. I tossed the ice cubes into the sink, and I discarded the glass inside of the dishwasher.

The day moved on without a single interruption. Not a peep from Sebastian, but the lack of communication wasn't anything unusual. I'd get some sort of reminder of his existence soon.

Everything was back in order on the bookshelf; the bathroom was sparkling clean, and our bedroom no longer resembled a teenager's unkempt room. I made the bed, cleared the floor of clothes, closed all drawers, and opened the blinds to let in the light. Our main living area had nothing overturned from my upheaval and everything was back in place.

Any remaining dishes in the sink, I rinsed out and started the dishwasher. The soft hum of the machine filled the room while I mixed up a batch of Sebastian's favorite cookie mix. I wasn't a baker at heart, but my mother had taught me my way around the kitchen. She knew I had to carry on the family legacy, and I needed to know how to please a husband. The outdated practice made me want to curse every man on this earth, but I had to do what needed to be done.

I had to save my family from ruin.

The Valencia namesake was a wealthy one. Big fortune meant high price tags and expensive everything. My family was one of the wealthiest in the city, but the fact of the matter was we were on the verge of bankruptcy.

Frank Valencia was a man made of money. My father had so much money, the notion went straight to his head. He figured there would never be an end to his limitless supply, but he was wrong. And my dad needed me to fix his problem.

As his only daughter, my mother had raised me for the position. Marry rich, become a trophy wife, and make our family richer. But in secret, save our status.

Status was everything to my mother. Gloria Valencia believed money held the key to happiness and love was for silly women. She married my father because he was rich, not out of affection. The same reason she had groomed me to marry Sebastian. Abusive or not, I couldn't let her down. Especially since she had no clue her husband had gambled us into destruction.

My father's gambling problem was our secret, and he didn't want my mother to find out. I didn't either, because the truth would destroy them. Somewhere along the way, my father grew to love my mother, and she was his entire world. I knew deep down she loved him too, but she was too proud to admit her affection. Too stubborn to even accept her heart belonged to my dad.

I loved my parents, and I'd do anything for them, but this was why I was in such a dire predicament: Marry Mr. Chamberlain and become his wife on Christmas Eve.

Suddenly, my phone rang. The loud, shrill ring was unwanted and had startled me. The wet batter from the peanut butter mixture splashed on my cheek and onto the countertop from the whisk. I swore out loud and cursed the person who called me. The last thing I needed was another mess to clean up.

Too late.

Quickly, I rinsed my hands and dried them on my dress. The caller was persistent, and I grew irritated. I reached into my pocket, pulled out my cell phone, and looked down at the screen. But my heart stopped cold.

Unknown caller.

I had almost forgotten about my stubborn stalker. Him and the unusual scar over his right cheek, with eyes as sooty as the ashes lingering around his soul. Those eyes would scare the crap out of an ordinary person, but me?

No.

I wasn't normal. I was far from it. Instead, I gave into fear.

The frightening scare that went bump in the night didn't bother me. I let fear corrupt me, terrify me, and I received a thrill from it. I stared horror right in its insidious face, and I wouldn't make a peep. And that's why this complete stranger who lurked in the shadows allured me to his darkness. He intrigued me in the most fucked up way, and my panties grew wet at the idea of him watching me get off with someone else.

Bastard.

Deep down, I was as sick as him. Distorted and messed up. But I wasn't weak. This sick fuck wouldn't win easily.

Ignorance was bliss, and I disregarded Sin's phone call. I pressed the red button, and he wouldn't even get to my voicemail. I wanted to send a message loud and clear. *Don't fuck with me, asshole.*

But as tenacious as he was, a call turned into another text.

Unknown:

My obsession is being a very bad girl.

His obsession?

No shit!

Me:

Leave me alone, you freak!

Sin held his grip on me to the truest of forms, almost as tightly as he wound his hands around my dainty neck. In his eyes, I bet I was his delicate flower. A primed rose ready for him to trim the way he wanted, but I wasn't. I was a weed bound to wrap around his precious rose and ruin the garden. I cursed the day Sin Cruz ever thought he could rule the rose bed.

Unknown:

I'm only a freak for you, sweetheart.

I punched my fingers into each letter as I typed and cursed ever going to the business party. I regretted my decision to lure a man into the darkness and attract a phantom right along with him.

Me:

LEAVE. ME. ALONE.

Unknown:

Don't take your aggression out on your phone, Liv. Take it out on me. God, I love watching you.

My eyes widened as I reread his message, and my hands trembled. The phone shook as I slowly raised my head and glanced over at the window. The glass was clear as fucking day because Sebastian hired window cleaners to keep it spotless. A job I wished he had left untouched, allowing the windows to smudge up. I wished a hurricane would blow through and splash mud all over the glass. Hell, even an unexpected Amazon delivery with curtains, for Christ's sake!

Instead, the sun shone through because it was a sunny, warm day. Cold fall temperatures never happened here. But the leaves had changed color.

Outside my condo apartment, across the street, a light breeze blew through the trees. The leaves fell to the ground and dusted the grass. The mass amount of tall trees mixed in with evergreens made it the perfect hiding place for my phantom.

Sin Cruz could lurk, watch, and wait. I was easy prey and had no way of shutting him out. He could eye me up in a single bite and I'd be a goner.

This asshole was too cowardly to face me as he hid in the shadows, standing behind a tree trunk and texting me threateningly. To hell with him.

With a sly smirk, I ambled my way toward the window and boldly stuck up my middle finger. If Sin was there, I wanted him to understand my message, and I wanted it to hurt. He needed to be as exposed as I was, and I wished I could see his face. I wanted to see the rejection from my stubborn will not to give in.

Sin played with me. He pulled on my strings. The same as a master would form his puppet. But I wasn't his pawn.

I was his worst nightmare. His greatest sin. A creepy doll who'd haunt him within his darkness until he left me the hell alone.

I shook my head, and I didn't believe a word he spoke. There was no way Sin was outside my apartment. He was trying to get under my skin, and I'd prove it.

Me:

Screw you, asshole.

Unknown:

Fuck. I'd love to watch you take that middle finger and come all over it.

Immediately, I gasped and dropped my hand from the window. My cell phone tumbled to the ground as shock rode through me and a chill as bitter as death shivered down my spine. My confidence flew right out the window, and I regretted my decision to question this lunatic.

Sin saw me. He lurked outside my front door. And he watched my every move.

I jumped to the side, away from my open window, and I heard my cell phone chime. Once. Twice. Three times. Each sound made me jump. My body quaked between fear and anger. I hated how scared Sin made me feel, and I loathed him for it. This wasn't me. Some silly woman getting the heebie-jeebies over some guy who gets his rocks off on it. But there was no escaping him.

My stalker, my crazed fan, wasn't going anywhere. I was forced all over again to entertain him. I had to play along with my masked psychopath.

Eight

Her Phantom

Sin

Goddamn it, my cock throbbed. My balls were tight and felt as if they were prisoner to her. Shackled behind bars as I took my time with her and enjoyed her need to disobey me. Everything inside of me ached to have her. Pulsated with a savage need for her.

Liv Valencia was a spitfire. She was my deepest, darkest desire. Pure temptation I could take, but our time would come.

For now, I'd hide behind this fucking tree trunk and watch her from behind her windows. The glass was clear for all the city to see, but only my eyes looked her way. Waited for her from inside of the fortress her fiancé had built for her, keeping her locked away for himself to have and fully control. But I knew she wanted to escape.

She needed to be set free.

My little obsession's time would come. I'd see to it. We may be at odds, and she could continue to defy me, but she'd come around.

I'd make her.

Liv thought she had me with her slow walk of confidence toward the window. Her sure will to fight back and not believe in the words I had sent her. She tested me when she shouldn't have, and I'd make her pay for it. But *fuck*... she was everything.

My fingers dug into the tree bark and a slight tingle of pain stung from the bark scratching me. The pain was no match for the torture ignited inside me while my eyes locked in on her seductive movements. The slacks I had worn, she made me regret. They grew tighter with each sway of her curvaceous hips and every bounce of her busty tits. I thought for sure my zipper would split. But I freed my erection and held my solid girth in my hand.

My obsession wouldn't get away with giving me the middle finger. I'd see that she obeyed her master. She'd bend to me and quiver for me. I was going to make her scream for forgiveness.

My fingers moved as I sent more texts and a surprise that I couldn't wait for her to receive. I held all the power, and if she was as smart as I thought she was, I'd have her right where I wanted her.

I tucked my cell phone back into my pocket and wrapped my hand around my cock when she disappeared from view. The motion of my hand sliding up and down my shaft would usually keep me aroused, but it wasn't enough. I needed to see her. I craved to peer into her big brown eyes and bury myself inside of her soul.

Liv made me want more. Need more. I became addicted to wanting more of everything when it came to her.

My hand moved faster as I waited for her response, and I held up my other hand with the most intoxicating sound: keys jangling against each other—two, to be precise—and the sweet sound made me harder than I had ever been.

I had a way in. She wouldn't even know I was coming. I was one step closer to making her ours.

Nine

Their Obsession

Liv

I sat with my back against the wall, my heart hammering against my chest, and I couldn't catch my breath. Sin was outside. He had found out where I lived, but that would be simple for him. Follow the breadcrumbs, leading right back to me. Stalk me straight down to the letter and there I'd be. Because I was going to marry his investor.

Damn it, Sebastian.

"Pull yourself together, Liv," I said out loud as I exhaled a deep breath and inhaled it back in. I repeated the relaxation technique. I had to gain back my control.

Sin Cruz stole my confidence from me, and I wouldn't let him continue. I was the type of person who sat with a bag of popcorn and enjoyed a horror flick on the big screen. I didn't sit there terrified, with a man's arm around me as I watched. The scare tactics didn't bother me. I loved the excitement of the chase, the loud music, and the excessive gore. Scary movies were a comfort, not a fear.

I wouldn't sit here now and let this shithead take a part of me away. I had to treat this as if I was in a horror film, with me as the lead actress. A woman who always beat her greatest fears. One example was Jamie Lee Curtis, who portrayed Laurie Strode in the classic Halloween franchise. Except my nightmare had a face and didn't hide behind a mask.

I gained the courage and crawled over to grab my cell phone but resumed my position behind the wall. My power slowly came back, and I knew I had to play smarter. Sin appeared to get off on my reactions, but if he couldn't see me, maybe he'd lose interest and find someone else to creep on.

My eyes peered down at the screen with my fingers ready to swipe, but I hated having to play his sick little game. Ten minutes had ticked by since he last heard from me, and I wondered if his patience had grown thin. I'd love to make the fucker wait just a little while longer, but I had no idea what he'd do. I'd better get this over with.

My finger swiped up, revealing one sentence, "I'm going to have to do something about your pretty little mouth, Liv."

And then another, "I told you not to talk dirty."

I remembered there was a third sound, and I dreaded opening the rest of the inbox to see what else he had sent. There were no more messages except one. There must be an image or video. Maybe Sin was the kind of freak who enjoyed sending a dick picture. I'd imagine he enjoyed the sight of his cock, and his ego was probably bigger than his dick. A teeny, tiny pencil dick where he had to adjust the angle of the selfie to enhance his small size.

Boohoo for Mr. Cruz.

It doesn't matter what he had sent because I still had to look at the notification in question. Because Sin was out there, and he was waiting. He knew the one secret I kept that would destroy everything.

"Fuck..." I muttered under my breath and opened his last message.

A video of me on repeat. The repetitive loop of a man I didn't even know eating out my pussy like a man starved, who had his last meal before execution. Except I was the one who faced a lethal injection. But the person holding the drug to ruin my life was the devil himself.

I stopped the video with my mouth agape as I groaned at a god who clearly didn't exist because he put me right on the path to a looney bin. My phantom had captured a video while he watched me last night and I let him. The biggest fucking mistake of my life. I knew he was there. I felt his eyes on me, and I still let him do this to me.

Sin would use this video as blackmail against me. He'd hold this over my head as cold, hard proof of my infidelity. He had witnessed with his own eyes that my upcoming marriage was a complete fraud.

Shit. I had to do the one thing I didn't want to, but Sin had forced my hand. I had to obey him.

Me:

Okay. You got my attention.

Unknown:

Good. Took you long enough to see things my way. Why the change of heart?

Fuck this fucker. Sin knew exactly how to get on my nerves and my fingers typed with a tremble of anxiety or anger. Which one, I wasn't sure.

Me:

It's not like you gave me much of a choice.

I bit my tongue. Literally. The taste of a pinch of blood in my mouth.

Unknown:

Good. You're learning. Now, stand up and let me see you.

Damn him. I didn't want to do as he instructed, and I hated the thought of his eyes on me when I couldn't even see him. But playing I spy with my little eye might be a good enough distraction from my undesirable fate.

I gained the willpower and stood up, taking a deep breath before I stepped forward. My world became bright and vulnerable. The openness of the window I once used to admire as I'd gaze out at the busy city street. But the view had turned into one I loathed in a matter of seconds.

Because Sin could see me.

Unknown:

Good girl.

I imagined a low groan escaping his mouth before he spoke those words to me, and the thought sent a shiver down my spine. A motion I was sure he could see while I couldn't even spot him. My eyes desperately searched on the sidewalk and across the bustling street. Not one tall dark-haired man in sight with a gloominess to him anyone could spot in the pure daylight. The scary scar was a sure giveaway of the terror he could inflict, but his face was incredibly gorgeous. Which only made me angrier. It was unfair for a man to look so good and deliver torment simultaneously.

Me:

What do I have to do to make this all go away?

I hated the question. Despised Sin for forcing me to comply. But I had no choice.

Sin Cruz held my fate in his hands.

Unknown:

I have a few things in mind. But first…

The dickhead left me hanging again. He strung me along in a chase where I was sure he'd win. But I'd fight him tooth and nail if I had to.

Me:

Such as?

Suddenly, my cell phone rang, and the sound startled me. My device almost dropped out of my hands as I glanced down and back outside before I answered the phone. Right on the fourth ring.

"Mm... That's my good little obsession answering when daddy calls," Sin groaned in welcome, making my skin crawl.

"What are you, my old creepy man now?" I asked with disgust.

"No. I'm your shadow daddy, Liv," Sin answered with a huskiness, wrapping me into his world. "And I want you to finger yourself because you were a bad girl."

"Fine, asshole. I'll touch myself tonight while you get your rocks off out there all alone," I snapped and quaked with rage. "Or maybe you should go home before your balls freeze up from the cold."

"Nah. You don't get off that easy, Liv," Sin breathed raggedly and my eyes looked toward the trees. "I'm here to watch you, obsess over you, and devour you."

Desperation took over me as my eyes scurried through the trees. I moved from one tree to another and searched for anyone with a phone up to their mouth. Hopelessly, I tried to search for the son of a bitch who continuously threatened me.

"Go on, sweetheart. Show me your middle finger again."

I did as he instructed, even though every fiber of my being screamed at me to disobey. Just to walk away and deal with the consequences of my actions, which had finally caught up to me. I knew they would someday, but I never imagined I'd wind up with this freak outside my window.

"There. You happy now?" I said and bit my tongue from cursing at him.

My dirty mouth had got me into this mess, and I wanted to get out of it. I wanted all this bullshit to go away and be some terrible night terror. A pure fantasy from watching too many horror movies, and this was my punishment. Not a living, breathing, walking, and talking nightmare.

"Not quite..." Sin whispered, and I heard a rustle on the other end. "I want you to slide that middle finger right between those beautiful pink lips."

Oh, this asshole was pushing it. But I could do the same.

"Which ones?" I asked.

"Fuck, Liv. I love it when you talk dirty, sweetheart." He chuckled with a rumble coming from deep within his chest and escaping his black heart. "But I'll let you take a wild guess."

"The lips you want wrapped around your dick when I'd much rather bite it off?" I asked.

Sin laughed, but the evilness of the sound crept up my spine. "Yes, those pretty lips. Go on. I'm watching."

My finger left the window, and I brought it toward my mouth. The slow motion was solely because I wanted to stop, but he'd take this entire situation as a seduction. Within the depths of his fucked-up mind, Sin would enjoy this. For himself and his obsession.

My wet hole captured my middle finger and slid inside with my lips securely wrapped around it. My tongue looped around the digit, coating it with spit and slipping it back out again. But I made sure I pulled it out with a loud pop just for him.

"Good..." Sin breathed and heat climbed up my skin. "Now be a good girl and stick that finger right inside your soaking wet pussy."

What the fuck?

Shock washed over me, floored that he wanted me to expose myself in such a manner where anyone could see me fingering myself. But I was more taken aback when I realized he was right.

My cunt was really wet.

"You can't be serious?" I asked, with hesitation.

But Sin answered right back, "Oh, I'm so fucking serious. I wish you could feel the way my cock is pressing up against my zipper right now, begging to be inside of your tight pussy."

I gasped at his words, but the sound only made Sin growl. The heated need seared straight through the phone line and sizzled to my toes. Goosebumps formed along my flesh as he drew a reaction from me I hated; my body had deceived me. My pussy loved his filthy mouth.

I argued, "But anyone can see me. There are tons of people walking around outside of my condo, Sin."

"I know. But that's the point. The thrill I want you to experience with the risk of getting caught. The fucking rush of adrenaline you'll have while you finger your cunt," he added with urgency. "But only I'm going to watch you."

"No. I won't do it," I refused and repeatedly shook my head.

"Then you'll suffer the consequences, Liv," Sin breathed with power. "I call the shots, remember? Do as I say, or I'll send the video to your fiancé."

Fuck. Sin had me. He wrapped me right around his wicked finger.

"You're a lunatic," I whispered. I couldn't disobey my phantom and lowered my hand down past my tits.

"Well, this lunatic is obsessed with you," Sin said with a grunt and a rustle of fabric.

I lifted the bottom of my short brown dress and was sure Sin would have a good view of my panty line. As I traced the black thong strap with the tip of my finger, I couldn't help but feel disgusted with myself for even doing it. I hated myself for picking this dress because I could've easily avoided showing any skin to the devil outside my door.

I tried hard not to enjoy the tingles I left on my skin as I pulled back my thong and dipped a finger inside. A shudder of pleasure soared through me, and I fought against any sound escaping my mouth. My teeth bit into my lower lip, and I tried to focus on the pain I inflicted instead of the bliss igniting inside of me. A conflict I battled with the fire of my desire, building low in my belly. My slit was slick and caused my finger to move faster.

But a moan escaped.

"Yes, just like that..." Sin groaned.

I kept the phone cradled against my ear, and I heard skin rubbing against skin. A smooth friction as the flame built higher, and if I wasn't caught up in lust, I'd curse at him. Because Sin Cruz was jerking off. He was getting off behind a tree while he watched me pleasure myself, peered at me, pleasing the ache he'd created deep inside of me, and I was ready to explode.

My cheek laid against the cool glass with my mouth agape. The ecstasy from my breath fogged up the window and my finger moved quicker while my thumb found my clit. The sensation was overwhelming, and my eyes fixated on the trees as I searched for him, longed for him when I knew I shouldn't, and I cursed the idea as I closed my eyes.

"You're being such a good girl pleasing your pussy how I told you to," Sin groaned as the rustling sound picked up pace and his breathing grew rapid.

Sin's groans shouldn't sound like the sexiest thing on this planet. The noises from this wicked man were straight from the devil. My pussy shouldn't throb from them, but the sinful bitch wouldn't listen.

I let myself indulge in Mr. Cruz pleasuring himself in the shadows right along with me. My shadow daddy. The man I despised with a powerful need.

"Show me those big fucking caramel eyes, sweetheart." Sin sighed with need.

I refused and I wouldn't peer the demon's way. He could blackmail me, toy with me, and tease me. But he'd never peer into my soul.

"Look. At. Me," Sin ordered out each word with the sound of him pounding his cock. "*Now.*"

My eyes flew open. The command was stern, certain, and forced me to obey. If I hadn't, I knew there'd be a consequence.

"Fucker," I gasped with hatred as the pleasure hit its peak, and I knew I'd soon collapse.

"Yes. Such a dirty little slut you've been..." Sin groaned, and I heard tainted, squelched sounds from the other end. "Fuck, I wish I could watch you taste my precum soaking the tip of my cock."

I sighed, "No way in hell."

Another long, drawn-out moan escaped me before I could even attempt to hold it back. I bit down again on my lower lip as my finger worked faster, and my pussy made noises it never had before. I was so aroused, my nipples perked against my dress, and I was sure Sin could see.

"Oh, Liv, you've been such a bad girl. But I want to hear you tell me how sorry you are before you come for me," Sin commanded.

"No," I said and bit harder into my lip.

I wouldn't apologize for something I meant to do. I resented Sin Cruz with everything in me, and I had fully intended on spitting in his face. Every word I cursed at him I meant, and I wouldn't take it all back. But I wanted my release.

My body craved a climax. A height of pleasure I had never known before. And the only way I could get there was with him.

"Say. It," Sin grunted out each word.

And my cry of forgiveness shattered me.

"Fuck, Sin! Fuck!" I screamed out my release. "I'm so fucking sorry!"

"Mm... Fuck." Sin grunted as the squelching noises grew louder, and I knew he had come all over himself.

Hopefully, he left an embarrassing white stain on his clothes.

Immediately, I felt shame for letting an evil man like Sin consume me in the way he had. He made me weak against the dominance he held over me. The leverage I couldn't take back, no matter how much I wished I could.

I let my finger, soaked with my release, slip from me. I rubbed the slickness between my fingers as I closed my legs, and they wobbled, on the verge of collapse. My body fell against the window as weakness took over, and I wasn't sure if I could ever get my strength back. Mr. Sin Cruz had stolen my energy from me and controlled my power.

"Come to my nightclub tomorrow."

"No," I answered with a shaky breath.

"That wasn't a question," Sin hissed out his order and dared me to defy him again. "Be at Sinful Saints nightclub at 8:00 p.m. sharp. I'll text you the address."

And as Sin had promised. He did.

I brought the phone back up and questioned him. "Why?"

"Because I want to introduce you to my best friend."

Ten

Their Obsession

Liv

The water from the rainfall showerhead trickled down on me and rinsed away all my sins. All the wrongful doings I had committed with my phantom while he hid in the shadows. While he masked himself and left me exposed to everyone.

I felt disgusted. Deceived by my body. I hated how he made me come.

Sin made me seek forgiveness.

I shouldn't be the one with regret. He should be. After all, Sin was the asshole stalking me. He preyed on me and there wasn't anything I could do about it. Unless I wanted Sebastian to find out about everything I had been doing and deal with his wrath. I was a strong woman, but I had a breaking point. I was only human.

Sin had sent me another text instructing me on how to dress. He had called it a "date" and in his crazed mind, he'd view the occasion as romantic. But there was no way I could romanticize any time spent with the devil.

A soul sucking hellion was more like it, and I was sure his best friend wasn't any better. No man could be if he spent time with a man as cruel as Sin Cruz. He was probably Lucifer for all I knew, and he must have been aware of Sin's harassing ways.

If he wasn't, he was a damn fool. But if he was, he was a man I didn't want to mess with. He might be even worse than Mr. Sin Cruz.

I exhaled a shaky breath as I let my nerves get the best of me and grabbed a towel to dry off. I wanted to be rid of the day I had endured and be clean before Sebastian came home.

For almost an hour after Sin left me alone, I waited for a phone call from my fiancé. Any text from him to inform me he had caught my indecent exposure. I even feared he'd come barging through the front door, but he never did.

And I still needed to cleanse. I needed to scrub away the smell—any scent of what I had taken part in with my phantom. Because I worried Sebastian would catch a trace of my risqué act.

I dressed in a cozy one-piece designer outfit for the evening and applied some light makeup. My highlighted hair dangled in a ponytail as I made my way to the walk-in closet and pulled up Sin's last text message.

Unknown:

Be a good girl. Wear a short miniskirt with black stockings.

I cursed Sin. Normally, I'd wear whatever the hell I wanted to. But this wasn't my choice to make. He held the cards and his best friend dealt out the deck. I was their winnings they'd collect and share at the end.

I picked out a black miniskirt, button-up purple blouse and black thigh-high lace stockings. I hid the undesired outfit behind some boxes on the top rack of the closet, out of sight from Sebastian. I didn't even want to leave a hint of what I'd been forced into. Not a trace of what I'd be up to tomorrow at *8:00 p.m. sharp.*

My ponytail swayed as I made my way out of the condo and toward my mailbox. The box was adjacent to the apartment and accessible in its own little building. I enjoyed the brief walk out into the sunset before nightfall came. The birds had calmed in the trees and the busy city streets wouldn't be in a rush for much longer. Any moment now, Sebastian would be home, and I still hadn't rounded up our mail. My last chore for the day to ensure everything was perfect for my fiancé's return home. A happy spouse made a happy house.

Complete horse shit.

Our mailbox was a fairly large size to fit parcels in, along with any bills or unexpected surprises. I took out the new mail key I had ordered earlier in the day that had been delivered by building management. Relief fell over me when the key worked, and the mailbox door opened easily. But a surprise caught my eye.

One white rose.

The only thing in the box with a few envelopes. I looked at the numbers beside mine and for a split second I thought I must've opened the wrong mailbox. But I hadn't. This was mine.

Despite being artificial, the rose was realistic in every sense. The petals were as soft as a rose and not a speck of dirt was on the purest part. The leaflets were small and came to a pointed shape. But the rose came without thorns.

I glanced at the mail that came with it, and every one had my address. This was, in fact, my mail, but there was no note indicating who this was from. Not a trace of ownership.

I locked the mailbox up with confusion reeling inside of my mind and headed back toward the condo. I'd take the rose straight to the trash first thing in the morning, hide it underneath disposed garbage so Sebastian wouldn't find the lovely gesture.

The front door key worked with no issue, and I entered the main hallway, but stopped dead in my tracks. Expensive brown leather loafers were on the floor and a suit jacket was tossed on the sofa for me to clean up. Sebastian was home, and he stared right at me. But his brown eyes swirled with anger.

"You're home early, darling." I beamed and swallowed the lump in my throat as I closed the door behind me.

Time to play happy housewife, even if the huge rock on my finger didn't signify marriage yet. Sebastian didn't care. I was his to control, torment, and do with as he wished because my family had made sure of it.

"I'm home right on time," Sebastian said as he took in the sight of me and stepped closer.

"I must've lost track of the time," I said as I peered at the clock behind his head. He was home half an hour early.

The logic of the fact didn't matter because I'd never be right in his eyes. Sebastian was. His answer was correct, and I had no reason to argue with that. If I did, abuse would be the result.

"It appears someone beat me home," he snapped, on the verge of a snarl. "Who is this from?"

"Oh, well, this is from your credit card company. There's a bill from the hydro company and—"

"Don't play dumb with me, bitch," Sebastian sneered and grabbed the rose out of my hand.

I jumped, startled by his outburst, but I wouldn't let him break me. Tears formed in my eyes, but I wouldn't let the wetness show. I had to numb the fear. The terror he raged to life inside of me, I pushed back down and buried the fright. I locked the door to my soul and wouldn't let the darkness inside. Even though his evil was right at my doorstep.

"The rose?" I asked and conjured up a lie. "It's from my parents."

"I don't believe you, you ungrateful whore!"

First came the slap with the back of his hand and then the pain. The throbbing ache pierced through me and knocked on the locked door of my soul. Threatened to invade my essence and wrap around the goodness I secured inside. But I wouldn't let him.

Sebastian wouldn't take away the last part of me.

My dignity.

The pride I had in being worthy of respect. Of true love and a happily ever after, once he was long gone.

I imagined Sebastian's death every damn day. Envisioned waking up, and he'd still be in bed. By my side, but stone cold as the darkness he let corrupt him. Sebastian Chamberlain, knocking on the devil's door in hell, couldn't come soon enough. But the time he met his maker had to wait because we had to be wed first.

For now, I let my head swing to the side and took several deep breaths before peering back at the evil in our home. A smile crept over my lips, and it hurt like a son of a bitch. But the pain was no match for the fight I had to battle daily.

"My parents informed me of their gift this morning, but you didn't call, so I could tell you it was coming," I breathed with fake happiness and felt utterly insane.

I had to ignore the slap of abuse and carry on as if the horrific event never occurred. Whether I was insane or not didn't matter. I had to stay alive.

"I didn't call because I was busy fucking my secretary at lunchtime." He glared at me with a heat so fierce it'd burn through flesh, and he held the rose at the tip of my nose.

Sebastian always made it a point to inform me of his sexual encounters. Another way he owned all the control and did whatever he wanted. While he let me wither away into nothing. But I got attention too.

A phantom or two. Multiple encounters of my own. Unlike my fiancé, I concealed my affairs.

"Gloria?" I questioned without a care, and a woodsy scent filled my nostrils. "I always liked her."

"Yes, she's sexy, unlike you. You're pure poison ivy," Sebastian insulted and popped the *P* on poison, resulting in spit splattering on my face.

I didn't flinch.

"You don't love the attire I wore for you today?" I asked.

Sebastian tilted his head to the side as his eyes roamed down my body. They burned through the clothes and made me feel exposed. Owned, uncherished, and used.

"It's hideous, and I want it tossed into the garbage," he answered as he pushed the rose into my chest and backed up a step. "But listen to me and listen to me good."

"I'm listening, darling."

"If you're fucking around on me, I'll find out," Sebastian warned, with his index finger pointed right at me. "I'll kill you in your sleep, smother you with your own pillow and no one would be the wiser. You'll die because you were a whore. Understood?"

"I understand," I whispered.

"I can't hear you, bitch."

Without warning, he slapped me again. This time with his large palm, and the force sent me backward down onto my ass. The pain radiated and pulsed as fast as my heartbeat, but I didn't dare to glance up.

"I understand," I answered louder and with more force.

"Good. Now get up, clean up my shit and go to bed," Sebastian ordered.

I waited until he left the room until the tears finally fell. The wetness was uncontrolled without him around and solely from the pain he had inflicted on me. The hurt I dealt with daily.

I believed Sebastian when he promised to kill me in my sleep. He might look like he was on steroids, but he was still bigger than me. My petite form wouldn't stand a chance against him smothering me in our bed and being rid of me once and for all. But Sebastian knew better.

My fiancé had me conformed just the way he wanted. A replacement for me wouldn't come easily. If death came, it'd be because he was in a blinded rage. The leading cause of related abusive deaths, and I didn't want to become a statistic.

I packed up Sebastian's crap, ready to toss his jacket outside and throw his shoes into a framed picture of us. Our smiles were completely fake for the camera, and the twinkle in our eyes was dull. We were a lifeless couple with no inch of love for each other, only hatred.

With the tears on my face, I wiped them away in the bathroom and took off my outfit. I obeyed my fiancé's word and tossed the undesirable clothing straight into the trash. But I thanked God the light was off when I made my way toward our bedroom.

Sebastian was sound asleep. He probably dreamed of money, chicks, and stuffing the rose down my throat. I laid down and prayed he wouldn't throw a pillow over my face and put an end to me.

Somewhere between the moment I laid my head down and pleaded for my life, my cell phone vibrated once on the nightstand. The screen lit up, and I peeked over in fear the disturbance had woken Sebastian. But thankfully, the device hadn't.

I heaved a silent sigh of relief. My attention turned back to my phone as I contemplated glancing at the message I had received. But I couldn't rest until I knew for sure what the text was about and looked at it.

Unknown:

Did you like my gift?

The single white rose was from Sin Cruz.

Not a chance in hell I'd keep the artificial flower. I'd toss it in the morning. If I even lived to see the daylight.

Eleven

Their Obsession

Liv

I made it.

Sebastian didn't suffocate me while I slept. There was no light leading me to the other side or to the flames in the fiery pits of hell. Heaven or hell didn't want me yet.

I simply woke up in bed.

A normal day was ahead of me, but deep down, I dreaded it. I had to get ready to see my phantom and meet his obedient best friend. I had no choice and had simple orders. But I gave Sin shit.

I texted Sin Cruz back with a special thanks for the disturbance yesterday. What he had seen as a devoted gesture had led my fiancé to become suspicious of me. His carelessness could have exposed my secrets. I had made the message clear to never pull a stunt like that again. But his response?

Unknown:

I had no intention of causing you any harm. But if any injury came to you, my little obsession, it'd be from my hand. No one else's.

Ha!

Right...

Little does my stalker know, which wasn't very *"stalker"* of him, Sebastian forced punishments on me almost daily. He had missed the slap to my face. Not once, but twice, all because someone had sent me a rose in the mail.

A shiver ran down my spine from Sin's threat and I couldn't help it. No damage to me, only torment by his hand. I knew in my mind he'd end Sebastian's life if he ever discovered the truth. But it was possible Sin already knew of Sebastian's abuse and simply bided his time to strike.

Shit.

Either way, none of the possibilities mattered because Sebastian Chamberlain had to live. He had to breathe until we made it to the altar. My world depended on him—otherwise, every hit, bruise, and emotional scar was for nothing.

I needed this plan to work, and no one would ruin this for me. Not even Sin or his best friend—the gorgeous man who I viewed on my desktop computer after I had done some payback of my own.

Saint Sullivan. Thirty-six years old. A man who appeared more refined with age; there was a twelve-year gap between us. Dusty brown hair with big, bold, sky-blue eyes. He could appear on the cover of any magazine—he was drool worthy. The only problem was, he hung out with the wrong crowd. Saint was probably as crazy as the man pictured beside him.

Sin Cruz. Thirty-eight years old. There was no need to go into detail because I had already, unfortunately, encountered him, and he was fucked-up. But the devil had made him sexy as hell.

A thrill shot through me as I sat there and creeped my stalker's website. A business page made for the nightclub Sin and Saint owned together called Sinful Saints. The pictures for the club displayed a nightlife full of strobe lights, wasted customers, and DJs. Their club was the hottest in the city, with others around the world. All thanks to my fiancé, their devoted investor. The business was successful and booming all within the past few years. I had never even heard of it, but I never had time to care.

My parents raised me to be proper, and exquisite taste was the only way. Not some club with STDs, drunk people, and loud music. Extremely distasteful.

I didn't need my parents finding out I was about to walk into a nightmare. All hell would break loose, and my fiancé would hear about my whereabouts. My location needed to remain hidden. Extra vigilance was key this evening. I was not only headed into uncharted territory, but into the lion's den.

My silky blouse brushed against my nipples, and I fully regretted attending braless. The material was cool on my erect buds, and I wanted to cover up. I knew Sin Cruz would spot my aroused points, but I went against my better judgment.

I pulled down the mini skirt that hiked up too much, but the black material crept right back up. I hadn't even set foot inside of the club, and I felt Sin's hands all over me. He tormented me and wasn't even within reach. The bastard was inside of my head and against my body because he made me wear this tight ass outfit. An order from his best friend. Both their fingers touched me, cursed me, and used me. Their tongues on me as they licked up every inch, each crevice, and feasted on me. Their eyes on me as if...

"Hey, lady, what the hell is the hold up?" A man yelled from behind me and laughed with his friends.

Startled, I hurried forward to catch up to the line ahead of me and snapped out of the nightmare I had wandered into. A daydream of monsters within the darkness, who wrapped me into their torment. I focused on the dungeon I was about to walk into.

"Name?" a bouncer asked at the front door.

Do I give a fake one?

My intention was for no one to know I was there. I wasn't Kim fucking Kardashian in any sense, but Sebastian made front page news from time to time. I had to be extra careful.

"Um...Can you keep a secret?" I questioned as I leaned in and pulled a $100 bill from my clutch.

"Sure," he muttered and yanked the crisp money from my grasp.

"Good." I nodded and whispered, "My name is Liv Valencia."

He eyed me up and down but tapped the man's shoulder next to him. The man who took my money whispered something in the other man's ear. Their faces were expressionless as the man with the shaved head stared at me and nodded. They both wore black jeans and black shirts. Nothing special to them. I imagined Sin gave a strict order for attire at his club for every employee. Wear dark clothing, black as a shadow. It was the truth about everything in this hell-hole, and the gloomy appearance suited him.

"Follow me. Mr. Cruz and Mr. Sullivan are expecting you."

Devils awaited my arrival and welcomed me into their lair.

How unfortunate for me.

I followed the shine from the back of the man's head as different colored lights reflected off it and the glare was intense. He must lotion that baby up before a night of working at the club. He was likely fond of spending time here, but I wasn't. I was out of my comfort zone, and someone pushed me into a world I wasn't meant to be in. Or maybe I was, and my parents had brainwashed me into believing otherwise?

The loud music blared into my eardrums to the point they might burst, and I felt tempted to cover them with my hands. A sure sign of weakness I couldn't afford under the watchful eye of a man obsessed. Somewhere, he lurked in his nightclub, and I had to assume he watched me. Crept on the sidelines and blended in with all the customers in their drunken stupor. He'd feed off any blemish and swallow it whole.

As the DJ played, the tune settled in, and I nodded my head to the beat—a rhythm my entire body wanted to give into, but I held back because I was raised not to. Never indulge in unacceptable behavior. Be a good girl and do as you're told. Appearance was everything. No man would want a wicked woman. There was no room for failure.

I wandered further into the club, past the bar, away from the stairs leading toward a second floor and down a hallway. There were mirrors everywhere, no wall was without them. Reflections of myself were everywhere. I imagined I'd find my phantom behind me with his hands ready to reach out and grab me to capture me in his threatening hold all over again. But the darkness never struck.

Sin remained where I couldn't see him, but I felt him all the same. He followed my every move, and I imagined his eyes all over me. In my hair, falling down my shoulders as his gaze touched every strand on my head. Locked on my lips as my teeth bit down on the bottom piece of flesh and I tasted blood. Down my neck, exposed for him to imagine his hands wrapped around, eager to take my breath away. As I walked, my tits bounced, and my nipples tingled under his lingering gaze. I imagined his gaze trapped on my ass as it swayed, though the motion wasn't intended for him. But he longed for me and obsessed over me no matter what I chose because I had no choice. No decision whatsoever as the bouncer abruptly stopped at a door, and I almost ran right into him.

I cursed up at the giant in front of me, and he glared down over his shoulder at me. A grumble of annoyance rumbled in his chest, and I swallowed hard as I took a step back. *Jesus.* He was wound up. *Bad.*

Dude probably hadn't got laid in months with that attitude.

"Sorry," I squeaked.

He ignored my dumb-ass apology and turned his focus back on the door. His giant hand turned the doorknob and opened it. The room inside was dark as Bigfoot signaled for me to step through.

Hesitation ran through me, and I took a step backward, but the grouchy man remained unimpressed. He wouldn't speak a word and grumbled at me until I took the hint. My heels stepped through the door and into the black hole with a light turned on over a chair. The metal seat was directly in the middle of the room and the flooring was dull. Everything about this room gave me the creeps. Straight up out of a horror film where the main character got tied to the chair and tortured for information.

Oh, hell, no...

Immediately, I turned around as the door slammed shut, and I heard a click. Frantically, I turned the knob as my heart raced and the organ felt like I'd vomit it out. Sheer panic coursed through me as I twisted and turned, but it was no use. The miserable bouncer with a hairless head as smooth as a baby's ass had locked the damn door.

"Hey, asshole? Open the fucking door and let me out of here!" I yelled and banged my fists against the door.

I heard nothing from the other side, not that I expected to. The only sound I heard was my breathing as my chest heaved and my blood pressure spiked. I pounded more forcefully on the door until the palms of my wrists hurt, and I realized it was no use. I was trapped. Stuck with my erratic, racing heart and some other sound shuffling behind me.

Shoes.

My entire body vibrated as I tried to gain control of the terror winning inside of me. Wisps of hair fixed to my lips with each unstable breath and my hands fell to my sides. I had to calm down. Any mistake would be made out of fear, but I had already made one and walked right into the devil's hands. Into his hot, sweaty evil palms, where I was about to learn my fate.

Slowly, I turned around, and I faced whoever was behind me, watching and waiting with such patience, it made my skin crawl. The silence was deafening as I glanced back toward the light and didn't see anyone. But I knew *someone* was there.

Their eyes roamed over me, and there was nowhere to hide. No place to run and no one to save me. I could bang on the door, but the notion was pointless.

Suddenly, a brown shoe stepped out of the darkness, and I almost jumped out of my skin. The other person in the room was a man. A tall man, from what I could see of his long leg extending outwards from the shadow he hid behind. The movement shouldn't have scared me, but the way he preyed on me beforehand terrified me. It had to be Sin. But something was off.

He was too quiet.

Sin would've opened his smart-ass mouth or let out an evil laugh, leaving my skin crawling with goosebumps. He had patience, but not this much. This restraint was overwhelming to the point I held my breath and thought my lungs might collapse.

I exhaled with one question. "Who are you?"

No answer. Not even a peep. Did this guy even breathe?

My instincts kicked in, and my gut reaction moved me forward a few steps. Which made him step into the light more and expose half of his body. An extremely large, intimidating form, and I swallowed all my courage. *Hard.*

A blue eye blazed at me with such an intense heat I thought I'd catch on fire and sizzle beneath his cobalt gaze that was sure to burn and ignite me into the inferno right along with him. Until we both burned out and turned to ash.

But I recognized this blue-eyed beast.

I gulped. "Are you Saint? Saint Sullivan?"

He granted me a single nod. No words. Not one introduction, unlike his best friend. But I was sure Sin wasn't far away.

Twelve

Her Phantom

Saint

She was fucking perfection. Everything Sin had described. I couldn't wait to get my hands on her.

"She's our fulfillment. The answer to every single one of our prayers," Sin whispered in my ear.

But God didn't speak here.

I only did the devil's work. And I'd enjoy every single second of it.

Thirteen
Their Obsession

Liv

Saint moved further out into the light until his entire massive figure was present for me to feast my eyes on. His picture didn't do him justice. They should list his height because he was huge. I was sure he was taller than Sin, and I thought *his* stature was domineering.

Mr. Sullivan wore a black suit with a dark button-up shirt underneath. He loosened a black tie and took it off while he studied at me. As he undid the top buttons of his shirt, a pendant glistened in the light, making the moment intense. The exact one Sin wore. The assholes not only loved to prey on me, but they had matching necklaces, too.

How cute?

He remained quiet, concealing his voice from me as he ambled forward, and I took a few more steps back. His face featured a bone structure made for a cover model, with that perfectly chiseled bad boy next door expression. Unlike Sin, whose face bore a scar carved into his skin and who glared at everything like he'd burn the world down. But Saint's stare made me quake with a volcanic heat that was ready to explode.

"So, no formal introduction from your best buddy?" I asked to break the tension.

But only a low rumble rolled through the air.

The sound could have been the air conditioner, a furnace, or even a noise from the music—anything other than what I knew I had heard. The hairs on my arms stood up with caution, my ears perked and my back hit the door.

A tiny gasp fell from me, and I swear Saint snickered. A cruel sound as evil as Sin's. Me being shaken up got his jollies off, too.

Lucky me.

"So what's your deal?" I asked as he took off his formal jacket and tie and draped them over the back of the chair.

Saint glanced at his arms and pushed up the sleeves of his shirt, revealing many tattoos covering them. The ink slid underneath his rolled-up sleeves, down his forearms, and stopped at his wrists. The tangles of veins popped out from his extremely muscular forearms and down onto his hands. They were masculine hands, forming into fists and unclenching as his blue-eyed blaze met mine again.

Jesus. Saint's one hand alone could wrap around my neck. Impressive.

"Hey, dickhead?"

Saint's lips curled into a wide grin, almost as sinister as this very moment, and my heart raced. Panic soared through me, and I ate my words. All the confidence I once held left me, and I turned around to try the door again. Wishful thinking of the door magically opening played on repeat in my mind, as if I had the ability to create some sort of goddamn miracle. When I didn't have shit. But I did have a bitching loud voice.

"Open this fucking door right now, Sin! I know you're out there!" I yelled as loud as I could and twisted the knob.

Banged once. Twice. Again and again. Nothing.

Then I screamed. A wild banshee wail for help. The sound echoed off the walls and right back into my eardrums until it stopped from a hand over my mouth. My eyes went wide in terror as the silent man muffled my scream and wrapped an arm around my waist. In response, I kicked out my legs and thrashed my feet. The heels of my pumps rapped against the door, and I tried twisting my body to gain control back. But it was no use.

Saint was gigantic, and I held little power over him. The struggle I put up only lasted a few seconds and he probably let me put up a fight. Only to get off on my poor effort.

I continued to scream against the hand Saint used to cover my mouth while he pulled me back further into the room. Far away from the door and my hopeless means of escape. There was no way out of this as soon as I walked through that door, and he knew it. I came here to save my ass, and now I think I only came here to discover true torture.

Unlike Sin, Saint covered my mouth so tightly I couldn't bite down. My backside was flush up against his solid chest, and I couldn't move my arms. My limbs were tucked tight against me while he held me in his firm grasp.

Saint was an angel of darkness—a fallen guardian who answered only to his unholiness. Sin. The devil peering in from the walls of hell as his worshipper wrapped his tarnished wings around me.

Satan's messenger pushed me into the chair, causing my skirt to fly up at the back. My ass cheeks made a loud slap against the metal because of the force, causing pain to course through my tailbone. The harsh motion cut the scream from me, and I shuddered with the back of my head against his shoulder. But the bastard still uttered no words.

Everything shook as I vibrated in the chair, and my nostrils flared with each unsteady breath through my nose. I remained silent while he breathed against my ear, and the same smell from Sin fell over me. *Cedarwood.* No whiskey, which I was grateful for. I didn't need a drunk asshole of Saint's size to mistreat me. But with his deranged state, he could be just as dangerous.

I came here to follow orders and put this situation behind me, but I feared this was only the beginning. A start to a fucked-up partnership I never wanted. Two psychos who'd haunt me until my death. This could be my end at the hands of this man while Sin wasn't far away, watching everything he had put into motion. He had set me up with a lunatic as crazy as he was and knew full well what this man was capable of.

Destruction.

Fourteen

Her Phantom

Sin

Liv put up quite the fight, and I knew she would. Our girl was argumentative as much as she was gutsy. She had a body that blinded all rational thought and a mouth that required a cock. Mine. Stuffed far up inside of her, her brain would shudder from a climax before her pussy. A wet hole Saint would willingly stick his dick in and let her tighten around him. A pleasure both of us would share as we'd come and fill her pretty little holes full.

Fuck.

I yearned to be in the room and much closer than this. I was stuck behind this wall that kept me from her and the excitement that built on the other side. Our bouncer had done a magnificent job and earned a pay raise. One I'd willingly pay for bringing our girl inside unharmed and right where we wanted her: away from prying eyes with no sound escaping through these soundproof walls, locked away for only us to enjoy.

Arousal spread through me, and my balls tucked up tight against me. I watched her squirm under Saint's hold. Her fight only excited me more. The thrill of gazing at her with nowhere to turn except my best friend made my breath accelerate and fogged up the glass, but my pulse thumped just as fast as she kicked her pretty feet.

Goddamn it. I cursed myself silently, so I didn't confuse Saint on the other side and wiped my hand to clear my view. This was a sight I didn't want to miss.

Her shriek opened up the gates of hell and reached for my soul. She wrapped herself around my essence while I gladly gave all of me to her. Liv was a soul-sucking slut who needed cleansing, and I'd love to purify her, starting with that pretty pink pussy.

Saint used force on Liv and pushed her down into the chair we used to torture those who crossed us. But not today. This evening was all about Liv. Our wicked one who shut the hell up, the fight leaving her body, with one harsh thump.

Good girl.

Even better was the perfect view I received from the angle presented to me. Our girl's thighs spread wide open, giving me a sweet view of her thong. Black lace puffed out from her cunt's lips, and the thin piece of fabric hid between the crevice of her plump ass cheeks. I was jealous of that G-string. I'd die to suffocate between those butt cheeks.

As if Liv read my mind, figuring out my eyes were on her cunt, she closed her legs. Locked them up tight and left me longing for another peek. Damn it. I wished I had telepathic abilities. I'd tell her to relax and spread those beautiful legs for me.

I was so fucking hard after seeing her wide open and in a confined state. I bet if I whacked my dick off this damn reflective glass, it'd make a solid dent. But she'd never hear a sound.

Not with the plan I had for her.

"Tie her up and make it tight," I ordered as I held my cell phone in my hand and smirked. "Because I want to watch our obsession squirm."

Fifteen

Their Obsession

Liv

"Please, please..." I begged in a muffled cry, blocked by Saint.

But I only heard, "Sh..."

The fucker could talk. Saint liked to play games as much as Sin. The wickedness was in both of them, but the sound of his voice made me clench my thighs.

The husky whisper against my ear did something to my belly deep down inside. The noise was harsh yet sweet. In my mind, I knew Saint was bad—a terrible person to get lost in—but my body was hooked and wanted to hear more. It was a horrible mix sure to confuse me, and I loathed myself even more.

I shouldn't want to listen to this freak talk. My ears shouldn't give a damn what Saint had to say. Another moment around him promised a fate sure to end in my demise.

Saint shook his head against mine, and the warning was clear. *Shut the fuck up or else.* My eyes widened in surprise as he let go of my mouth when he could've taken his tie and stuffed my loud mouth full, but he didn't. His mistake.

My boisterous cry filled the room and rang out for help. The sound ended as quickly as it had begun when Saint clamped his hand back over my mouth. This time with such harsh force, my lips pressed into my teeth. The slight taste of blood warmed my tongue, and he shook my head with a frustrated grunt. His hand was so tight my mouth puckered together, and my cheeks hurt.

Saint's other hand wrapped around my wrists and squished them together. The force was powerful and stung from them being completely bound against each other. My nostrils flared against his hand, and my mind raced.

What was he going to do to me?

Why did they choose me?

How could I get out of this?

The answers were obvious, but I refused to listen. I wouldn't give up this easily. There had to be some way out of this, even when I felt this was the end.

Suddenly, Saint gripped my cheeks tighter. Tears pricked my eyes, and he forced my attention to him. His nostrils opened and closed like a bull in heat, with his blue eyes smoldering right at me. His index finger reached up and tapped my nose with another warning as he shook his head once more. He reminded me, *don't fuck with him.*

Immediately, I nodded. The vibration of my acknowledgment shook me right down to my feet, and I was ready to listen. If I didn't, there would be dire consequences.

Saint slowly released his hand, ready to strike if I played him again. My eyes trained on his hand as his fingers spread wide and they danced, almost teasing, but I knew of his threat. *Don't try anything stupid.*

My breathing came out heavy as his hand disappeared behind me and his suit jacket fell to the floor. He kept my hands bound, but something wrapped around them—a fabric that was soft against my skin until he pulled it tight, and I gasped. Saint's tie knotted around my hands, and he bound me to the metal chair.

But he let go, and I didn't move a muscle.

Saint was too close. Too near I could hear his wild heart beating inside of his chest. The vision of me strapped to his chair must excite him, entice him to do wicked things to me no man should without my permission, but he'd never get it.

I trembled in the seat I didn't want to be in. My ass was numb. The pain went away after Saint's rough mistreatment—a punishment I received for getting out of hand while trying to escape, but there was no running from Saint Sullivan. No freedom from his mass destruction.

I stared straight ahead because I wasn't willing to give Saint attention, only if I had to. But I couldn't help peeking at him out of the corner of my eye.

Saint brushed his hand down my hair with care and ease as he admired his masterpiece. He studied each lock as if the silky strands were a delicacy he deserved and let them fall back onto my shoulder. I trembled from his unwanted touch and pressed my lips together in disgust. He had the inked wings of an angel on his forearm, but in my mind, I saw them tainted black. Engraved by the devil's work because there was no way this man was any saint. He presented himself as tarnished, mean, and overbearing. A true monster sent to torment me until I bent to his will.

"Mm..." Saint groaned as he smelled up the side of my head, and it took all the effort in me not to bash my head upside his.

I remained still, as motionless as I could, considering the circumstances. Even though Saint had earned a strike from the woman he held captive against her will. But the move would be stupid.

This chair had my hands tied to it, and even if the door unlocked, it would be hard for me to escape. This metal chair was heavy. I couldn't drag the seat all the way through the club and toward someone who gave a shit. Hell, the bouncer was probably back by now and stood guard on the other side of the door. I'd have to deal with the bastard who locked me in this mess all over again, but I'd put up a hell of a fight. He deserved a clunk with this chair over the side of his head after I gained super strength from the adrenaline rushing through me. Maybe a bite too from my mouth, covering his hand as he'd reach out to stop me. Or...

The thought of my imagined plans of escape left me when Saint rounded in front of me. I could smell his aroused heat, and the scent made me press my thighs tighter. Lust and cedarwood. A dangerous combination.

Saint's eyes bored into mine, and the sound of my wild heart racing filled my ears. The noise pounded in my head, and I was sure my pulse fluttered at the base of my neck. He'd see my unwanted arousal, even though I was mad at my body. I didn't want to be turned on by this fucker and whatever his deranged plan was. I hated him and wanted him to let me go.

My eyes trained on Saint as he fell to his knees in front of me and confusion swept over me. He kneeled there, peering straight at me, and didn't move. His height remained dominant over me as I sat confined to the chair. He compelled me to look up at him and left me completely at his mercy.

"What the hell are you doing?" I asked with narrowed eyebrows.

Saint only responded by titling his head to the side, not uttering a word. His eyes left mine and traveled down my body. They didn't stop until they landed on my legs, but it was my turn to be speechless.

I watched with horror as his evil grin returned and spread across his lips. His blue heated gaze locked on my closed thighs, and he got down on all fours. Slowly, Saint crawled to me. He moved on his hands and knees like an animal in heat—turned on by me and ready to destroy me in every sense of the word.

Sixteen

Her Phantom

Saint

I wanted my face buried in her cunt. To choke on her juices and not come up for air. I wanted to wash away in her climax and never return. I'd die a happy man.

Jealousy seared through me when I had watched the video of her with someone else. I was envious of the man eating out the woman I was hooked on from the moment Sin's eyes landed on her. The very second my eyes found her, too.

She was gorgeous. Black hair past her shoulders with a touch of blonde. Perfect for pigtails while I'd use them as handlebars as she bobbed her head. All the while, gazing up at me with her dark brown eyes while she sucked on my cock. *Fuck.* She'd be perfect.

Unlike my raging boner pulsating against my pants. The friction of the zipper was almost unbearable. I needed to jerk off after this and remember all the things I did to her. All the ways I had made her scream, all for me. For us.

Liv had me hard. Wet in my pants with precum; I wished she could see. I yearned for her to know how much she had affected me. But not yet.

This was about her.

We'd make her come in my mouth. Show her a world she had never known and treat her unlike any other man had done before. She was ours to control, ours to have. Not anyone else's.

But I wanted to kill the man in that video.

Crush his throat with my one hand and watch him struggle until life left his ugly eyes. Constrict his windpipe until his head popped off like a dandelion and chant, "*mama had a baby and its head popped off.*" But his eyes would be bloodshot, lifeless, and he'd be braindead.

I'd feed his head to the cows.

He was a lousy fucker who barely got our girl off. He couldn't handle a woman like Liv, who squirmed in the metal chair in front of me with a feisty need to disobey. I enjoyed how she fought me in order to gain back her control. The vision excited me, enticing me to break her and make her comply.

I was her darkness, and she was our greatest sin. Together, we were a force to be reckoned with, and no one was a match for us. We'd be unstoppable.

So here I was, down on my hands and knees, crawling toward the floodgates of heaven. A utopia I wanted her to spread wide for me and welcome every murky shade of me, but I knew she'd require some help. And our little obsession would give me the introduction I had always waited for. My first encounter with her pretty pink world. But I'd be damned if it'd be my last.

Seventeen

Their Obsession

Liv

"No... No!" I choked out and kicked my feet.

Saint only nodded his head; he didn't have to speak for me to understand his full intention. I knew what would happen, and I wanted no part of his dirty plan. This was madness. He was insane.

"No, get away from me, asshole!" I yelled at him, but he continued to crawl.

Saint reached my knees, and I held them together. Clenched them tight with my heels flat against the floor. But I was no match for him.

"No! Fuck off, fucker!" I snapped at him.

I felt anger, fear, and hopelessness all at the same time. Tears burned my eyes as Saint forced my knees apart and opened my world for me. He demanded his way inside, and I tried everything to keep him out.

My legs thrashed, and I prayed one of my heels lodged straight through an eyeball, but he caught hold of my thrashing ankles. Gripped them tight and pulled until my ass jerked in the seat. He compelled my back to arch to his will and aligned me, so he was in perfect proximity to my wet pussy. As he placed each of my legs over his shoulders, I could feel my thong becoming drenched.

"Stop. Don't do this..." I panted hopelessly, and I kicked the back of my heels into his backside.

Saint let out a groan so deep the sound tore into me as he looped his long arms around my legs and trapped me in his hold. I shouldn't like the sound of the unwanted husky noise as the vibrations pulsated into my feverish belly and left an achy pit. A heat flew through me, and I hated myself for desiring him. Loathed everything about this man who was going to force himself on me. I didn't stand a chance. I wouldn't let him destroy my soul, but my pussy was in for mass destruction.

I twisted my body with all my might against his powerful strength. My will to not give up was strong, but I only earned Saint pushing my knees upward. The chair scraped along the floor from his force, and I gasped, with my knees up, mere inches from my cheeks.

And Saint's face was only seconds away from mine.

Fiery indigo eyes swirled with need, making me lose my breath. My lungs constricted, running out of air, as he stared into my soul and forced his way inside. His breath was hot on my lips as his tongue reached out and touched mine.

Oh... Gross!

I turned my head away from his dampness and he let out a deep, throaty chuckle. I panted and avoided his stare. The only option I had in this uncomfortable, cramped position.

But the asshole didn't stop there.

No. Saint pulled back enough to zero in on my cunt. He bowed his head and grazed his teeth across my clit. I held back a moan, daring to escape, and stuffed the sound back down with a hard swallow. His teeth nipped at the flesh, and I bucked with the need to break free. But the notion was hopeless.

All I had succeeded in was pushing my cunt closer to the bastard's face. The move wasn't in my favor and only made Saint grunt with approval. Fuck me.

A tiny gasp broke free from me as he ripped my thong open, and the smell of my arousal filled the air. The warm scent was against his face and Saint groaned at the bliss of my pleasure. The asshole ripped my panties in half with his teeth!

Saint kissed my pussy, and I crumbled inside. A shudder coursed through me, and I fought against it with all of my might. I panted from above through flared nostrils and held back any sounds, wanting to break free. I had only brought this fight on by being stupid enough to walk into a dark room with one light. I had only landed here because I tried to save myself from Sin's god-awful threat—his stern warning against not following directions—and I'd live with the consequences.

I hated myself. I despised Sin. But most of all, I loathed how good Saint's mouth felt on my pussy.

"Fucker..." I breathed right as his tongue licked up my slit, and I couldn't stop a moan from escaping.

A shiver ran down my spine as Saint's hot breath caressed my cunt after his insatiable torment to my most sensitive spot. I couldn't fight the tears in my eyes as one slipped loose while I withered beneath him. He took his teeth, running their sharpness over my clit. An untamed groan came out of him as I thrashed against him, but he held me tight. My responsive skin sent quivers to my toes as he sucked it into his mouth and released the flesh with one loud pop.

"Oh!" I cried out, unable to conceal the blast of pleasure.

My sound of satisfaction only rewarded Saint and encouraged him more. I cursed myself as he granted me with a slide of his tongue over my slit. The torturous pleasure once again pulled a sound from me and made my eyes roll toward the ceiling.

A delirious passion coated me and wrapped around me. The intoxicating need built more and more inside of my belly. The sensation was ready to burst. I almost lost sight of the fight I needed to put up against Saint, but I regained my focus. I grabbed hold of all the refusal I had left.

I sickened myself. Repulsed at my deceptive body for feeling anything other than pure hate. This bliss wasn't for me and not something I'd willingly give. Not to this deranged, delicious man. Never.

Saint must've sensed my push back, and his tongue entered me. It pushed deep inside of my wetness, and I cursed at him. He groaned against my pussy and the sensitive area responded for me. My juices coated his tongue and let his skilled muscle wiggle in further. The vibrations from the sound he produced were my undoing. It was an evil I hated more than myself because he had made me, forced himself on me when I didn't want this, but he left me with no choice.

Damn him.

Slowly, he withdrew his tongue, but Saint didn't stop there. He licked the entirety of my entrance right up to my clit and attacked the skin with his teeth. Enamel scraped, nipped, and dragged. He pulled my clit between his teeth until a feral cry fell from me, and my head fell back.

Uncontrollably, my eyes rolled back again, and I clamped my mouth shut. My hands balled into fists as I fought the climax climbing higher and higher inside of me. I was ready to tumble over the edge, but I maintained my balance. It was a wobbly edge as Saint sucked my clit into his mouth, and he covered the delicate flesh with his entire tongue.

The muscle played a wicked game as Saint swirled, licked, and whirled his torturous heat. He took me to a place I'd never been before. No man had ever reached here because he was a beast. An animal sent to eat me and swallow me whole.

My hips bucked in surprise of his tactful tongue diving back inside of me, and I was out of control. The force pushed my pussy further into his face when I didn't want to. Saint's nose rubbed against my clit as he fully feasted on my cunt. He was savage, a wild man fully intent on making me come. His face buried against me as my hips had a mind of their own and rode against his mouth.

I suffocated Saint. I hoped he died, and my pussy sent him right back to where he came from: hell.

Die, motherfucker. Just fucking die.

"Fuck," Saint groaned, his first muffled word and the delicious sound was my unfortunate downfall.

Deeper and deeper I fell into the darkness. Trapped in my phantom's world. Until he set me free and released me from his chains.

A blast of pure euphoria shot through my body, and I cried out as I never had before. The sound strangled as I tried to contain the bliss, but the frenzied climax wanted no part of it. The sensations within me longed to be heard.

I lost the battle I had fought hard for, and my cries of pleasure filled the room. My thighs were no longer confined as they fastened his head between them, and my hips thrusted my slit further into his face. My orgasm blinded me, and my nails bit into the palms of my hands. Pain radiated from my self-inflicted injuries.

I lost myself and fell over the edge. The pleasure he'd made was impossible to resist as the fire deep inside of my aching belly blazed into a wildfire, and I plummeted off the cliff to escape it. But there was no running from Saint Sullivan's forced bliss.

Eighteen

Their Obsession

Liv

Saint had captured me. Forced me into hell right alongside him and the devil himself, Sin Cruz. Saint's master, who called the shots.

My ears stopped pounding long enough for me to hear a noise. The sound of the doorknob unlocking, and I held my breath. My lungs burned with the need to breathe after the dirty sensations had coiled through me, spun me tight, and plagued me with a new commotion. Fear.

My head shot up just as Saint peered up from my pussy with my juices around his mouth. The slick wetness glistened on his face, and my body shivered at the sight. My nightmare phantom with his head between my legs, squeezing my thighs and wiping the palm of his hand over his mouth. He smirked wickedly as he licked his hand and didn't waste a drop. The taste of me was far too precious, and I hated him with utter disgust. But the asshole looked delicious as fuck.

I snarled, "I hate you."

Saint's response was a harsh slap to my pussy. My mound jolted, and pain radiated from the sensitivity of my clit. Pleasure replaced suffering, and I bit my lip to conceal a moan. It was more satisfaction than he deserved.

"And we fucking love you," Sin answered from behind Saint.

My blood boiled at the sight of Sin Cruz as he leisurely stepped through the door and let it click shut behind him. I eyed him with a glare of pure rage mixed with terror. I thrashed against my binds and kicked out my legs, but Saint regained his hold on me.

"Love? This isn't love, asshole. You let this freak force himself on me!"

"No, I didn't Liv. You came here of your own free will," Sin answered as he tried to confuse me and turn my words against me.

"Yeah, after you threatened me," I snapped.

Sin came closer and tsked. "Liv, Liv, Liv...I told you I loved to watch."

Sin watched me as he ambled by and out of sight as he untied my hands. The tie fell to the floor and there was only one restraint left. This insane barbarian between my legs.

"Yeah, watch me get fucked."

"Saint did just that. He fucked your pussy with his mouth..." Sin breathed as he stood near me, and his scent surrounded me. "And you rode his face like such a good girl."

My breathing quivered as I watched his hand travel down toward my cleavage, but Sin never touched me. The heat radiated off his hands as he traveled further in a downward motion, and he stopped right over my center. The sweetest spot of me and my core, which I had no desire for him touching. *Ever.*

"Soon, Liv, I won't just watch. I'll touch you and taste you myself," Sin warned and snapped his fingers for Saint to get up.

Saint grunted at Sin's command and swatted his hand away. He stood up and the two men loomed over me as they glared at each other. A miscommunication brewed between them and tension mounted. A stand-off I didn't want to be any part of, and my eyes darted toward the door between them.

I was the one who got violated. But here they were, fighting over their prey.

Men.

The idiots stared at each other with all the testosterone fused around them. I glanced at them and the door. The unlocked door was my only escape out of here. I was small enough to squeeze between the two of them while they preoccupied themselves with their stupidity.

My heels planted on the floor and time slowed down as I weighed my options. Stay here and get further repulsed by my body's deception or make a run for it?

I dashed for the door. Darted right through the middle of their silent argument, which was creepy as fuck, and ran for my life. But an arm clamped around my waist and stopped me cold.

"Let me go, you buffoon!" I shouted as I kicked my legs and my fists pounded against a muscular arm.

Saint had me in his grasp while Sin grabbed my chin with so much force it hurt. He squeezed tight until the fight left me and tears blinded my eyes. But I didn't let them fall.

This fucking asshole would love to see me cry.

"As much as we desire a good chase..." Sin said as he reached inside of his pocket and pulled out a necklace. "We have more important matters to discuss."

I snapped, "Like what?"

I glared into his cold dark eyes and wouldn't show him the fear I held inside. My hatred for him intensified as he made me despise something I used to enjoy. I loathed them both.

"Our little agreement," Sin said.

"More like blackmail," I hissed against his hold of my chin and fought Saint all over again.

I thrashed, kicked out my legs and prayed to kick Sin in the nut sack, the heel of my shoe digging into his flesh, causing him to wail out in agony. But my imagination got carried away.

Sin caught my heel in his large hand, and the force made my knee bend. He angled me perfectly, pressing his body up against me and sandwiching me between the two men. Their heated breaths were on my skin, and I hated myself for liking it.

"Quit your fucking squirming, Liv or I'll fuck you blind..." Sin warned as my belly pressed up against his massive erection inside his pants. "Right here. Right now."

Immediately, I caved. Sin could whip out his cock and hold true to his promise while his friend let him. I stood no chance of winning with my panties torn in half and a fucking mini skirt, exposing my bare cunt to him.

"Okay. I'm listening," I whispered through clenched teeth.

"We want you to do exactly as you're told, Liv," Sin instructed as his eyes burned into mine with possession and Saint's hard cock throbbed against my back. "Be our good girl and don't misbehave."

"Or else what?"

Sin threatened. "Or your video not only goes to your fiancé, but straight to the press."

My eyes widened, my heart raced, and my blood rushed to my head. I couldn't let them do this to me—use me, violate me, and own me. There was only one way out of this: I had to play along.

"Fine."

"Let her go, Saint," Sin ordered after a second passed and his fucking lap dog released me.

Well, in hindsight, Mr. Sullivan was more like a great fucking Great Dane rather than a puny dog. *Damn it.*

Saint towered behind me and didn't budge, with his body flush against mine. Sin let go of my chin and released my leg from his rough grasp. A bruised handprint would form later, and I'd have to conceal the contusion from Sebastian. Or earn some more black-and-blue marks from the wrath of him.

"Are we done here?" I asked with bravery and almost ate my words. "Sebastian will become suspicious of my whereabouts anytime now. I can only hold up a lie for so long."

"We can't have that, can we, my little obsession?" Sin whispered as he brushed the hair from around my neck and placed a necklace around it. "But we want you to wear this."

Saint took the clasp of the necklace from Sin's hands and secured the chain in place. He let my hair fall over the top of the clasp while gently running his hands down the strands. His fingers combed through with ease as if I was the most precious enjoyment in the world.

"What is it?" I asked as I gazed down at a silver rose pendant and back up at Sin.

"It's our gift to you. Every time you look at this pretty face in the mirror, you'll think of us," Sin breathed as he caressed my cheek, and I flinched at his touch. "But I want you to remember one thing."

"What's that?" I questioned.

"Never take it off," Sin warned me with a soft kiss of death to the tip of my nose, making me shudder with terror. "Because if you do, we'll find out."

And I pondered if I should call their bluff.

I did. I called Sin and Saint's bluff. Screw them both.

The rose pendant was no longer around my neck and was hidden inside of my jewelry box on my nightstand. I didn't want to look in the mirror and think about last night's event. The sheer torture I had to endure at the hands of two men who were completely out of their minds. Worst of all, I didn't want to see their faces and recall how much of the torment I had enjoyed. The thrill of Saint's mouth became my unwanted undoing, while Sin had observed from wherever the fuck he was.

I applied my foundation with a smokey eyeshadow to match my dark state. My emotional well-being was in an upheaval, and I had chosen an outfit to match. All dark shades of black from my ripped charcoal jeans, black crop top and gray knitted cardigan to go over top. I'd make a stop at the nail salon to get my nails painted black before I made a trip to the grocery store. I wanted to get as far away from my phantoms' present as possible.

When I had unclasped the necklace from around my neck, a sense of freedom washed over me. The sweetest sound was the jewelry box's lid slamming shut because I knew their gift was tucked away inside. Those damaged men couldn't control me, and they'd never own me. I'd make sure of it.

I didn't care if they saw me through the window without the stupid rose on. I didn't care if they saw me walking down the street without it. Sin and Saint could burn in hell for all I cared, and I'd never wear the piece again.

I was on cloud nine but fuming with rage at the thought of those two bastards. The overcast puffy cluster of clouds turned into smog from my hateful reflection. My repulsion made the happy cloud a chaotic thunderstorm bound to produce a tornado of mass destruction.

My provoking attitude of vengeance followed me right out into the kitchen as I made myself my usual morning coffee with extra sweetener. The sugary taste got rid of the bitterness inside of me and the warmth fell through my body. The caffeinated kick made me forget the two men corrupting every thought for all of one minute before I heard my doorbell ring.

I wasn't expecting any company, and my eyes flew toward the window. My mind reeled as I set my coffee down on the countertop and I peered out the big window. Rain trickled down the glass as the gloomy day made it harder to see my front porch. I could barely make out the figure of a man dressed in black with a hood draped over his head and his back turned toward me. I couldn't glimpse his face, but it was bound to be a delivery.

What the hell had Sebastian ordered from Amazon now?

The doorbell rang again, and I huffed, "I'm coming!"

This dickhead was persistent. A nuisance I wanted to go away so I could get on with my day and get my errands done. Everything had to be in order for Sebastian's return home or I'd deal with his fury from my disorganization.

The doorbell rang repeatedly as I hurried toward the front door, pulled at the doorknob, and plastered a smile on my face. When all I wanted to do was whack the wooden door right in his face. Catch the asshole by surprise, make him learn a lesson and suffer the consequences of his annoying behavior. A nosebleed would suffice for him—

"Good morning, Liv." Sin interrupted my overactive imagination and stood with his body leaning against the doorframe.

"Sin?" I gasped with surprise, and my eyes darted to Saint strolling up behind him.

I panicked. My instant reaction was to lock them out. I closed the door with all of my strength, only to be disappointed when it didn't slam shut.

Sin held the door open with his large hand and tsked, "Not so fast."

I held the handle in my grasp as Sin towered over me with his black hood on. Raindrops dripped off the fabric. He was soaked, and the water from the storm formed a puddle at my feet. He was cold, calculated, and in total control. His hot breath fanned against my face while his dark eyes fired with annoyance, and I shivered in his presence. Not from the chill coming in from outside, but from Sin. My extremely displeased phantom.

"What the fuck do you want?" I asked.

Another hand grabbed the door while my eyes widened, and Saint ripped the door handle from my grasp. The doorway flew open, and I took several steps back as Saint welcomed himself inside with a growl. But a rose pendant dangled from his hand.

Saint dripped raindrops further into the entryway as his blue eyes blazed at me as he held the same necklace I had hidden upstairs in my bedroom. He wore a leather jacket, not suited for the wet weather, but the bad boy image made him delicious. He ran a hand through his hair, water fell down his face and over his frustrated stare piercing into me.

I stumbled backward and hit a table behind me. The contents on the table wobbled, almost falling to the floor, and the sudden shift in my environment made me shake like an earthquake.

How the hell did they get the pendant?

Sin stepped through the door and stood beside Saint. Together, they held a solid front and blocked my way out. I could bolt for the stairs and barricade myself inside of a room, but I knew deep in the pit of my stomach they'd break the door down. I couldn't afford another lame explanation for Sebastian, which only led to another slap in my face. But I could clean up the damn mess they made from their muddy boots all over the floor.

Sin glared. "I thought we told you to never take this off?"

Sin pointed at their gift to me. The silver rose pendant of my doomed fate shimmered from the light in my house, and a lightning bolt flashed from behind their darkened figures. A sudden flicker from the loss of electricity made me jump from their wicked presence. A sight straight out of a horror film as thunder clapped. I should make a run for it, but I stood my ground.

"How did you get in?" I questioned them with a glare.

"You left your window open, sweetheart," Sin answered simply.

The realization hit me in full force, and I wanted to scream at them. I wanted to tell them to get out and never come back. To take their damn gift, rip the chain in two, and shove it up their asses.

Sin and Saint had invaded my home and strolled right in like they ruled the place. Broke into my place of privacy while I thought I was alone and acted as if they owned me. Staked their claim on me and wanted me to put their goddamn necklace back on.

No way.

I didn't recall leaving any windows open. The forecast had called for rain, and I wouldn't want to let in a draft. I'd never leave a window cracked with these two maniacs on the loose and stalking me twenty-four seven.

"No, I didn't. You're full of shit," I snapped.

Suddenly, both men reacted and stepped forward with two large equal thumps. In full unison, they worked a gasp of surprise from me, and my fear encouraged them to close the distance between us.

"Want to make a bet?" Sin challenged with a wicked smirk, his whiskey breath hot on my face.

Their cedarwood scent mixed and entangled me in their heat. The delicious looks from them made me wet and my thighs clamped together in remembrance of their madness. My body desired them to be this close to me, but my mind fought the urge to give in. A full out war raged inside of me, and I didn't know who'd win the battle.

"No. Because I will lose," I admitted.

"Did you hear that, Saint?" Sin asked as he licked his lips and peered over my body. "Our girl is learning."

Saint groaned as he grabbed the back of my neck and forcefully jerked my head to stare up at him. I let out a yelp and held his stare. His grip was tight against my scalp and he pulled at the hairs at the nape of my neck. The pain bit at me, but I refused to cry. Instead, I pressed my lips together and panted through flared nostrils.

Saint was like a caveman, holding the necklace up to my face. He grunted at me and gestured toward the chain with urgency. I didn't react. He didn't appreciate the lack of response and yanked me closer. His eyes glared into my wide ones until I took the necklace from his hand. A zing of electricity from the brush of our fingers coursed through me, and I didn't give a damn if he felt it, too. The touch meant nothing, and he sickened me to my core.

I'd give Saint what he wanted. I'd give them both what they desired and had broken into my home for—this stupid chain around my neck. Instead, I should pick up the phone and call the cops to arrest them for breaking and entering.

"Fine. I'll put your dumb necklace back on," I muttered with disgust.

"Turn around," Sin ordered.

I huffed with frustration but did as he commanded. My backside was to them as I felt fingers in my hair and a shiver ran down my spine. I wasn't sure whose hands held my hair, but they did it with care as their precious chain returned to its rightful owner.

I dared a glance back and asked, "Why are you doing this to me?"

Sin brushed hair behind my ear and whispered, "Because we're both fucked up. Broken, shattered like glass, and no one can break us because we're already broken."

"That's a screwed-up analogy."

Sin chuckled softly against my ear, and his fingertip trailed along the skin, straight down to my earlobe where he gently flicked the flesh, and my pussy pulsated for him. I despised him so damn much.

"But our little obsession breaks, too. We're all cracked pieces wanting to be put back together in this fucked-up world. A cruel, damaged place where evil can be just outside your door. Watching and waiting. Hooked to the one thing that can put us all back together. You," Sin added.

"I can't save you," I breathed as I jerked against their hold and turned away from Sin, but Saint's body was right up against me. "You are both too far gone for redemption."

"We don't need you to save us, Liv. You're our missing piece," Sin said huskily as his hand traveled down to my neck and touched the pendant between my cleavage. "A shard we've been searching for and we'll do anything to keep. You could cut us and make us bleed, but we'd never leave your side. We are yours forever, and we'll make you see this all in time."

"You both are fucking crazy," I said as I clenched the table ledge and it dug into my thighs. "I'll never be yours. I can't stand you. Hell, I don't even like either of you."

"Well, we sure as hell like you, Liv," Sin groaned as he grabbed my hand and forced me to touch his erect cock hidden in his pants. "When we find something we like, we want it. No matter how much we shouldn't take it, it's ours."

A rumbling moan climbed up my throat, and I wanted to clamp my mouth shut before it escaped, but I was too late. The sound had no business having a mind of its own, and I hated everything about this.

Sin's firm dick against my hand made my pussy wetter than it ever should be, as he rubbed my palm up and down his massive shaft. I should grab his crotch and twist, producing pain instead of desired satisfaction. But I wouldn't stand a chance.

Sin was cruel with his punishments, and I knew this firsthand. With Saint right on my tail, there was nowhere to go and no place to hide. This was a discipline all its own.

"I'm. Not. Yours," I argued with extra emphasis on each word as beads of sweat formed on my forehead, and I fought them from within.

Saint's dick rubbed against my butt cheeks and the friction of him made me delirious. The smell of our arousals mixed and created a thick fog over the room. Forced passion and the smell of rainfall lingered within my nostrils. Nature versus desire created a dizzy swirl over me, but I clenched the table harder to hold myself steady. Weakness wasn't an option. I had to maintain some kind of control and couldn't give in.

"Oh, but you smell like you are, and your pussy is our plaything. A toy we shouldn't amuse ourselves with because we're told not to. But we tend to not listen," Sin breathed with a soft chuckle in my ear. "And we enjoy winding you up."

Twenty

Their Obsession

Liv

Saint's hands brushed down the sides of my body. He started at my shoulders with a gentle caress as he made his way down over the sides of my breasts, lingered on my waist until he bit his fingers into my hips. The force pushed me down while he groaned in my ear and pressed my most sensitive area against the pointed corner of the table.

"What the fuck are you doing, Saint?" I questioned in panic. "Please let me go."

My pleas went unanswered because Saint didn't speak a word. His breath only panted in my ear as he moved my hips back and forth, while the friction against my clit formed an achy pit in my belly. A coil of lust spasmed inside me and wanted to break free. He wanted to own me again and make me come. All within twenty-four hours.

"We can make you come anywhere at any time," Sin answered me when Saint wouldn't. "Don't underestimate us because the moment that you do, we'll have your pussy dripping for us."

Sin was right. I was soaked, hot for them both, even when I hated them. I was bothered that they could make me react this way and force me to the realization that they owned me.

They watched me, blackmailed me, and wanted me. Followed me with a passion and possessed me, but they would never have my soul. They'd never own my heart.

"You're both fucking psycho assholes and can burn—" I couldn't finish my sentence as a feral moan escaped my mouth.

Saint roughly pressed me into the pointed corner, causing pain, but a blissful heat chased after, and I gyrated against the point. The quick shift made me grab Sin's cock and he let out a husky grunt. The sound had my eyes rolling as my head laid back into Saint, and his firm chest muscles welcomed me. His body fit perfectly with mine and I cursed him for it.

I bit my lip until I tasted blood and knew I couldn't let them do this to me again. I couldn't let them make me come. Every part of me urged me to let go, but they pried away this sexual heat from me once more.

Sin growled, "You'll burn right with us, Liv."

My hips thrust faster, causing the contents on the table to tumble over and fall to the floor. I peered straight ahead, but that was a grave mistake. I noticed my reflection in a forgotten mirror, and my eyes burned with lust. Behind me, Saint watched me, his dark indigo eyes transfixed on my body as mine followed his gaze down to my bouncing tits. Each time I gyrated against the corner of the table, my entire body jerked, and I bit my lip harder, desperately trying to conceal any sound from escaping.

"Fuck," Saint groaned as he let go of my hips and worked his way up to my tits.

Saint's enormous hands cupped my plump rack, and I sizzled at his touch. My erect buds pointed against my crop top and Saint pinched each nipple between his fingers. He pulled at them until the motion was painful and I cried out. Which only made him enjoy me more, and I circled the pointed edge faster to override the pain.

"Fuck. You," I panted out each word and stared into Saint's eyes.

Saint only smirked and pressed his cock further into my ass. His dick was huge. He throbbed against me with each wave of my behind, and the grinding only made him harder—solid as a rock, the same as Sin's rigid dick still in my hand.

"Now, Liv, don't get nasty. Our girl has been doing such a good job," Sin praised against my ear as my eyes shot to his.

My pussy trembled with a fiery need and evil stared me right in the face. His dark eyes swirled with lust as he licked up my ear and sucked my earlobe into his mouth. Only to bite down and give me more pain, which I masked by producing more pleasure. Saint noted my need to hold back and only squeezed my tits tighter, causing a scream to tear from my lips. The cry was half muffled, half wild.

I was untamed, lost in their monstrosity and unable to escape.

"Fuck. Don't do this, please..." I begged as I panted and felt my release right at the edge.

Any moment now, I'd tumble over and fall to my death. Another part of me would break off for them to steal when I desperately tried to keep them from taking another piece. It would be just another shard of me they'd own as they collected every bit to make us whole.

Sin popped my earlobe from his mouth. "You don't want to come? To feel everything we do every single time we look at you?"

"I don't want to feel anything for either of you." I glared at him as I fought my body and slowed my gyrating pace.

"Wrong answer," Sin growled as he grabbed my hip closest to him and pressed my clit further into the pointed edge.

"Oh, fuck!" I cried out as pain bit into my sensitive area and the sensation stung, but he soothed the hurt with each harsh thrust of my hips.

I closed my eyes, unable to gaze at the men who brought me so much pleasure mixed with pain, and pressed my lips together. My climax built higher and higher. Saint let go of my tits and helped Sin bring me into agonizing bliss. Together, they rode each wave with me until my entire body spasmed with a force I'd never forget, and I fell over the edge.

A feral scream left me as I took over and rocked against the table, banging into the wall. My pussy walls clenched tightly, and my release roared through me. But no one caught me as I fell to my death.

My phantom's had vanished all within the blink of an eye.

No one held my hips, no muscular man was up against me, and no cock was there for me to clench. I was alone, riding out my orgasm against a table I was sure Sebastian had bought for himself. My juices spilled onto the corner. The crotch of my jeans was all wet as I panted and came down from the high and there was nothing but utter doom.

Damn them.

I opened my eyes to see my flushed face staring back at me and my door wide open. Quickly, I stepped back from the destruction created by the two lunatics—the insane men who wanted me to see I was theirs.

Sin and Saint owned my body, this much was true. But my soul was under lock and key. There was no way for them to gain access to my racing heart. I loathed them with every fiber of my being, and that'd be the only thing I'd ever feel for them.

I hurried to the door as fast as my wobbly legs would carry me and slammed it shut. My heart pounded in my ears, and I cursed them for ever getting inside and leaving me feeling this way. I radiated with pent up sexual tension even though my body had claimed its release. My body couldn't get enough of Sin or Saint when my mind wanted nothing to do with them.

I sighed regretfully with frustration, locked the door, and made my way around the main floor of my condo to check all the windows. They were all locked up tight. Not a single one was open. I raced up the stairs two steps at a time, and I checked all the windows. But only found one of them was wide open.

My bedroom window.

I closed the window with a hard thud and checked the lock to ensure it wasn't broken. Only rain had seeped its way inside through the screen and made a mess on the windowsill. The mechanism was in pristine condition, and I retraced my steps from the morning in my mind.

I cleaned up the unwanted rainwater and mopped up the muddy puddles those assholes left. The contents on the table I neatly organized, and I prayed Sebastian wouldn't notice the wet stain left by me. Thinking back on my morning, I could've sworn I'd left the window locked and had never opened it.

Or was I losing my mind?

My phantoms must be rubbing off on me.

Twenty-One
Her Phantom

Sin

Liv had no idea we could see her. We watched our little obsession and every move she made. We weren't hidden in the shadows or lurking behind those damn trees by her place. We were right up close and personal, dangling from her necklace.

Our feisty one had put up quite a fight, which made her release painful, but she was the one to blame. She still kept herself from us, hiding inside a shell we desperately needed to crack open and crawl inside. Liv only made us force our way in, and we had to make her hurt to bring her toward her truth.

She wanted us. Our little obsession needed us. Just as much as we desired her.

Liv's pain brought her pleasure. An agony we were more than willing to soothe. But if I was being honest,

I'd drown in her pain because it brought her that much closer to bliss.

The car ride back to the club was tense while our dicks were fully rock hard. The sensation hurt a lot and blue balls were dropping over the horizon. My balls were tight up against me and the friction made me wince in agony, but everything was worth it for our girl. Christ, the moans from her almost had me coming in my pants, and if it wasn't for our quick departure, my come would be seeping through my zipper.

Saint had argued with me for a hot minute before I won and hid away inside an enclosed spot. I watched Liv from a screen inside of our club while she retouched her makeup. She reapplied red lipstick we had successfully ruined from her biting her damn lip. I only lasted a whole two minutes before I came all over her sweet as fuck face. My jiz leaked down and made her look like she had shed some tears. Waterworks I'd love to see tear up in real time with my cock gagging her from deep inside her tight throat.

Fuck. I couldn't wait to do it for real. To see Liv open her pretty mouth for me. She'd stick out her tongue and let me jerk off onto her sweet taste buds. My ejaculation would be the death of me. But I'd rise from the dead for her, just to do it all over again.

"Hurry the fuck up, Sin. My balls are busting out here!" Saint hollered at me from behind the door.

"Yeah, yeah. I'm all done. Fuck. Anxious much?" I yelled back as I wiped up my mess and watched her take off her top.

Fuck me. Of course, Saint gets to watch the good stuff.

Saint hurried inside, grabbed me by the shoulders, and he heaved me out of the room. I only caught a glimpse of those sweet-ass perky tits before he slammed the door in my face. *Goddamn it.*

"Enjoy the show, asshole!" I huffed through the door and only heard Saint grunt.

Fucking asshole got to bury his face in Liv's pussy and now he gets to watch her undress? Jesus, was I down on my luck. But all in good time. I'd get my shot.

Besides, Saint did all the work while I sat back and watched. The thrill of the chase was what I loved. I enjoyed watching our girl squirm and be disobedient as fuck. Liv Valencia was our dream come true, and we'd share her for the rest of our lives. We had to make her realize it, bend her to our will, and she'd see the light, shimmering off my come caked on her wicked wet tongue.

Shit. There goes my cock again.

Suddenly, the door opened as Saint zipped up his trousers, and he wiped the sweat beads off his forehead with the back of his hand. The perspiration had built up from his need to get off all over our girl's tits. Another place I desired to come all over as my balls grew tighter, and I got the urge to jerk off again.

"Sin, man, you've got to see this," Saint said as he stepped aside, and my eyes left his.

"Finally. What the fuck took—" but I ate my words as I saw Sebastian's face on the screen.

No longer was I greeted with the pleasure of our obsession, but a man I solely despised. Sebastian Chamberlain was a fit-looking motherfucker who I'd love to sink my fist into. He'd earn the beating all because he was with our girl. He didn't deserve her, and we did. We could give her the world and bring everyone to their knees, including this greasy bastard.

"What the fuck is that?" Sebastian questioned Liv as he pointed toward the camera hidden against her chest.

"He better not fucking touch it," Saint huffed with hatred.

"He better not fucking touch *her*," I seethed through clenched teeth.

Liv was ours. If he so much as laid a hand on her, he was dead. Sebastian, our dear investor, was her fiancé, but she was our future. Our everything. We...

Slap

He fucking hit her. Right in the face. All I could see was red with rage as my blood boiled to an erupting point, and I was ready to fly off the handle.

He. Fucking. Slapped. Our. Girl.

"Goddamn bastard," Saint growled.

Saint felt my pain. The rage within us rose, and I was ready to grab the television screen and throw it against the two-way glass. But what good would that do? We weren't willing to lose sight of the one woman most precious to us.

"He's abusing her," I breathed through clenched teeth.

I punched the mirror with an angry grunt and shards of glass fell to the floor. The pain numbed itself, masked by my hatred of this man—a person I could slice open with a piece of glass and watch him pass out, but my knuckles bled instead.

Saint held his composure, but his fists clenched, and I saw blood seep from between his fingers with his nails digging into his skin. The crimson color trickled to the floor, and we'd left a mess. But not as messy as Sebastian Chamberlain's face was going to be after we were done with him.

I felt Liv's pain as she explained, "I bought this for you because I thought you'd like it?"

A big fat fucking lie, but that was our girl. Liv held her head high after Sebastian had struck her to the side. She stumbled. The camera went blurry, but she didn't stand down. She didn't cower at his feet, and she didn't even beg him to stop.

"Like it? I hate it!" Sebastian yelled at Liv and threw his arms up in the air. "Why would you waste my money on that?"

Sebastian spit at her and cursed as he turned away. Sebastian left her like used garbage, even though she was everything this world needed. All the pieces of her made the darkness brighter, and she was worth it. Worthy enough of respect. Not this scum of the earth who deserved everything he had coming.

As Liv walked into the bathroom and her mirrored teary-eyed reflection stared back at us, we knew we had to stop him. We had to end the abuse her fiancé inflicted on her behind our backs and kept it secret from the world. Sebastian was evil, more vile than us, and we'd make him beg to meet our maker. Satan. The devil who created us.

Because no one touched our girl. No one would make her feel pain. Only us.

Sebastian, your clock was ticking. Ticktock, ticktock. The poor man could be in the wrong place at the wrong time. An unfortunate incident of breaking and entering would suffice. It was only a matter of time before he met his untimely demise.

Twenty-Two

Their Obsession

Liv

Shit...

I spilled my coffee all over my outfit!

This day wasn't going my way. Sebastian had unexpectedly taken the day off work after a business trip, and I'd rather not be home while he was. But the last week without him had been bliss.

No name calling directed my way, not one hand laid on me, and my stalkers had even gone quiet. I almost wondered if they were arrested for harassing someone else—I wouldn't be surprised. I was sure they could afford bail. Maybe they had unfortunately died and I had gotten my wish, but I highly doubted it.

What the hell were they up to?

I had quickly gathered my purse and dashed out of the house before Sebastian could wonder where I was off to. I hadn't even known where I was going, just that it had to be anywhere other than home. Yet here I was, headed back because of my stupidity.

I had ordered my favorite, a coffee with extra sweetener. After a losing fight with the door on my way out of the shop, the morning brew had splashed all over my dress. I barely got a sip because the coffee was burning hot. Clearly, I wanted to wear the caffeinated drink instead. My skin crawled with anxiety as I turned my key in the door and pushed it open. Bugs felt like they inched all over me, and I gave myself a mental shake. I'd only be ten minutes tops, and I'd be gone like the wind. But I wished I could climb through the bedroom window instead of walking right into the devil's den.

Sebastian was nowhere in sight as I tiptoed toward the stairs to avoid him at all costs. Heat started at my toes and worked its way up my body as I hit the stairs, but I heard a rustle from the kitchen. Papers moved and the damn stair creaked below my feet, causing me to halt on the spot.

I knew the fucking creaky floorboard was there because I had them all memorized throughout the place. I had to live with a man as dangerous as my fiancé inside a home where I should be safe, but I never was. Not as long as I lived under a roof with a man I despised.

Beads of sweat formed on my forehead, and I cursed myself for even coming back. I should've bought a brand-new outfit and tossed this one in the trash. I would have saved myself from the awful position I had gotten myself into and had no way out of except to haul ass.

I held my breath as I heard footsteps and knew Sebastian would be around the corner any second. Quickly, I tiptoed up the stairs in a flash. This time, without making a sound, managing to avoid him.

How?

I'd never know. All that mattered was I had made it. He didn't know I was inside, and I'd be out in a flash.

Once I tucked myself away behind my bedroom door, I blew out the breath I had concealed. I kept the door unlocked in case Sebastian came in, and I'd make up some excuse for my return home. But I prayed he wouldn't step foot up here.

When Sebastian took his days off, he'd get plastered off scotch, laze around, eat junk food, and do whatever the hell he wanted. I even had to prepare supper for his lazy ass! He'd only come upstairs when he was ready to pass out drunk in bed.

Once I caught him watching porn from his laptop at the dinner table while I made his favorite meal and he jerked off. I wasn't expecting to see such a disgusting sight, and I wanted to throw up the bile collected in my throat right into his meal. He had ordered me to get the fuck out as he was about to come and his come had spilled into his hand.

Sebastian had lunged at me out of rage, knocking over his chair, and he'd made sure I never did it again. My face had earned a smack with his sticky semen-smeared hand. It was a moment I wouldn't soon forget, and I'd never make the mistake again.

I took off my overcoat and placed it on the bed along with my purse as I walked toward the bathroom. I pulled my dress up over my head and closed the door behind me. The more barriers between me and the monster downstairs, the better. I ran the tap on low, very hopeful he wouldn't hear the running water, and cleaned my stomach with soapy water. I cleansed myself of the coffee smell and felt less sticky.

There. Much better. Now, to get out of the bathroom. I had to find something else to wear. I'd be on my way in no time and Sebastian wouldn't have a...

A hand covered my mouth as I came out of the door, muffling my scream, and I clawed at the arm to free myself. My fingernails scratched but my attacker held on tight as my eyes went wide and my body filled with fright. I kicked out my legs as my attacker pushed me upward off the floor, but a force knocked me forward and we fell straight onto the bed. I feared the person above me was Sebastian until a cedarwood mixed with whiskey scent filled my nose.

Mr. Cruz.

"Mm… I love the feeling of you trapped underneath me, Liv," Sin whispered in my ear as he placed a leg between my thighs and forced my knees to bend. "Caught by your phantom and completely at my mercy."

I couldn't move even if I wanted to with my legs tucked up underneath me and his heavy weight on top of me. All in one day, my worst nightmares were back. Sebastian, Sin, and Saint. Saint, I gathered, wouldn't be too far behind. But I couldn't decide which one was the greatest night terror of them all.

A noise came from near the window, and sure enough, I watched Saint climb through. I crowbar in his hand and the realization dawned on me. They had pried the window open and broken in!

Fuckers!

Anger pulsated through me, my nostrils flared, and a quiver ran through me when Sin moved my hair out of my face. Saint's eyes landed on me, and they changed from darkness to lust within a second. He wandered over toward the bed and my eyes couldn't help themselves as they landed right on the crotch of his black jeans. My eyes widened at the sight of the large bulge constricted behind his zipper, and I swallowed the hard lump in my throat. The sight of me aroused Saint, and Sin was no different.

I felt the massive size of him pressed up between the crevice of my ass. My pussy throbbed, and I whimpered as Sin rubbed his dick against me. The G-string thong was no match for the sinful ways of Mr. Sin Cruz.

Why did I bother coming home?

"Do you promise to be quiet if I remove my hand, little obsession?" Sin asked in a hoarse whisper.

I simply nodded. There was no point in screaming. There was nowhere to run and hide. I found myself trapped in my bedroom with two obsessive and unhinged men, ready to do whatever they wanted with me. Bend me to their will, force me to crawl to them, and break me all over again. They could have their way with me because they were in control and Sebastian wouldn't save me. He'd feed me to the wolves. He was far worse than my unhinged phantoms.

Sin drifted his hand away and whispered, "Good girl," when I didn't make a sound. Instead, I laid there until he lifted his weight off me and I scurried off of the bed. Far away from the madmen who had broken in.

"What the fuck?" I asked in a breathy, low tone. "Is stalking not enough for you? Now you're breaking into my place?"

Sin ambled his way around the bed with Saint close behind him as my tits bounced from unsteady breaths. The lacy bra I wore matched my thong, and their eyes never left me. Deep blue and extra dark eyes roamed over my spilled cleavage, over every curved inch of skin, and back up to my plump, wet lips. They devoured me, ate me up in one whole bite, but wouldn't swallow me. They'd savor my taste for the rest of their lives.

"We aren't here for you, sweetheart. You're not supposed to be home," Sin answered as he stood in front of me and Saint joined him at his side.

"I was out to get a coffee at the café, and it spilled all over my dress. And..." I confessed as I realized I was rambling, but it wasn't any of their damn business and I shook my head. "Wait a minute. If you're not here for me then—"

"We're here for your fiancé..." Sin interrupted with a smirk. "But if we would've known we'd find you here wearing this... Well, we would've come a lot sooner."

"Sebastian?" I breathed quietly with a soft giggle. "He's not worth breaking the law for."

"It's worth it for you," Sin responded with a glint of anger in his stare. "He hurt you."

They knew? Of course, they knew Sebastian abused me. They watch me night and day, for Christ's sake!

Suddenly, I felt exposed. My arms crossed over my skin to hide the shame I felt from them knowing the truth. No one else knew of the abuse I had dealt with for so long. Not one person could put a stop to Sebastian when he was at his worst, and I could not defend myself. There was no point in protecting myself against a man who had all the power because the next beating would be far worse. He'd make sure of it.

The humiliation was unbearable. I trembled under their prying stares and the walls were closing in on me. But they were no better than Sebastian.

They had forced themselves on me, made me do unforgivable things against my will. These monsters had blackmailed me into their arms when all I wanted to do was hide from them. Their darkness had consumed me and added to all the mortification.

I shrugged my shoulders and snapped, "So? You two are no better than him."

Sin moved in the blink of an eye, and his hands were on either side of my face. He squeezed my head tight within his hold, and my cheeks pressed together as my lips puckered, leaving them to be used at his disposal. He stuck out his tongue and licked my bottom lip straight to the top one.

"Stop it," I muttered. "You're hurting me."

"But we bring you fulfillment," Sin explained as his eyes bored into mine. "That's the difference between us and him. We love to bring you pain but bask in your bliss. Sebastian only hurts you, and we're here to kill him for it."

Twenty-Three

Their Obsession

Liv

"Kill him?" I whispered in disbelief.

"Yes, Liv. We won't stand for *anyone* causing you harm," Sin admitted and let me go.

The twinge of pain subsided as I rubbed my cheeks and stumbled backward—further away from the torment they brought me until my backside hit the wall. A small gasp escaped me when I realized there was nowhere to go. No place to hide with Sin and Saint towering over me as I cowered in a corner. I was on high alert because Sebastian was in the house and my ghosts cornered me. He couldn't find out; he couldn't learn my secrets, and I'd be damned if these two idiots ruined everything for me.

"You can't kill him," I whispered.

"And why the hell not?" Sin asked with a low groan as he clenched his fists at his sides. "No one touches you but us."

"You didn't seem to have a problem with it before? Why start now?" I asked as I tilted up my chin with sass.

Saint gave a grunt of frustration and Sin breathed, "Point taken."

"Yep," I whispered with a pop of the *P* and nodded toward the window. "Now you can both leave and not let the window hit you on the way out."

"No can do, sweetheart..." Sin disagreed as he shook his head and nodded toward me. "But you can turn a blind eye to what we're about to do and let us take care of him. Then you'll be free of that scum forever."

As much as I wanted my dirtbag of a fiancé dead, I needed him alive even more. The Chamberlain name was my family's way out of ruin. Our marriage was the key to saving everything, not his demise. Even though he wholeheartedly deserved these two lunatics beating his ass to a pulp and slitting his throat for everything he had put me through. All the sleepless nights, strikes to my body, and invisible scars on my heart.

"No, I need him alive," I breathed adamantly.

Sin growled. "But he deserves to die."

The only way to get through to these two made me want to dive into the cold ocean. Let hypothermia set in and numb my body until I couldn't feel a damn thing. Until I didn't have a need to touch them.

Electricity zinged through me when both of my hands reached out and touched the men who had taken so much from me. They had stolen pieces of my humanity that I would never regain, and they held them captive forever. Their demeanors softened as my hands caressed their cheeks, one jagged with a scar and the other prickly with stubble. Their groans of need filled my ears—they'd howl at the moon like wolves would if they could. They were dead set on feasting on their prey, little old me, who tamed them with my touch. I provided contact they had never expected of me, but longed for, and I had caught them off guard.

"Sebastian *needs* to stay alive. Understood?" I pressed.

"Mm..." Sin moaned as his eyes fluttered closed, and he turned his head to look at Saint.

His best friend met his gaze, and they silently agreed as they peered back at me. The softness left them, and they were back to their old creepy-ass selves. Their stares hardened and their eyes blazed full of lust. A needy greed they shared for me, and I shivered under the fiery blast of heat.

"Understood. But we don't like it one bit," Sin whispered through clenched teeth.

"I don't care if you don't fucking like it. This is my life, not yours," I whispered with frustration and removed my hands from their faces.

Instantly, Sin and Saint grabbed my wrists, and pulled me up against them. They wouldn't release me, as their fingers squeezed harder to tame my disobedience. My heart raced in my ribcage and the noise filled my ears. They wouldn't let me go, no matter how hard I tried to escape.

"And your life means everything to us. From this beautiful, intelligent brain of yours..." Sin shot back as he tapped my head and slid his hand downward. "Right down to your fucking slit."

A gasp escaped me as Sin slapped my clit, and Saint harshly pulled me forward and wrapped his hand around my throat, moving his body flush against my backside. I struggled in his firm embrace, but it was no use. I couldn't break free.

"Let me go, asshole," I said through clamped teeth.

"No can do, Liv..." Sin said as he tilted his chin downward, his eyes blazed and a wicked smirk spread across his lips. "Looks like our plans have changed."

Sin trailed his fingers up my bare navel, and he drew sweet circles. My skin prickled with goosebumps, and my body's reaction to his touch made him sigh with pleasure. Saint tightened his grip around my neck, restricting my airway, and I wiggled to break free. My attempt only made him groan and squeeze tighter until my bulgy eyes teared up with the need to breathe.

"Fuck, Liv, you're so beautiful when you shed drops of pleasure," Sin whispered as he wiped the tears from my cheeks and licked them away. "I can't wait to see those tears release while you gag on my cock."

Fingers traveled down my cleavage, peeking out of my bra, and Sin slapped my tits. A constricted yelp flew out of me as the pain stung, but he replaced the wince with pleasure from his demanding tongue. His wetness lapped over one breast and then the other. A torturous ache formed in my belly and coiled tight. Saint loosened his grip, and I gasped for air.

I choked out, "What are you doing? Release me."

My chest heaved into Sin's face as he took full delight in the situation, his breath hot over the inches of flesh he had already discovered. A quiver ran through me like an earthquake, and my legs trembled as Saint breathed heavily from behind me.

No one listened, too lost in their own desirous torment of me. I lashed out again, grabbing Sin's hair and pulling at the roots. My pushback only tugged his face off my tits for a split second, and he dove right back in. An evil laugh vibrated against my skin as his lips skittered back on the path they had chosen and the ache in me grew wild. But he stopped right above my nipple.

"I'm going to mark you as ours," Sin said right before he bit into my flesh.

Twenty-Four

Their Obsession

Liv

Without thinking, my back bucked against Saint and disgust mixed with lust, confusing my head. It was a natural reaction to pleasure, but in my mind, I knew the sensation was wrong. All vile and dark, and it made me as sick as them.

"Ours," Saint groaned from above, his breath hot over my ear.

Sin moaned against me while his teeth dug in, creating deep impressions, and his mouth sucked. He was drunk off me like I was a drink he couldn't get enough of. The suction subsided and his teeth let up, but they grazed over the wound he'd inflicted. A claim he was proud of, as my mouth opened, but only a silent yelp came out. Drowned by his tongue dancing over my flesh and he repeated it all over again to my other breast, streaking me with bite marks and hickeys all over my aching tits.

My hands scraped into his scalp and held on tight. My nails dug into his hair follicles and my fingers pulled his hair strands hard. The harder I yanked, the more marks he left. He bit me again and again, leaving bruises on my breasts.

A feral cry crept up my throat, and Saint sensed it. His other hand covered my mouth to hide my uncontrollable scream and the hand around my throat forced the air from me. A man with no remorse attacked my tits, leaving shameful blemishes, while his best friend forced me to shut up.

His buddy created a masterpiece for me to remember. A landscape of horror across my chest that I'd see for weeks, and anyone who tried to take me would run from the ugliness. My beauty was now embedded with sin.

Kill me.

Please, just do it and get this life over with. Squeeze me tighter until my eyes become bloodshot and terrified of the unknown. Let the light take me and lead me away from the darkness they had entrapped me in. Release me from this immorality.

As if they heard my plea to escape behind heaven's gates, they let up. Saint let go of my neck and Sin stopped his claim on me. Uncontrollable shivers rattled over my body and Sin's wet lips tracked over the path he'd left on me.

I panted against Saint's hand, and my nostrils flared as my vision became clear again. They could've killed me! I hated them so much.

"Assholes!" I breathed against Saint's hand.

Sin lifted his head from my chest, and his cheeks were flushed from being suffocated against my bust. My hands let go of his hair, and I took my chance as my hands clawed at his face. I was a ferocious cat, ready to gouge his eyes out and make him feel the pain he'd just given me. My nails connected with his cheek, and he didn't even flinch. I yelled with all my might, but Saint only pushed back and covered any sound.

"We like it when you fight back, Liv..." Sin growled as his face hardened. He glanced at Saint and he restrained my hands. "I think our little obsession should receive a punishment. Don't you think so, man?"

"Yes," Saint hissed in my ear.

Rather chatty today, aren't we Saint?

"Here. Hold her hands," Sin ordered as he angled my limbs backward and pain shot up my arms.

I winced from the bones being forced in the wrong direction, and I thrashed against their bonds, but I was no match for them. Sin grunted with frustration after he freed one of his hands and slapped my clit. My back arched at the pleasurable sting and made the fight in me come to a halt.

Saint bound my wrists together behind my back but kept me close with the heat from his body radiating off mine. Beads of sweat formed on my forehead as Sin rubbed my clit with two fingers against my thong. His face was inches from mine as his hot and bothered breath fanned my face, and I wanted to headbutt him—break his nose and make him bleed—but I had to focus on not letting my hips rock from his taunting tease.

So, I got mouthy with him instead.

"Not in a watchful mood today, are you, Sin?" I asked.

God, I should learn to keep my mouth shut. I only made the situation worse for myself, but these two assholes brought the worst out of me.

"No, I'm not. I want to play too," Sin answered and grabbed my hip bone.

Sin's fingers bit into my skin until I yelped, but he covered the noise with his mouth. His tongue dove in and blindsided me with a spark we ignited from our tongues' collision. An unexpected head-on crash that he had created. A horrific event I shouldn't want any part of, but our tongues licked and lapped. Lights blinded me behind closed eyes as time passed by and we revisited our accident all over again. A time loop, an illusion to the point of madness.

My moans and his grunts filled the room as my hips rocked against his fingers. His other hand was in my hair, providing gentle caresses while my body trembled. Sin had me blissfully shattered as I let him devour me and he left my lips bruised. I burned from our sinful friction until he tore his mouth away and reality hit me when Saint grabbed my ass cheek in a bruising hold. *Fuck.*

I was breathless, my eyes wide open. Unable to form a rational thought after an earth-shattering kiss that should've never happened. Another piece of me stolen by my phantom that I'd never get back.

Sin retreated.

His dark, blazing gaze of desire never wavered from mine, as his mind reeled as much as mine did. Our kiss was chaotic. A mixture of hatred, pleasure, and desperation. I hated him. I hated Sin so damn much.

"Cat got your tongue?" I asked because I couldn't shut the fuck up.

I had danced with the damn devil. Lived through the experience with my two left feet and one of them should go in my big fat mouth. My stupidity had won this dance-off.

"No. But you still need to learn with a punishment," he breathed as he reached behind him and pulled something out of his waistband.

A gun.

Twenty-Five

Their Obsession

Liv

My mouth fell agape with shock, and I whisper shouted, "You have a—!"

"Sh..." Sin shushed me as he held the weapon up to my trembling lips and silenced me. "The gun's for added measures."

Sin tapped the head of the gun off my lips while Saint ran his hand from my ass up to my tit. He trailed his nails all the way up and made my body quake with need, but I fought the desire coiled up inside of me. I tried to ignore the pent up frustration I didn't want to release, but my attackers were sure to antagonize me. Pressure me to erupt.

"Open. Up," Sin ordered out each word as he dragged the nozzle down my lower lip until I obeyed him. "Good girl."

"Shoot me, fucker. Blow my fucking—" Saint harshly squeezed my tit, and I shut up.

My mouth opened wide, and Sin pushed the gun inside. My teeth chattered against the nozzle of his weapon as my lips wrapped around it, and I was ready to die. Tears blurred my vision, but I didn't let them fall. These insane jerks didn't deserve them.

Snot leaked from my nose uncontrollably, and everything in me trembled. I had lost all hold on reality, and I was ready for everything to end. For this nightmare to go away and finally let them free me to heaven.

"Suck on it," Sin commanded.

My nostrils flared as Sin pushed the gun in more, and I involuntarily sucked on it. Slowly, he pushed it back and forth. The agony of the dire situation made me dizzy, and I'd have fallen over if Saint hadn't held me so damn close. A black haze fell over me until Sin released the gun from my mouth and trailed it down my chin. Leisurely, he ran it down my neck and toward my chest. The saliva caressed me in a torturous way and my heavy breaths heaved in and out of me.

"Sebastian's downstairs. He'll hear everything," I muttered out of utter panic.

Fully ready for Sin to fire a bullet into my chest.

"I don't care if he's there," Sin said.

The weapon didn't stop between my breasts as it traveled down to my stomach. The motion made me nauseous, and bile crept up into my throat. Projectile vomit was ready to explode, but I swallowed the hard lump back down.

I wouldn't die in my puke.

"One sound from that gun, and he'll call the cops," I whispered.

"Oh, trust me. My gun won't make a sound," Sin breathed as he leaned in and pushed the gun into my navel. "We'll have to keep you quiet. Won't we?"

The fucker touched my clit and rubbed until my lips parted. No sound came out as Sin kissed them and dropped the nozzle of his weapon lower. He'd bring me pleasure while ending my life. Fuck him.

But Sin replaced his hand with the barrel of his gun.

Sin kissed me and ate my moan as he pressed his weapon against the sensitive area. Saint forced his fingers underneath my bra and cupped my naked tit. He kneaded my nipple until the bud stung, and I flinched against his tease. My need coiled tighter inside of me as the tip of the gun slipped further and pushed between my thighs.

Sin's tongue flicked over mine, and he bit my lower lip. *Fuck.* He drew blood.

The metallic taste was inside of my mouth as he grabbed my lip between his teeth and let go, only to kiss me again. Feverishly and furiously, he attacked me, but I let him. Repeatedly, we spiraled further down where there was only us. Sin devouring me alive with his gun nearing insanely close to my entrance and Saint making me lose all rational thought, playing with my tit.

Sin pried his mouth from mine. "Fuck. Such a good little slut weeping all over the barrel of my gun."

"Please, please don't—"

"Don't what? Do this?" Sin interrupted as he removed the gun from my pussy and fired off a shot.

And wetness squirted at my clit.

"Oh—" my whimper cut short with his hand covering my mouth.

It's a fucking water gun! It looked just like a real gun!

Who the fuck does that? Who'd take a water gun and point blank threaten me with it? My crazy stalkers, that's who.

They had some nerve—

"Oh, fuck!" I whimpered into Sin's hand.

Sin unleashed more spurts of water, and the coolness mixed with my heat created a zinging blast of pleasure that buzzed through me. My thong was wet, but I soaked the G-string well before he got me wet.

Abruptly, Sin stopped his tormenting tease with the water gun and stepped back to peer at me. I quaked with spasms as Saint groaned in my ear and continued with his pleasure on my hard nipple. I couldn't believe that the skin didn't cut him, given how erect I was.

Sin Cruz loved to watch. His eyes were obsessing over me. He yearned to bring me painful bliss.

"Saint," Sin ordered as he gripped the bottom of my leg and hoisted it upward. "Grab her ankle."

"Please, no. I can't—"

"Sh...Yes you can, sweetheart." Sin shushed me with his gun back on my lips. "You can and you will stretch your world wide open for us."

The smell of my arousal mixed with his cedarwood scent clouded my judgment as Saint stretched my leg high and held me by my ankle. He forced my leg to bend at an uncomfortable angle, and I yelped, but Sin concealed the sound for me.

"You won't be needing these," Sin said as he ripped my panties wide open and they dangled from my pussy by a thread.

I trembled, my cunt bare and exposed to my unhinged phantom, ready to experience his sick game. A game I wanted no part of, but they forced me with my leg held high and fully spread wide.

"Please, I'm sorry, I—"

"Shut the fuck up, my slutty obsession!" Sin ordered against my face and puckered my lips together with the force of his hand. "Suck."

And I did.

I took the head of the water gun into my mouth, and I sucked it between my lips while Sin watched me. Saint pinched my nipple with satisfaction for my obedience and brought me some form of pleasure through the humiliation. In and out, he pushed the gun until its slickness pleased him. The squirt gun lowered back toward my pussy—to a place I didn't want it to go.

Sin stared me in the eyes as he squirted water at my clit, and he squeezed my puckered lips harder to keep me from releasing a blissful cry. Instead, I whimpered against my lips and shut my eyes as the tip of the gun slipped back over my clit. Repeatedly, rubbing the flesh until I was on the verge of climax and bright stars blinked in the darkness.

Abruptly, Sin stopped the tortuous friction and my eyes popped open. Only to catch him staring down at my exposed cunt, weeping for him. A big mistake on my part as he gazed back up at me and granted me a delicious, devilish grin. His hand loosened its hold against my lips, traced a finger down to my chin and titled my gaze downward.

"No," I snapped as I pulled my chin from his grasp and he only repeated the process.

Sin forced me to stare down at Saint touching my extremely sensitive tit and he demanded me to peer at his water gun as he squirted my clit again. I bit my lower lip until I tasted the wound Sin had inflicted on me, reopening it after he had bitten me. The blood was my sole focus to conceal the blissful torment he tried to take from me.

"Yes," Sin growled.

The sound was animalistic, loud and fierce, to the point I was frightened. Not by him, but by the man downstairs. Afraid he had heard Sin's call of the wild and would come charging up the stairs.

But Sebastian never came.

I exhaled the breath I had held in. A soft whimper came out as Sin glided the tip against my clit again. Over and over, he forced me higher—to an altitude I couldn't come down from unless he let me. I wasn't sure anymore if I ever wanted to come back down.

"Oh, fuck, please don't—" My words left me when I watched in horrific passion, as Sin pushed the fake weapon past my folds. The barrel of the gun buried inside of me, and it was enough to make me wither.

Twenty-Six

Their Obsession

Liv

Sin lingered with the gun between my walls as my eyes widened, and I tried to piece together what was happening to me. There was a toy water gun inside of me. My pussy liked the pleasure of it, but its exterior brought me pain. A combination that was hard to wrap my head around, but Sin didn't give me any more time to think.

He shot me.

This time, point blank inside as my body jerked from the stimulation and my eyes rolled back. My head followed as Sin let go of my chin, and I rested against Saint—the man, who wasn't an angel and who hid behind his dark mask as he held me close and my pussy clenched.

This situation became completely messed up. So fucking wrong on every level. Everything about this twisted pleasure had me hating myself more than I ever had before. Because... I liked it.

Sin pulled the gun out of me, but he didn't waste time and plunged it back inside. A deep wave of desire ran through me, and my mouth opened wide, with Saint kissing the sound I made away. His head bowed low to take me and bring me into his tormented home. A place I got lost in as his tongue swirled with mine, and I lashed back at his heat. Every bit of me wanted to fight him and stop him from making me spill my release. I'd do it and not let them take another piece of me, not let them steal what never should be taken in the first place. My dignity.

Sin killed me softly with his gun. The size of it stretched me more than I ever imagined possible, but Saint bruised me with his lips. A kiss so fierce, I cried out against his mouth as he sucked my bottom lip between his lips. The blissful pain blinded me as Sin worked the gun faster until he slowed the pace and forced Saint's mouth from mine.

"What did this teach you, Liv?" Sin asked hoarsely, and Saint gave a low rumble of disapproval toward Sin.

The sound was primal, like an angry bear not willing to share his prey. Sin wanted a piece of me as much as Saint. They wanted to share their meal until there was nothing of me left.

"That you are a cruel bastard," I sneered from trembling lips.

Sin pushed the gun in more until the tip hit my sweet spot and my heart beat in my ears. Repeatedly, he nudged to the hilt while a wild moan worked its way up and Saint captured my mouth again. He kissed me senseless while his hand cupped my tit, his thumb rubbing my nipple. This insanity had to end!

I pulled my mouth from Saint's and pleaded in a loud whisper, "Okay, okay, stop. Please!"

"No. Not until you learn not to disobey us."

"Fine. I won't try to gouge your eyes out," I whispered hurriedly as my climax grew, and I couldn't hold it back for much longer. "Happy now? Is that what you wanted to hear?"

"Yes," Sin hissed as he kept the gun inside of me and fired some water again.

"Oh..." I whimpered as I clamped my mouth shut to conceal my cry, and he pulled the squirt gun out, but left the tip in.

With an agonizing slowness, Sin moved the tip back and forth. The motion left me panting as my back arched and my eyes rolled. Saint licked at my mouth while Sin slapped my clit, and an overbearing tongue sheltered my yelp. He lapped over my mouth again and again like he couldn't get enough.

"Oh my God, please, fucking—" I was unable to finish as Sin's fingers vigorously rubbed my clit, causing me to come with two more pumps of the gun.

Everything exploded as an untamed scream tore me apart inside and my mouth covered Saint's. Uncontrollably, I kissed him, and he welcomed me inside. His tongue licked at each sound wave of wild bellows as they ripped through me, and my toes curled from the force of my release.

"Mm...Such a good slut with your tight pussy weeping all over the punishment that brought you pleasure," Sin whispered huskily in my ear. "It's fucking beautiful glistening with your come, isn't it?"

Sin kept the tip in while Saint bit at my cheek, but not bruising, unlike his best friend. I peered down at the weapon Sin had used on me and felt nothing but shame. I was still uncoiling from the aftershock of what they had done to me. But I was too numb to answer him.

"Well, Liv?" Sin asked again.

"It's insanity," I snapped and meant every word.

As true as my answer may be, it was the wrong one to voice. My opinion didn't matter, my voice didn't matter. I was a dumb bitch who seemed fearless.

"No, this isn't insane..." Sin breathed as he gave me a wild look and pulled the gun from me, tossing it on the bed. "You haven't seen madness yet, sweetheart."

"I don't care to, either," I snapped back.

Something altered in Sin's eyes and the wildness left, but this new awakening lingered. Madness swirled in his dark charcoal eyes as his pupils dilated and a new direction unfolded. The change in Sin sent a chill right down my spine.

"Let her go, man."

Immediately, Saint dropped his hand from my ankle. The loss of blood circulation had made my leg numb, and it fell to the floor with a thud. I couldn't stop the noise and prayed that Sebastian had the television on full blast.

Saint's hand fell from my ravished boob, and I pushed the cup of my bra back in place. They gave me space, but not as much as I was comfortable with. Both men stood tall over me, caging me in. Sandwiched between them with their raging boners from the orgasm they forced from me.

Again.

"Really?" I asked in a low whisper and pointed at the gun on my bed. "Now you let me go after you used that thing inside of me without my consent?"

"Yep," Sin answered as he popped the *P* and nodded his head.

"You fucking bastard." I glared with hatred at Sin and slouched down on the bed. "Get out."

Tears of rage bit at my eyes as I peered up at the men who continued to show me their worst, and I kept giving into them. They coerced me to the point I didn't recognize myself anymore. Without them, I was a battered woman trying to pick up the pieces, but with them, I was fearless. A woman who snapped back in the eyes of danger and was full of desires I never knew I had. These assholes kept the pieces they took from me and locked them tightly away in their broken world. A place they wanted me to join because I was theirs to keep. Forever.

What the hell was wrong with me?

"No," Saint whispered harshly.

"Yes," I snapped back.

Sin reached out and touched my face. The worst part? I didn't fight back. I let him.

The caress Sin granted me was gentle, it was almost sweet. A soft touch I couldn't deny after all the force he'd used on me. I almost craved this tender side of him, but it was awkward at the same time because I wasn't used to him this way. I had become used to his roughness; I'd grown accustomed to the sharp edges he had shown me. Not this lovable character who stared into my eyes and wanted to own my soul.

"But we aren't done with you yet," Sin whispered as his mouth turned up into a wicked grin, and the evil ass was back.

I flinched away from him and twisted around on the bed. Desperation fell over me as I pulled my knees up and tried to scurry to the other side of the room. Escape them and run toward the bathroom to lock myself inside. This was the ultimate plan. Create a barrier between us, praying they'd leave the same way they broke in. But my idea took a face plant.

My face met the mattress as Saint and Sin grabbed an ankle, pulling me back toward them. I fought, kicked, and I would've screamed if it wasn't for the damn man downstairs. My feet thrashed like a floppy fish coming out of the ocean as I tried to break free. The fins were my arms, wobbling in the sheets of endless waves as I pulled on them and tried to unchain myself from my captors. But I was too weak.

"No, no, let me go!" I whispered in a frightful shriek.

Sin only released a low laugh full of evil and said, "Keep it up, little obsession. We love it."

"No, fuck off, fu—" One of them slapped my bare ass. The pain smarted and made me eat my words.

"No way, sweetheart." Sin breathed heavily behind me and bit down on the back of my juicy thigh.

I bucked my back in response, squeaked into the bedsheet, and another slap met my behind. The sound was louder than the last, and I knew Sebastian had to have the television on full blast. There was no way he couldn't hear the sounds these two idiots made me create otherwise. Whether it be the strikes against my flesh or the moans they made from tormenting me.

Saint grabbed my hips and flipped me over on the bed. My legs continued to kick at them until the thrashing stopped from his firm grip, locked on each ankle. Sin reached down, grabbed a handful of my hair and yanked me until I sat in a seated position. I had no time to scream while my strands felt like they were being pulled from me. The harsh movement made my scalp throb in pain as Sin kneeled down beside me until he was at eye level with me. A crazed look was in his eyes as I watched the skull dangle from the black thread of his necklace. He glared at me for my disobedience, and I knew he wouldn't let me go soon.

"Liv, Liv, Liv..." Sin tsked and shook his head. "I promised you madness. Remember?"

I didn't answer him. Only stared into his eyes full of darkness, swirling with delight at my struggle and lusting over all the ways he'd make me experience pain. Because the pain brought me pleasure, and they lived to hurt me.

Sin yanked my hair and forced me to answer. "Yes."

"Do you know what our madness looks like?"

Christ. This asshole must love the sound of his voice. He never shut the fuck up!

"No. And I don't want to."

"You. Are. Going. To." He hissed out each word in my face and stood up as he pulled at his zipper. "Saint. Let's show her what real men are made of."

Twenty-Seven

Their Obsession

Liv

Panic took over me as I lashed out and clawed at the air. Desperately, I tried to gain back control while Sin wound my hair around his hand and freed his cock from its restriction. I fought with all I had until my eyes landed on his enormous shaft as his jeans hit the floor. He stepped out of them and kicked them to the side, but I couldn't believe the size of him.

His cock was giant! He wouldn't fit anywhere in me!

Next, the sound of Saint's zipper caught my attention, and Sin stroked his cock in his hand. Sin grunted with pleasure as he watched me react, and his sounds had my pussy drenched all over again. *Damn him.*

Disgust ran through me as Saint's dick sprang free, and my revulsion turned to admiration. Bewildered by the sight of his dick, which was as big as Sin's.

They must own a dick pump or had penis enlargement surgery. There was no way I had two crazed stalkers with giant dicks the size of ten-inch eggplants! I bet their flaccid cocks were the size of a typical man's erect cock.

I snorted. "This can't be natural."

I had a stupid fucking mouth on me. I was as bad as Sin. Unable to shut up.

"All natural, Liv," Sin answered as he yanked on my hair and inched my face closer to his mushroom head dick. "I told you we'd show you madness."

My mouth went dry at the sight of his tip. The width of the mushroom shape was huge, and the ridge curved smoothly over, connecting to his veiny shaft. The perfect hump to elevate a climax but bring pain with the ungodly size of him.

"Keep that fucking thing away from me." I glared, pressing my hands against his thighs and trying to push away from him.

Fuck! Sin could poke an eye out with that thing! He could screw my eye socket if he'd even fit.

"Shut up!" Sin roared as he harshly slapped his cock off my cheek. "I'm through with watching you and fully intent on keeping you quiet."

I yelped, but I bit my lip to conceal my surprise from his cruelty and blinked my eyes. As Sin laughed and slapped me a second time, I bit harder, causing a new spot to tear open on my lip, the taste salty and metallic. My pussy throbbed when it shouldn't have, and I clenched my thighs together as I tried to stop the ache awakening inside. My cheeks heated with embarrassment or arousal—which one, I wasn't sure anymore. They had a way of confusing me and making me hate myself even more.

"Let me go, ass—" my words departed as Sin pulled my hair toward him and cut me off.

My lips had nowhere to go but to ride up the long length of his girth. He rested my cheek against his torso and kept my hair tightly bound in his hand. I couldn't move. I had nowhere to go and couldn't open my mouth or else I'd bring him pleasure. The one thing he wanted from me, as my wide eyes watched as Saint stroked himself while watching us. His eyes hooded with lust as his chin tilted down and precum drizzled from the tip of his cock.

He was ready for me. They both were, and I had to make a split-second decision. I opened my mouth and bit down on Sin's dick.

"Oh. Fuck," Sin grunted out each word and let go of my hair as he grabbed the back of my neck. "Sweetheart. You can't wait for a taste of Daddy. Can you?"

Bad choice.

The white impression from my teeth only lasted a second before they disappeared, and the head of his dick jumped. The sick bastard enjoyed the bite I'd meant to inflict pain. I was hopeful my teeth would draw blood, and then I could make a run for it, but I had no such luck.

My decision only made everything worse as Sin gripped the back of my neck and made me gaze up at him. His dark eyes were fused with heat and desire, with the scar wrinkled on his cheek from his evil curled grin. His white shirt was unbuttoned as he stared down at me, and his gaze held a promise—a threat—to make me regret my choice because it had only made him want me even more.

I glared. "You disgust me."

"And you excite me," Sin shot back and shook my head till my vision turned fuzzy. "Now. Open up."

"No."

"I said..." Sin hissed and rocked me with each word. "Open. Up."

The bed creaked below me from the force, and my eyes crossed. My pressed lips loosened, and I opened them, giving in. I had little choice unless I wanted him to throw me around like a rag doll.

"Good girl. I want you all wet for me, Liv," Sin breathed as a trail of saliva slipped from his mouth and fell down into mine.

Without warning, Sin pushed me more into the bed with little time to react as he followed me and pounced on top of me. My backside pressed further into the mattress as my arms worked beneath me as I tried to get out from underneath him. But it was no use when my head hit the headboard.

Sin laughed. "Our little obsession thinks she can escape her shadow daddies?"

Saint grabbed my ankles from underneath Sin and pulled my body downward. A half shriek escaped me, but Saint cut the noise short when he maneuvered my face to be below Sin's dick that bobbed against my forehead, with his big balls dangling at my mouth. His crotch was inches from my face as he wasted no time and dipped his balls inside of my surprised mouth.

"No!" I squealed with my voice muffled by his giant nut sack.

The asshole tea bagged me!

Sin popped his tight balls out of my mouth right before I chomped down and bit him like a shark under attack. My jaws snapped at the air as Sin reacted fast and hopped over behind me while Saint flopped me over onto my stomach. The motion knocked the wind out of me, and I lost track of where my arms or legs were. But my phantoms knew and placed me in the position they desired: on my hands and knees, with Sin in front of me while Saint was at my ass, fully exposed to him as he had my legs spread apart and my pussy wide open. The hot smell of me wafted up into his face and made him groan.

I moved my hands and tried to shift my knees, but I couldn't budge. All I accomplished was my hands pulling at the unmoving bedsheets under Sin's weight. Saint held me trapped with his hands on my hips and his fingers dug into my skin. More bruises would form from the brutal force he inflicted as he backed my pussy further into him until I froze because the tip of his large mushroom head poked at my entrance.

"So, here's the plan, sweetheart," Sin said from above me as his wicked laugh filled my ears, and he continued to talk filthy to me. "We're going to stuff you full. I'm going to fill your pretty mouth, and Saint's going to get his dick wet in your tight slit."

"No! You are too fucking big!" I panicked in a high whisper with widened eyes. "You both won't fit!"

"Yes, we will, Liv. You were made for us." Sin encouraged me as he stroked my head and wouldn't listen to reason. "Your mouth and cunt will stretch to accommodate the shadows who worship you."

"I can't do it!"

"Don't worry. You can take us because you are our girl."

"No, please, I—"

"Sh..." Sin whispered as he forcefully yanked my chin, and I had to look up at him. "As much as I love to see you beg, I want to fill you full of our come even more."

"Wait—!" I shrieked, cut short with a dick-slap to the face.

"Such a defiant little slut. I thought I told you no more begging." Sin breathed heavily as he caressed his cock against my cheek and raised an eyebrow at me. "For now."

I rolled my eyes. "I know, I know. I disobeyed you. Blah, blah, blah."

"And now you're mouthing off?" Sin smirked and slapped me again with his dick, his precum slick against my skin. "I fucking love you, Liv."

"Me too," Saint said from behind me and slapped my ass cheek.

I whimpered, and my plump skin recoiled from the hit. My backside bucked as my fingers clenched into the sheets, and I bit my lip. All over again, pleasure pierced through me when it shouldn't. A shiver ran up my spine, and Sin met my eyes as he held my chin tighter until it hurt. Tears filled my eyes from the mix of anger, pain, and lust. A combination no one should have to feel, but here I was, stuck at their mercy while they were ready to stuff me like a turkey with no regards to my feelings or limitations.

"Once again, fuckers, this isn't love. I hate you for holding me against my will and making me do things

I'd never do," I snapped at them with the heated reminder.

"But you are, Liv. You're doing everything asked of you," Sin said as he placed the tip of his dick on my lips. "Stick out your tongue and lick me."

I shook my head with the tip of Sin grazing against me. My eyes squeezed tight as some tears escaped, and I hated myself for letting him see them. The beads of wetness fell to my mouth, pressed firmly together, and greeted his tip.

"Do it, darling," Saint voiced from behind me as he slapped me again and squeezed my flesh.

A muffled whimper escaped me, and I shuddered from the havoc Saint rained down on me. My ass was surely red after the harsh slaps he had left, and the area was sensitive. He didn't care as he grazed his fingers over the beaten skin and left me with his own bite mark.

"Mmm!" I cried out in pain as Saint claimed me, his teeth leaving a lasting impression.

Saint skirted his teeth over the blemish as more tears fell from my eyes, and I could see lighter movements behind my closed eyes. The sound of Sin's hand stroking his dick in front of me filled my ears, and he grabbed a handful of my hair. He aimed and was ready to dive in as soon as I opened my big mouth to let him inside.

Asshole.

The tears wouldn't stop falling as black mascara smeared and Saint bit me again. Repeatedly, he left impressions on my behind as I thrashed against him, and my ass jiggled in his hold. He loved to see me squirm as his dick pulsated against my slick slit and he growled with each chomp.

"Enough, Saint! You greedy fuck!" Sin ordered as he yanked my hair and pressed me further into his tip. "I want my fill too, man. Screw her so she'll open wide for me, and we can share her."

"In a minute, asshole," Saint huffed as his teeth scratched down my swollen skin and his dick left my entrance.

I exhaled through my nostrils in relief as they flared with each heavy breath and silently thanked Saint for finding the light. He'd stop this madness and let me go. There was still some good left in this broken man, and he'd stand up to Sin. There might be a spot in heaven for Saint after all.

"What the hell are you doing, man?" Sin asked in pent up frustration.

"I'm seeing what paradise tastes like," Saint replied as his breath fanned against my pussy, and he licked up the entirety of my slit. "Her desire is as close to heaven as I'm ever going to get."

Fuck. The asshole made me quiver deep down into my core. The feeling of his tongue giving me even an ounce of pleasure after he'd dealt me pain was a relief. But I hated to admit it.

"Goddamn it, Saint, would you fuck her brains out already?" Sin huffed.

Saint growled, and his stubble tickled my slit. "Fine, fuck."

"Oh my God, no I—" my protest, equal parts fright and passion, was cut short as Saint nudged his cock inside of me, and my eyes flew open.

Twenty-Eight

Their Obsession

Liv

Sin took his shot and stretched my mouth. His huge mushroom head was not even an inch in, and I already felt like he wouldn't fit. My lips wrapped around him as both men groaned, and my belly ached from the sounds they made. My cunt throbbed with tension from Saint's massive girth as he pushed in more, and I thought I'd burst.

"Ah!" I moaned against Sin's cock and the vibrations made his dick twitch.

"Fuck. Such a good slut taking our big cocks, inch by inch," Sin growled with satisfaction and looked down at me. "Now to make our girl see teary-eyed shooting stars."

"Uh-Uh!" I panicked with a dick stuffed in my mouth as Sin inched in more and Saint followed suit.

Sin pushed my head further down as he let out a long, pleased grunt and my mouth filled with saliva. The liquid swept out the sides of my mouth as he forced me to take him deeper and my eyes were bugging out of my head. Fresh hot tears brimmed in my eyes but wouldn't fall as I stared up at my enemy and bit down as much as I could on his cock. But his girth was too broad, and my teeth only ignited more pleasure.

"Yes, sweetheart, just like that. Such a good girl grazing those pearly whites along my shaft." Sin groaned with pleasure as he thrusted his hips up to push deeper into my throat. "Ah. Fuck. I love it when you do that."

Saint gave me a small thrust from behind and filled me fuller than I had ever been before. Pain mixed with passion as my walls stretched and my pussy fought against him. But the restriction only made him determined as he grunted and shoved his way in deeper.

They had plunged into me bare. No protection. They failed to discuss with me if I was on birth control or ask if I had an IUD. These fuckers didn't care. It wouldn't surprise me if they wanted to get me pregnant and keep me tied to them forever.

Finally, with one agonizing, blissful plunge, they buried themselves in me.

"Oh God—" Sin hit my gag reflex, cutting short my cry with a *gwock* sound from deep inside my throat.

More sounds filled the room as Sin thrust into my mouth repeatedly and never set me loose. He stuffed me full as my tears fell and my phantom's face blurred. All I heard was his grunts of pure satisfaction, of his girl taking his cock so well and Saint groaning his chants of praise.

My pussy clenched, and Saint throbbed as he drove into me over and over until my head bobbed on its own. Sin let go of my head with a wicked smirk on his face as he watched me take his cock greedily. I feasted on him as pleasure soared through me and Saint helped me ride the waves. He thrusted faster and faster as my mouth gobbled up Sin.

"Our girl even sounds like a stuffed turkey."

Sin's evil, low laughter echoed throughout the room and mixed with the sound of my ass cheeks clapping against Saint's thighs. Hatred and lust mixed inside of me as Saint slowed his pace. Their long lengths were back to torturing me as one thrusted all the way into the hilt until I thought my pussy would erupt. While the other one caught the shove and plunged their dick deep into my throat. My eyes bulged with each push until they rolled and I choked.

"Yes, darling. Good girl. Just. Like. That," Saint grunted out each word as he thrusted and a feral moan ripped up my throat.

Sin popped his dick out of my mouth as a sound tore out of me, but he concealed the noise with his tongue. His hand puckered my mouth together as he licked over my open mouth. The motion was wet and sloppy as he drove his tongue inside.

Sin kissed me with a fierce need as Saint drove wildly inside of me. He buried himself again and again as our skin smacked. My climax grew higher and higher, but I loathed them for it all. My body responded the way they promised it would. I stretched wide for them and grew accustomed to their massive sizes. Girths I thought I couldn't handle, but I was wrong. They felt far too good stuffed up inside of me, and I ached for Sin to join Saint. To fill me full all over again.

"Yes! Yes!" I cried out into Sin's mouth as he ate up my cries of passion and our tongues swirled to a deadly beat.

These men were going to be the death of me. They'd stuffed my body until I ceased to exist. But they'd be sure to own me, even in the afterlife. They would always haunt me.

Sin tore his mouth from mine. "Enough."

Sin forcefully whipped my face with his wet dick, causing me to open my mouth wide in surprise as he abruptly cut off my yelp and plunged back inside. Quickly, he gathered my hands into his and forced them behind my back. The new position caused my head to fall forward, and the tip of Sin's dick hit my gag reflex. Wet sounds of protest came from my throat as my eyes bugged out of my head and Sin jolted upward. He buried himself in my mouth until I thought he'd hit my brain and fucked it. Saint grabbed my wrists and bound them in his grasp as he pulled me back.

"What the fu—" my protest silenced as Saint gave me a hard thrust and my body jerked in his hold. Saint slammed into me repeatedly, and the sound was music to my ears as my mouth went wide and an animalistic moan escaped onto the head of Sin's cock. He didn't waste a beat and shoved himself back into me as they rocked me back and forth. In one wet hole and out the other. Our climax grew as the sounds we made grew louder and the men couldn't help themselves. We couldn't stop the pleasure we all felt as they shared me, and I couldn't deny them any longer.

"Such. A. Good. Slut," Sin grunted each word as he thrusted, and I gagged on his cock. "Show me your pretty tongue."

And I did. I showed him my tongue as he pulled back, and he was the first to erupt. Saint slowed to an excruciating pace as he let Sin blow his load on me, and I tasted his warm come as he jerked off into my mouth. The taste of him was surprisingly sweet as I drank him up, and I knew I'd soon regret my decision.

They gave me no time to contemplate my latest mistake as Saint hoisted me back up and he picked up his sweet pace. Sin bared my tits and covered his mouth over a nipple. I bit down on my lip and concealed my cry as Sin lapped his tongue in circles around my erect bud. A coil wrung tight deep inside of me and was ready to burst, but I held back.

I wasn't ready to give another piece of me to these assholes. I was unprepared to spill my juices all over my phantom's deliciously skilled, ten-inch cock. He couldn't have me. They couldn't make me.

As if sensing my apprehension, Saint slapped my ass. Once, twice, and three times. He rounded a fourth harsh smack and somewhere in between his lashings, Sin covered my mouth. He concealed the whimpers I let out as Saint went on a rampage. Over and over, he slapped me like I was his bad fucking girl. My behind would have a nasty red welt at the end of all of this, the skin on the verge of bleeding. The pain he inflicted was nipped away by pleasure as he thrusted and slapped.

Sin bit at my nipples, sucked and licked until I was on the edge of insanity. Every inch of me exploded with pleasure, as I couldn't stop my release, even though I had fought damn hard. They had beat me into submission, and I gave into them.

"Yes, yes, yes!" My muffled cry came out as stars flew, and I stared down at my phantom feasting on my tits. "Fuck you, fuckers!"

My back arched, my nails dug into the palms of my clenched fists, and my eyes rolled. I rode out my climax as Saint grunted with my tight pussy walls clenching down on him, and he, too, hurdled over the edge. He rode me hard and fast as he rattled the entire bed frame.

"Fuck!" was the only word he uttered as he spilled his seed inside of me, and I prayed the asshole was full of dead sperm.

Even though I was on birth control, I still worried and felt his come warm me from the inside. Those tiny pills could fuck up. One slight slip, and I'd be pregnant with a baby I wouldn't want. I couldn't afford to miss a single goddamn pill.

"Assholes," I panted as Sin removed his hand from my mouth, and he met my angry stare.

Hot tears filled my eyes as the shame creeped back in, but I wouldn't let them spill. I had cried enough tears of tormented bliss for one session with them, and they didn't deserve to see me do it again. But humiliation was the least of my worries.

My soul was on the line with my heart following close behind, and my phantoms had worn me down.

They took from me another piece I couldn't get back, but I had let them.

They had broken in and were fully intent on killing Sebastian until plans changed because of me. I had touched them intimately when I knew better. I had pushed them with my big mouth, and I'd known what they'd do.

Sin and Saint wanted me, and they weren't willing to let me go. Owning my body wasn't their only priority. They wanted my heart, my mind and my pretty little soul.

"You were perfect, sweetheart," Sin breathed as he fanned my lips with his warm breath and brushed my hair behind my ears. "Frazzled, tight, and willing."

"Willing?" I questioned as Saint's dick dripped come on my ass and my juices leaked down my thighs.

"Yes," Sin hissed as he pecked my lips, and his eyes never wavered from mine.

"Have you lost every marble in your fucked up head?" I asked and wiggled in Saint's hold, but he wouldn't let me go.

Sin whispered, "I'm a rather intelligent person, Liv."

"You have yet to prove that," I huffed.

Sin laughed. "Oh, how you wound me."

Sin held a hand over his heart sarcastically, acting as though I had hurt him. The muscle sat stone-cold behind his ribcage and didn't beat as his actions reflected his lack of emotion. Sin Cruz was a deranged psychopath.

"I can't hurt someone who's dead inside." I glared at Sin and hoped he choked on my words. "Cold, calculated, and cruel, without a beating heart."

"Trying to hurt us only makes you more like us. A vicious cycle we'll get lost in together until you admit you need us. Until you confess your love for us, too," Sin explained as he held my face in his hands and kissed my nose.

Before I could lash back, Sin let me go and snapped at Saint. He released me and gravity landed me back on the bed. I gathered any strength I had left and scurried away from them as they went to the edge of the bed. They gathered their pants and briefs but wouldn't take their dark and possessive eyes off me. In another cruel tease, they slowly dressed and zipped up their pleased cocks inside of their pants.

My being vibrated from the shock of what I had endured, and I clung to the headboard. I'd been violated all over again by two men who were ready to hide back in the shadows until they felt the need to strike. To consume me, use me, and abuse me, but I lived through each blow.

Every attack caused my fight to weaken, and I gave into everything they dealt. They'd continue and wouldn't stop. Not until I fully submitted to them and gave them all of me.

"I'll never love you," I breathed as they went back to the window and Saint blew me a kiss.

I pretended to catch the affection in my hand, and, to his disappointment, I smashed it onto the mattress. Saint growled with disapproval as he climbed out the window and vanished into thin air. Mr. Saint Sullivan deserved nothing from me after everything he had put me through.

"You will."

I glared. "No, I won't."

"Yes, you will. After your heart shatters, and we piece it all back together. We're counting on it, Liv, but you are the one who is unsure, judging by your pulse racing a mile a minute," Sin said with certainty.

I gazed down at my wrist and held two fingers against it. Sure enough, the beat against my skin was erratically throbbing, and I double-checked with my fingers against my neck. My pulse quickened even more with the realization Mr. Sin Cruz was gone.

Was Sin right? Will I seek refuge in them? Could I give my heart to them?

No. There was absolutely no way. It was not possible after everything they had done.

Tears burst from my eyes as I let them fall after my shadows left me alone. I curled up in the fetal position and wept for the person I once knew. A woman who'd let no man control her, but I had let two. I used to be the one in control of the men I had chosen, but Sin and Saint had chosen me.

Darkness engulfed me as I fell into myself. I dashed down further into my soul as I tried to make sense of each tormented encounter with them. I had wanted to forget, but I couldn't. They lived within me night and day. Devoured me until there was little left, with my heart beating wildly in my chest, and I wasn't sure of anything anymore.

Twenty-Nine

Their Obsession

Liv

The next morning, I woke up to the sunshine creeping through a small gap between my blinds. The sunrise greeted me as it touched the unmade bed on Sebastian's side and drew my eyes to the sun's rays. But the broken window reminded me of everything I went through hours ago.

My hands skittered over the tarnished markings my ghosts had left on my skin that wouldn't vanish anytime soon. I was damaged, but they had made me feel alive. A fucked-up mixture I didn't want any part of, but it was too late.

I had closed the drapes last night because Sebastian couldn't notice the pried open window created by Sin and Saint. I didn't need another devil breathing down my neck and leaving more lasting impressions. Two were good enough.

Yesterday, this bedroom was my sanctuary. I kept hidden away for most of the day after the assault I had endured at the hands of my phantoms. Their attack left me mixed up, and a confused mess because I still craved them. Yet I hated them. Loathed everything they had made me do and put me through, but I couldn't stop thinking about them.

"Fuck," I muttered as I sat up in bed and grabbed my cell phone from the nightstand.

I knocked over the book I had been engrossed in last night before I had crept downstairs to sneak a bite to eat. Sebastian wasn't a worry after I caught him with a scotch in hand, stumbling around the living room and hollering at the television as if his life depended on it. The coast was clear as I grabbed some leftovers and proceeded back upstairs.

The novel I read was a dark romance about a man obsessed with a woman he wanted and the lengths he'd go to all for her—all the unhinged things he'd do to her and all the people he'd kill because of her. The fictional story reminded me of the men who stalked me, but I was envious. This bitch only had one stalker while I had two. Two deranged, addicted, and gorgeous men. *Goddamn.*

My heart beat out of control at the thought of them and my response to their torturous pleasure. The taunting teases they skillfully granted me when I was unwilling, but Sin and Saint had made me willing. Their delusions had become my delicious reality, and they weren't going away.

The clock had struck half past midnight when Sebastian had flopped into bed, and I felt the shockwave of his body weight. Deep snores followed immediately after his head hit the pillow and he passed out drunk. I had expected this when he hadn't asked me for supper, and I knew he must have been completely drunk, passed out on the downstairs sofa.

I was secretly grateful I had missed an unwanted altercation with him, and the situation had turned out great for me. Not so much for him. But the bastard had earned a raging hangover.

A smirk widened on my face as I peered down at my device for the daily news and a light breeze caught my attention. The blinds swayed from side to side and an early morning chill came from the window. Goosebumps raised on my skin, and I rubbed my bare arms to warm them, but I was relieved Sebastian had left early enough for work not to notice the brisk morning air.

Scratch that. Overlooked or was still intoxicated? I'd go with him being wasted.

I had closed the window; I was sure of it. To the best of my ability, I had pressed the window down and there hadn't been a breeze creeping through. No crack for air to...

Wait a minute.

As I crept further forward to investigate, I noticed something colorful behind the blinds. The drape blew to the side and revealed a paper coffee cup from the café I had visited the day before. The same place I had spilled my morning brew all over my dress. Curiously, I pulled the curtain aside, and I found something shocking.

Two white roses on the window ledge.

A soft chime sound came from my cell phone, catching my attention, and I peered down at a text message.

Unknown:

Can't have our girl go without her morning cup of java. Especially after yesterday's spill.

Startled, I looked up from my phone and out the window toward the trees. Sunshine beamed through and blurred the view. The bright light was hard on my eyes, and I had to turn away before I went blind. Black stars danced as I blinked and knew Sin was out there watching and waiting in the damn trees with Saint by his side.

Now they brought me coffee too?

I appeased them by grasping the hot coffee as steam blew with my morning breath, and I took a small sip. The sweetness bit at my bitterness. My disgust quickly turned to softness as their gesture pulled at my heartstrings and got even sweeter when I realized the coffee had extra sweetener. The way I liked it.

Assholes. I'd have to get the damn window fixed ASAP.

Thirty
Her Phantom

Sin

"Here pussy, pussy, pussy." I cooed as I called for the pesky little cat to haul ass and come over for the pet we both knew he wanted. "Good pussycat."

My hand gently stroked the cat named Rocko, who Saint had let in from the street. He gave him a place to stay in our shared penthouse inside of our club. The one on the second floor and in the far back of the nightclub. A space we called our home sweet home.

Wait. Back up a bit. Sweet wasn't the right word to describe it. More like *spooky*.

Our home spooky home.

The place was fucking haunted. We turned the cheap, rundown building around for the better and gave it a facelift. Unknown to us, the property used to be a hospital for the city. A sure hit to be cursed because hundreds of people would've died here. But we fit right in and got along with whatever fucked up shit still lurked within these walls.

The feline purred as I brushed along its soft coat and it snuggled in closer. "Hey, watch the outfit, kitty cat. Your damn fur will be all over it."

I didn't like the fucking felines who roamed around the place, but Saint loved to give stray cats a home. This cat was a pest that wouldn't screw off, but I didn't mind him. The rest though? They were needy little shits.

There had to be up to ten clingy cats in this joint! There could be more, but who the fuck knows?

I lost count after the last pregnant puss strolled her prissy ass in here and had her litter of kittens. Now those were freaking cute, but they grew up and got hissy. Nope. Not for me.

Somehow Rocko, this playful little fucker gnawing at my finger, fit right in. He stayed and never left. The others came for the variety of wet foods Saint left out every day and quenched their thirst at the water fountain I ordered online. I only got the damn kitty fountain for those hissy fits because it was Saint's birthday. Not out of the kindness of my heart. I didn't know what else to get him because he already had everything, including a kitty litter box.

I got up from the black sofa and made my way toward the back patio door, which led out onto the balcony. Everything was out on the sheltered deck from patio furniture, a grill, cat food, and the fountain with stairs leading down into the park. The same public woodland where we enjoyed watching Liv on the other side. Where we crept in the shadows and blended in with these damn cats.

Rocko was right at my heels as I stopped at the door and peeked down at my leg while he rubbed up against me. The little puss lived rent free in our eerie space, but it was time for the asshole to screw off. I wiggled my leg and opened the built-in cat door.

"Shoo, you pesky shit," I hissed at the cat as he scurried through, and I brushed the fur from my dark pant leg. "You'll bring me bad luck."

I didn't need misfortune tonight. We were creating our own luck. We were about to do the devil's work.

"Are you ready to go, man?" Saint hollered from the other room.

I shouted back, "I've been waiting on you, asshole!"

Footsteps stomped up behind me, and I turned around, only to see Saint come down the hallway. He dressed in all black with a skull mask to conceal his identity. He looked creepy. The appearance would do for this evening.

"How do I look?"

"Like you're ready to become someone's worst nightmare," I answered.

Saint chuckled and patted my shoulder. "Well, that's what Halloween is all about. Scaring the shit out of people."

I followed beside Saint as we made our way through the penthouse, and I admired our Gothic taste. Everything was dark and eerie how we wanted it. A true masterpiece, perfect for us, with large gargoyle statues and creepy pictures hanging on the walls instead of lame family portraits. Shady and somber was our jam. The trick-or-treaters would love it in here, but I wasn't about to let the little fuckers in.

"Fucking kids will crawl the streets begging for candy like they do every year," I grumbled as I locked up at the penthouse and held my mask in my hand.

Saint snorted. "You're a dick man."

I grunted with annoyance at Saint as we stepped into the elevator, which took us straight down to the main floor, and we walked until loud music thumped in our ears from the club. Sinful Saints was the place to be on this festive All Hallows' Eve. We hit the beat and drew in a frightful crowd. Scary clowns, bloody dolls, vampires, witches, goblins, and ghouls. There was the odd angel, fairy, and even a sexy-ass cop. But those ladies had nothing on our girl.

We pushed through the crowd and made it to the front doors of the club. I nearly tripped over some clown's enormous feet as I stumbled forward and pushed him out of the way. The short motherfucker cussed at me, but backed off once he saw how pissed off I was. I fixed my leather jacket as my chest puffed out and the scrawny asshole was on his way. I was about to fuck the dude up before the night even began and I got to the best part.

"Now *he's* a dick," I huffed.

"No, man. You are."

"What?" I shrugged in disagreement and gazed around at the kids combing the street. "Kids go from door-to-door chanting Trick-or-Treat and the little demons get what they want."

"It's tradition," Saint said as he plucked a giant candy bar from the basket I'd instructed the bouncer to leave out for Satan's spawn.

I grabbed a chocolate bar and huffed, "They are a nuisance."

Saint laughed as he crunched down on his bar and said midchew, "Put your mask on. It's go-time."

"Don't mind if I do."

I put on my disguise and stepped into character as I walked down the stairs. A little kid dressed up as a ghost veered out in front of me and was eager to get to the sweets I had left out. But I scared him with a loud boo.

Startled, he jumped with a scream and his fright sent a chill through my bones. The sound made me smile, but I secretly tossed the candy bar I had taken for myself into the ghosts pillow case. Cute little shit deserved two.

After all, I didn't need the extra calories. I had to be in the fittest shape for our girl. She needed another round where we sent her straight to pound town.

Saint leaned over and whispered, "Not so mean after all."

I only grunted as we made our way toward the new black Mustang we had purchased. We needed an upgrade after our old rust bucket was ready for the scrap yard. The new car suited our expensive lifestyle much better than the old piece of shit Saint wanted to hold on to because it held sentimental value. *Bullshit.* Out with the old and in with brand spanking new.

I hit the key fob, and the car sounded with a sweet-ass chirp. It was music to my ears as I slid into the sleek leather driver's seat and Saint fell into the passenger seat beside me. The vehicle had a brand-new car smell, and the scent filled my nostrils with delight. *Fucking sweet.*

I sparked the engine to life, and some bitch screeched through the speakers. The loud ballad music wasn't my style, and I fumbled for the volume control. *She sure had some vocal cords on her. Jesus Christ!*

"There. That's better," I said as I put on *Animals* by Nickelback and stepped on the gas.

This was the perfect song to fuck Liv to. Her moans would be music to my ears as we'd drive into her, and she'd arch her sexy back to every thrust. *Shit.* I was hard, but now wasn't the time.

"Hey, man! Ease up!" Saint exclaimed as the tires squealed and the Mustang's tread created a burning smell. "We don't need the cops on our ass."

Saint's seatbelt locked in place as the car swayed before the tires regained traction on the pavement and we took off down the street. My excitement was too high to be bothered by the damn police. I was ready for everything we were about to accomplish and excited to hunt our prey, but our usual meal wasn't on the menu tonight.

No. This asshole was far more dangerous. Too unpredictable for our precious Liv and the scumbag needed to break.

"Fuck off, Saint."

Saint grunted at me but remained silent. He worried too fucking much. Me? I was a risk-taker, an adrenaline junky. Ready to dive right in and have my heart beating a mile a minute in my chest. As much as the muscle was hammering now. I was pumped and prepared to pounce.

Damn, this baby had some speed.

Unfortunately, I slowed down as we rounded the corner and Liv's condo came into view. I decelerated to a painstakingly steady creep with the car rolling forward, and I parked tucked away in the darkness as children walked on the sidewalk. I cut the music as we sat across the street, and I peered into my side door mirror. My scream mask stared back at me. The stabby slasher mask was a frightening sight alongside a skulled disguised monster—both up to no good. We slouched in our seats, watched, waited, and we were ready for our plan to take action.

But an hour passed.

We were on standby as I contemplated breaking the damn door down, fully prepared to drag the fucker out on his ass and screw some shit up. Forget our idea and let's...

Surprisingly, to my most delighted shock, the juice-head we had been waiting for walked out the door. He peered down at his cell phone and extended his arm out in front of him. A loud whistle sounded from his pressed mouth as he hailed down a taxicab.

"Follow him," Saint grumbled from beside me, full of anger.

"It would be my pleasure."

Thirty-One

Her Phantom

Sin

We followed Sebastian to the older side of downtown. Where the crime rate was high and dirty shit went down. A place where he didn't fit in, and I wondered what he was up to.

No kids walked down the streets, but they weren't empty either. Homeless roamed, hookers were getting stoned, and pimps drove in flashy vehicles. Expensive ones like ours so we blended in, but it was a goddamn mess down here.

Without warning, the cab jerked to a stop. I watched as gas fumes coated the dark night on the other side of the street and the hormone-induced donkey got out of the taxi. He threw his arms up and tossed some money at the driver. The door slammed shut, and the cabbie gave Sebastian the middle finger.

"Jesus. The asshole causes havoc wherever he goes," Saint mumbled beside me as Sebastian pounded a fist down onto the roof of the cab and it took off.

Its tires squealed, but Sebastian couldn't care less. He turned his short, broad frame toward the alleyway. Dim lighting shone down on it, but he walked into the dark. Bastard will be sorry he did.

"*A-hm, ha-hm, ha-hm...*" I hummed as I turned off the car and got out.

Saint hummed along as he exited the car and fell in step beside me. "*A-hm, ha-hm, ha-hm...*"

We were night crawlers in action, stalking our mark—an egotistical jerk-off who feared nothing as he walked toward his fate and into a crime infested corridor. But he'd soon experience terror from us.

Saint and I wandered from the edge of the alleyway, spying from behind a brick wall. Sebastian met with a highly suspicious character wearing a black hoodie. Tattoos littered his hands as he passed him some pills in a plastic bag, and Sebastian handed him a wad of cash.

I knew it.

The donkey does roids. He pumped himself full of pills and didn't pump weights at the gym. The asshole was a blown-up balloon full of hot air and we'd pop his ego flat.

The drug dealer made the exchange and left our prey with his illegal substance. The man with the hood over his head paid no attention to us as he strode out of the alley and down the sidewalk. Dollar bills circulated in his pea-sized brain until he met up for his next deal. Hopefully, a big drug bust.

Sebastian was too busy popping his pills as we came out of hiding and blocked the way he came. Saint stood beside me, and we locked our eyes straight ahead on our target. His drug addiction consumed the idiot. Time to gather his full attention with our favorite song.

I sang in a low unrecognizable tune, "*A-hunting we will go, a-hunting we will go...*"

Finally, the fucker looked up. He didn't even hide his pills, and within the dim lighting, I could see beads of sweat forming on his forehead. Good. He was nervous.

"What the fuck do you want?" Sebastian asked.

But we didn't answer and took one step forward.

"What do you want? Candy?" Sebastian questioned in annoyance and stepped toward us. "Well, I don't have any! Now get lost!"

Saint glanced over at me and crooned, "*heigh-ho, the derry-o—*"

"Get the fuck out of my way, you lunatics!"

Lunatics?

This asshole called *us* crazy? Oh, he was about to meet his worst nightmare.

We quickly moved forward a step with a grunt, and the jackass jumped. Startled, Sebastian moved backward like a stray dog with his tail between his legs. Phony-ass bitch.

"Okay... Okay... You want money?" Sebastian asked as his voice trembled, and he extended his wallet. "Here. Take it."

I shook my head.

"Okay, um..." He shoved his wallet back in his pocket and extended his drugs. "Here. Take my pills. I can get—"

I grunted and shot forward until a squeak echoed down the alleyway. Sebastian stumbled and lost his footing, falling to the ground. Saint laughed as Sebastian scurried back to his feet, and he repeatedly searched behind him. There was nowhere to go and no place to hide. He had no choice but to meet his fate.

We cornered our little donkey at the dead-end, with our masks surely giving him a fright. In the process of his pointless escape, he dropped his roids, and we trapped him up against a tall chain-link fence.

"P-please... I could give you anything you want. Just let me go. I—"

Not so big and tough now. Are you, Mr. Chamberlain?

I snapped my fingers, and he shut the fuck up. My head tilted to the side, and I watched as the fucker pissed himself right in front of us. I bet he wet his bed as a kid.

The lighting was enough to catch the embarrassment he felt cross his face. The shame he had excited me; it was a rush I had been impatiently waiting for, a thrill I took great pride in as Saint reached out and clenched his throat, his hand wrapping right around his windpipe.

"Fuc—" Saint didn't let him finish as Sebastian gasped for air, and he struggled against his hold.

But he was no match for my buddy.

His hands could thrash, he could kick his puny legs, and he could fight. Saint would only squeeze tighter until he broke his trachea, but I'd love to watch. To observe as his eyes filled with fear of his oncoming death. All bloodshot and gross while they popped out of his head from the force. His face would turn red, and his mouth would be wide as he clung to hope for a breath of air. Then his body would go limp with the struggle he tried to keep up gone. Lifeless. Dead.

But I had no such luck.

So, I continued our song. "*A-hunting we will go, a-hunting we will go...*"

Saint sensed the end and let go. Sebastian dropped to the ground as he brought a hand up to his throat.

The other held up his weight on the asphalt as he panted at our feet. We peered down at him as he probably gathered his whereabouts after he almost blacked out.

"Jesus Christ!" he choked out. "You could've fucking killed me!"

Believe me. We want to. So fucking bad the idea of your death pained our souls.

"*We'll catch the jackass and...*" Saint added.

"What the—AH!" I stomped on his left hand, cutting short his tangent and causing him to cry out in pain.

I sang, "*Crack some limbs...*"

Sebastian cracked like a twig. The delightful sound of another bone breaking filled the nighttime air as Saint stomped on his right hand before he could even hold himself up. The howls of agony were music to our ears as we heard another crack when his face hit the ground.

We bent down as Saint grabbed Sebastian by the hair, and we admired his ugly gravel-beaten face. The shitbag mumbled something incoherent, and I spit in his face. His low-life, useless existence deserved an end, but we couldn't yet. We'd make sure he suffered in the meantime, and our girl could live without fear of him.

"*And never have him hurt again.*" I ended our song with a punch to his face and it was lights out for Mr.

Sebastain Chamberlain. He went limp, and at least I got my one wish. But he deserved far worse.

"Grab his wallet. Make this look like a robbery," Saint said as he pushed his face into a muddy puddle and flipped him over as if he was a rag doll.

"Got it."

We peered down at the prick who hurt Liv with our fists clenched, ready to strike again, but we held back. This was all for her. To protect our girl from this monster who lived under the same roof as her. If she wouldn't let us kill him for her, then we'd bide our time until we could. Sebastian was a dead man walking with broken hands, and he wouldn't be able to use them to hurt her anytime soon.

Thirty-Two

Their Obsession

Liv

I awoke to the sound of creaks in the floorboards. Foggy from sleep, I blinked several times, my eyes straining to see the light, but nothing came. My pupils adjusted to the dark room when I heard the sound a second time.

I inhaled a sharp breath and held it while I stayed still. Afraid to move in case I missed the noise, I was sure it came from the other side of my door. I was a cat on high alert, and the hairs stood up on the nape of my neck. My eyes widened as I waited for another creak, but all I heard was my fast-paced heartbeat.

Nothing. My mind must've imagined the disturbance, the racket all in my head. A bad dream my subconscious made up after all the crap I had recently been through. My brain desperately tried to make sense of the fucked-up feelings I had for my stalkers. It was seriously screwed up—a mix between hatred and want. A need I should never have for men who were forceful, dominating, possessive, and completely out of their minds.

Creak.

There was the sound again! I knew it! I wasn't crazy, and the noise wasn't all in my head. Sebastian had left in the middle of the night, and I knew the disturbance wasn't him. He never creeped around the house like this and moved with a steady rhythm. Not thuds that made a lump form in my throat and my nerves race out of control.

I was curled up in bed, too frightened to move, with the bed sheets pulled up to my nose as I breathed heavily. Fully intent on suffocation instead of letting whoever was out there get me.

The groans on the floor had turned into footsteps, but there wasn't just one. There were two sets of steps. One lighter and one heavier. The lightweight steps tried to conceal themselves, while the solid ones gave a steady stomp.

I shot up in bed when I heard them come right up to my door. My eyes locked on the doorknob as I watched the knob slowly turn. And I made a beeline for the door.

Scurried for the solid fixture without another thought as the bed sheets tangled around my waist, and I fell to the floor. My feet kicked to free myself, my hands pushed me up off the floor, and I slammed my body up against the door. I clicked the lock with trembling hands as my pulse hammered against my neck, and my hair sucked in and out of my mouth with each hurried breath.

"I know you're there! Get the fuck out of my house before I call the cops!"

Dumb. Really stupid, Liv. Me and my big mouth.

Silence greeted me. Not one peep from the intruders on the other side, who were likely frozen at my words and judging their next move.

I quaked with shudders and couldn't stop my reaction to the intrusion I had awoken to. Blindsided and awoken from a deep slumber in full panic mode. Fight or flight. But the only direction to run was right out my window.

Shit.

I turned around with my back against the door as I listened for any more noise and peered around my room. Desperately trying to find anything to plunge, strike, or gouge my intruders with. Instead, my eyes landed on something else.

Two fake white roses.

They sat perfectly centered, waiting for my attention, with the sheets bunched up around them and a note laid beside them at the foot of my bed. I had missed the artificial flowers in my horrific scurry and the fear quickly turned to rage. These weren't any criminals, they were my phantoms.

Assholes!

How did they get into my condo?

Once again, I was at a loss because the doors and windows were all locked. I had triple-checked after Sebastian had left, and I knew all too well they'd be back. I wasn't taking any chances, so I'd fixed the damn window.

I snatched the note off the bed and read their torturous words,

Roses are red,

Violets are blue.

Obsession lasts forever,

And so do these roses

Meant just for you.

Jesus.

My heart hammered into my throat, and I swallowed the hard lump. My gulp was loud, but my emotions were fierce. Their note struck something deep inside of me and tore away at another tiny piece of my soul—ripped at my essence and tried to pry it wide open, but I wouldn't let them tear me to shreds.

Another small piece of me was gone. Stolen by their words, and I hated to admit their move was smart. Unlike their usual dumb tactics, just as stupid as these artificial roses. Cheap fuckers. They couldn't even afford the real thing. Must be bankrupt. Served them right.

I grabbed the roses from my bed and stomped into the bathroom, hauled them straight into the trash can. Angrily, I tore up the note and loathed them for invading my privacy and disrupting my sleep. A crude reminder of how mean they could be while my heart beat wildly from their attempt at a sweet gesture.

"Fuckers! I know it's you!" I yelled as trudged to the door and placed my ear against it.

The stillness should have brought me peace. The silence was deafening as I ripped my ear from the door and huffed in aggravation. I peeked at my alarm clock. It was half past two in the morning. Witching hours. My phantoms fit right in with the ghosts. How inviting. But I reeled with another thought.

Where the fuck was Sebastian?

Whichever bimbo he was with must be good in the sack because he had lost all track of time. His dick was rather small, and she probably couldn't get her lips wrapped securely around his ugly stick. Unfortunately for her, she'd have to pretend to enjoy his company for hours to get a penny out of him because that was all Sebastian Chamberlain was good for.

Shadows moved through the crack at the bottom of my bedroom door. The dark figures swayed one way and then the other. Until the darkened outlines were out of sight.

I held my breath and unlocked the door. Nothing happened. There was no sound or movement from the other side, not even one attempt to force their way inside.

Were they gone?

I highly doubted it.

Carefully, I opened the door until there was a small gap I could see through. I scanned from left to right. No one was there. But a creak came from the stairs.

I made a mad dash for the stairwell. "Ah-ha!"

To my surprise, I was the only one there, alone at the top of the staircase, peering down into thin air. Slowly, I took the steps two at a time with my heartbeat pounding in my chest, and the muscle felt like it might explode. The sound was inside my eardrums as I made it to the bottom floor.

"Sebastian will be home any minute now! Get the hell out!"

Goosebumps crawled over my skin, starting from my legs, all the way up my chest, and extending out toward the back of my hands. The unknown was unnerving as I crept toward the kitchen in a fearless fashion. But on the inside, everything crawled with dread.

I knew I shouldn't. Alarm bells rang out in my mind to run and head back upstairs, but my legs wouldn't listen. Either I was too fucking curious if they were still there or incredibly dumb. Likely both, but I stopped, and my eyes widened when they landed on a frightening sight.

Two colossal figures with masks on both faced me. The pair were in spooky spirits. One was disguised in a skull mask, holding a baton, and the other was Ghostface from the *Scream* movies, and he held a knife.

They were equally a horrific view as they stood incredibly still and didn't move a muscle.

"Phantoms? Is that you?" I asked as I caught sight of the butcher block and sidestepped.

They didn't answer me but swayed in the same direction.

"I hated your gift."

The skulled figure didn't appreciate the comment and steadily tapped the baton against his palm. The soft tap against flesh was the only sound I heard as I took another step, wanting to arm myself. I was defenseless with each man armed. The fight was unfair, and the odds of me escaping this were scarce.

"I knew it's you, and you both disgust me. I despise the pair of you more than I have anyone in my entire life. More than Sebastian." I glared, and I wanted to hurt them.

But the last part was a flat out lie.

Sebastian was the root of all evil, not my ghosts. Yes, they forced me to do unspeakable acts with them, but it brought me pleasure I never knew I could feel. I'd discovered explosive, erotic, feral needs that I hated to want. I'd made animalistic sounds I didn't even recognize and couldn't tame, even if I tried. They consumed me; Sebastian ruined me. There was a difference I clearly saw, but I'd never admit the truth to them.

"You'll never have me because I belong with Sebastian."

The words were bile in my mouth and made me sick to my stomach. Sebastian repulsed me, but I needed to preoccupy them. I required a split second to reach out and lunge for a knife.

Fiercely, they growled and studied at each other. The sound hurt my ears, pierced into my heart, and stung like a venomous snake with its scaly skin wrapped around me. The sensation squeezed me tight, refusing to free me, but I released myself and ran for the blade.

Suddenly, a hand gripped the back of my neck. "Ah!"

I reached for the butcher block and my hand touched the handle. I fumbled to get a grip on the handle, but the death lock around my neck jerked me forward and away from my weapon. The commotion caused a knife to tumble out onto the island with the butcher block falling to the floor and I squeaked as I met a solid chest. I peered at the face of the disguised slasher.

"Fuck! Let me go!" I yelled at the masked man.

Slowly, the asshole shook his head from side to side, and I squirmed in his hold. The grip only grew tighter and bruised my skin and pulled my hair. The disguised jerk's dick was hard against my belly, and the smell of cedarwood mixed with whiskey excited me. A fiery pit swirled in me because this was what these fuckers do to me. They awakened emotions I couldn't deny no matter how hard I pushed them away, and even with their identities concealed, they still did a number on my pussy.

Ghostface took the tip of his blade and brought it up to my neck, but my hands remained at my sides. My rapid breathing made my tits bounce as the steel ran over my tank and skittered across my navel. Slowly, the sharp tip nudged between the drawstring of my silk pajama bottoms, and he cut the thread in half.

Instantly, my bottoms fell to my bare feet, and I gasped at the sudden escalation of the situation. I was now half-naked in front of both men while the slasher ran the knife back up my skin and underneath my tank top. Tingles ignited while fear should have made me quiver, but I was turned on. I hated the feeling, but liked it all at the same time. My body remembered all the ways they could make me feel, all the unwanted desires they sprang to life. The assholes knew how to please me, but first they must cause me pain.

"Slice me. Go on, do it. End this torturous intoxication you both put me through," I hissed with need and reached up to touch the handle.

The fucker fought me; I'd caught him off guard as his breathing picked up a notch. He didn't expect me to react in such a dangerous way, but they brought out the worst in me. A feverish feminine brute who was confused, but her mind was fogged by lust.

My phantom groaned as he gave up the fight, and I inhaled sharply as the blade skimmed the surface of my skin. The cut wasn't too deep as the steel tip ran up the middle of my abdomen and blood trickled downward. Drips slowly pooled into my belly button and fell down below. The red surely mixed with the juices my pussy had produced from my untamed arousal.

I released the pressure on the knife as my phantom stopped skimming the blade across the surface and trailed over the top of my white shirt. I watched as the bright stain ran from one hard nipple to the next. The blade teased me as I bit down into my attacker's flesh, and he snarled when my teeth clamped down. The sound ignited a fiery need in the pit of my stomach, and I released my teeth from him as I felt hands on my ass. They squeezed tight, and I instantly bit down again while the slasher hissed from above. His massive erection pulsated against me.

I freed my mouth from him and breathed, "Again."

The knife trailed back down toward the cut I had helped him inflict on me, and the masked jerk behind me slapped my ass. The motion made me arch my back, and the blade drew fresh blood, but from a tiny nick right beside the longer cut. A whimpered hiss escaped my lips with my head thrown back and my eyes wide open, trained on my phantom's disguised face. I found the long black hooded eyes to be a horrific sight, but they fired me up. Underneath all my layers, I kept a wild creature hidden, but I was a sick fuck. I was as screwed up as them, and I didn't realize it until now.

"Enough!" I exclaimed, but the blade cut short my realization as it departed from my skin and propelled me backward—into the arms of my other phantom.

Thirty-Three

Their Obsession

Liv

Ghostface slightly tilted his head to the side as the mask moved downward and slowly back up. He admired his work and my body being all fused up. Pent-up sexual tension surged from me as I panted with unruly, wispy hairs sucking in and out of my mouth. I quivered, but not out of fear. Out of undeniable want that I hated to admit was there, but it was all I could feel.

I examined the slasher the same way he had me and took in his dark attire. A black V-neck shirt displayed his ink and made him deliciously dangerous. His muscles were pronounced they bulged from under his shirt. The man was incredibly ripped in black denim jeans and black boots that he wore in a leisurely, untied manner.

"Did your mother never teach you to tie your shoes?" The question blurted from me before I could stop it.

Call me stupid, call me foolish. Hell, call me a dumb bitch, but this was what my phantoms did to me. They made me lose all hold on reality, questioning all my morals and seeking only them. I was on the brink of collapse and, piece by piece, I'd fall, bound to perish with their arms around me, never letting me go. But it was within their embraces, they'd piece me back together, leave me begging, and make me whole.

He peered at his feet and ignored my stupidity, but I could envision a sexy grin on his face. One I'd want to hit until he grabbed me by the throat and made me bleed again. Maybe slice deeper and make this pain go away—the never-ending ache they granted me that exists right between my damn legs.

Instead, Ghostface looked up and calmly leaned forward. His motion was cruel and excruciating as thoughts ran wildly through my head. He touched the tip of his finger against the end of the blade and pricked it into his skin. I watched as he didn't even flinch, and his blood mixed with my own that was still left on the steel.

Sin pointed the blade at me and said, "Be a good girl and open your pretty mouth for Daddy."

I clamped my mouth shut, pressed my lips together and wouldn't open up. If memory served me right, they'd stick something in there. So, I zipped up tight.

Saint harshly gripped the back of my neck until I peered up into his skulled disguise, "Don't fight us now. Open up, darling."

"Mh-mh," I answered with a closed mouth and shook my head.

"Fine. Be a sassy brat," Sin snarled with irritation and grabbed my face.

His fingers dug into my cheeks and pressed them together. I maintained my reluctance, but he forcefully opened my mouth. Saint exposed my wet hole by shoving the black baton between my lips, causing my eyes to widen. He pushed the wand right down until the end hit my gag reflex and my eyesight grew watery. Saliva pooled up and dripped out from the sides of my mouth while the men groaned at the sight of me. All slippery and extremely wet.

"Assholes!" I choked out with a cough when Saint removed his baton from my mouth.

Sin only let up his hold on my cheeks for a second while Saint let go of me and before I knew it, Sin gripped my face again tightly until I winced from the pain. He didn't stop there and pulled me forward toward the island while he walked around to the other side. I squeaked as he yanked me until my chest hit the countertop and I faced him. His mask was only mere inches from my face as I felt the heat come off him.

I was dizzy, delusional, and stuck. Trapped with Sin's blade back against my delicate flesh and the sharp steel nipped at my neck. The tip ran along my thudding pulse until the blade rested along my curved neckline. He could slice me open if he wanted to. Kill me on the spot and my phantoms could bask in all my red, fiery blood. But I knew I wouldn't get that lucky. Because they wanted me alive, where my blood flowed through me and they'd make me drip whenever they desired. Or whenever I made them. Which made me fucking crazy.

"Spread your thighs, little obsession." Sin ordered from behind his mask.

"No," I breathed through puckered lips and clenched my thighs together.

"Yes."

Sin's hiss brought on a rough slap to my ass cheek, and I whimpered at the pain. My chest heaved and tears bit at my eyes while lips kissed the bruised skin as they soothed away the pain. Briefly, my legs unclenched from the motion and Saint pressed my knees into the island. Powerfully holding my position so I was wider for him, and I was sure he'd get a good view of my waxed asshole.

"Perfection," Saint growled with need.

My hand clenched the one side of the ledge while the other searched around for something to grab onto. Anything to hold while I dealt with whatever these men had planned for me. But I felt something cold with a sharp blade.

A knife!

Without hesitation, I gripped the handle as if my life depended on it and used any ninja-like reflexes I prayed I had and brought the blade up. Sin didn't move, he didn't flinch, as I pressed the steel up against his neck. The moment was electric, intense, and unexpected.

"Make him stop or I'll cut you where you stand."

Sin only laughed a wicked sound and asked, "Are you going to make me bleed, Liv?"

I swallowed. "Yes, if I have to."

"Yes, good girl..." Sin hissed huskily as his words crawled over me and the blade nicked his skin. "Make me bleed. My blood only fills my heart, but I'd die for my soul to belong with you. Forever."

Red oozed through the black fabric of his costume and my eyes widened as Saint slid something between the crevice of my ass. He made me vulnerable with his threat as I came to realize the piece drawing nearer to my asshole was the baton. The wet slickness of the weapon slid closer and closer to the unknown.

I watched Sin with fright, pent up anger, and sexual tension. I couldn't turn away as Sin's crimson colored blood slowly trickled down the blade, but he didn't move a muscle from the pain and only hissed with pleasure. He liked this shit. He got off on it, but I did too. We were two fucked up creatures holding each other at knife point. Ready to slit each other's throats for a pleasurable pain while his best friend wrecked some kind of havoc on my ass.

"*Make. Him. Stop.*"

"I can't and I won't," Sin murmured as his knife slightly cut my skin and stung me. "Because your pain brings us closer to owning every single hole your body has, and we love to see you hurting, my little obsession. But you also love our pleasure."

"No, I—" My argument cut short with a low animalistic moan in its place as Saint pushed into my tight ass.

"Fuck. Yes," Sin breathed with satisfaction.

"Shit, I'm too tight! I've never done this before. I—"

The baton moved further in, and I clung onto the ledge while my taut ass felt the pressure mount. The wand was a foreign object, and it didn't belong inside a hole I had never used for anything like this in my life. But the hole stretched wider while my eyes rolled, and a pleasure mounted unlike anything I had ever experienced before.

"That's it, darling," Saint groaned from behind me and licked his tongue up the entirety of my slit. "Relax your pretty ass."

Saint's breath was hot against my cunt as he found my clit and dragged across it with his teeth. I cried out and moved my ass upward, only to push the weapon further into me. My toes curled against the tiled kitchen floor, and my heart pounded in my ears as my body hummed in pure ecstasy.

Once again, I hated myself for feeling this way. They brought me nothing but pain, yet made me more alive than I had ever been in my life. They had me do things I never dreamed of and forced me to feel the unknown. They demanded everything I never thought I had in me, but they proved I could be as wicked as them.

"You're taking this baton so damn good, Liv," Sin breathed with need as he traced the tip of his blade over my lips and across my cheek. "We can't wait to watch you succumb to one of our dick's stretching your pretty asshole."

Saint pulled the baton outwards, leaving me with nothing but the tip inside of me. He tortured me with his mouth on my pussy, and I found myself grinding my entrance back into his face. Which he gladly accepted and feasted on me. His tongue plunged deep inside and swirled around vigorously until I screamed out his name.

Fuck. I had never uttered either of their names out of pure passion. But Saint felt so goddamn good.

Thirty-Four

Her Phantom

Saint

Jesus Christ and all that was unholy. The way she called out my name made me weak in the knees. I was damn lucky I was already down on them or else I'd crumble.

She tasted like honey and her moans made my dick buzz like a bee. I sucked her clit into my mouth and flicked my tongue hurriedly to hear her whimper my name again. I grazed my teeth over the tender flesh until she cried out, but my name never came.

I now had a powerful addiction to hearing her scream my name. A crazed obsession took over me, and I knew she needed more. Liv needed her asshole filled back up and left brimming full.

Since she stretched sweetly the first time, I didn't go slowly the second. She took what I gave to her as I pushed the baton all the way in, and she bucked against the force. Her body's response was all the invitation I needed, and I buried my face back in her cunt.

The juices from her pussy gushed all over me—I could practically take a shower in it. Her slickness was all over my nose, lips, cheeks, and nighttime stubble. I coated my tongue with her come and my mouth couldn't get enough of her sweet gushes. Our girl could squirt into my mouth, and I'd gladly take her like a champ. I'd take anything Liv Valencia threw my way because she was all ours. Her sweet ass and her cunt could attest to that fact.

I worked the wand back and didn't even have to push it forward because she accepted it herself. Our girl rode this pleasure like it was meant for her and she gave in. She spread her legs like a good girl all on her own and let me screw her with my tongue while pounding her tight little ass.

"Saint," she moaned on repeat, and the sound made me want to come in my pants.

I gave her what she craved while my balls tightly pressed up against me and filled with my come. My cock hurt from the friction of my zipper, but the pain was worth it. Anything for our girl.

"Yes, ride his face, sweetheart," Sin spoke as she moved faster against my mouth and my tongue enthusiastically probed her. "Come all over him like you know you want to."

Suddenly, she cried out with an untamed howl at the moonlight streaming into her kitchen. Her shrieks of release rang out while her pussy walls clenched down around my muscle, jerking fiercely inside of her. I pumped the baton back and forth in her tight hole as I watched the round flesh being penetrated repeatedly. Her plump ass cheeks jiggled, resembling waves, and I wished I had an extra hand. I'd continuously slap her bare ass until it became bruised and beet red. But I knew she'd love the brutal blows as much as I'd love inflicting them.

And I cherished each drop of the greedy need she gave to me as she came all over my face.

Thirty-Five

Her Phantom

Sin

Liv's perky tits could bounce. *Fuck.*

I was a goner.

She was our sinful goddess, dripping in her own blood.

Liv came for us like she had been waiting her entire life. Saint had earned his name from her mouth, but I hit the jackpot when she came with my name screaming from her lips. Her eyes were wide and rolled back, her back arched, and her tits rippled with each eager thrust. She rode out her orgasm unlike anything I had ever seen before, and my dick paid the price. But it was a small cost to wage in the reward we sought.

Her.

Liv's heart, mind, body, and soul. We'd win everything piece by fucking piece. I was confident about this.

Disoriented, Liv collapsed against the countertop, and I let her go. She dropped the knife she had held against me, and I wondered if she'd even remember how it wobbled against my throat. How much it trembled in her grasp long before she let herself go and her body shuddered with pleasure. Or how she couldn't hold on to her need to fight me with my friend's skilled mouth playing with her much too eager slit.

Saint removed his weapon from her once she had completely fallen into our darkness and he peered at me from over the top of her nicely shaped ass. His chin, nose, mouth, and cheeks gleamed with her wet juices. Her come was all over my best friend's face and that was all the answer I needed.

We were so damn close.

She was worthy of every fiber of our being, every dirty thought we obsessed over and all the absolutions she deserved. Our dark hearts were hers and she held them in the palms of her hands. She could ruin us, shut us down, but never, ever stop the love we have for her. Because she consumed our every fucked-up decision, our wicked souls, and our goddamn filthy minds.

Our little obsession was worth every single thing in the entire universe. Her willingness to give into the painful bliss we gave her brought us one step closer to her becoming ours forever.

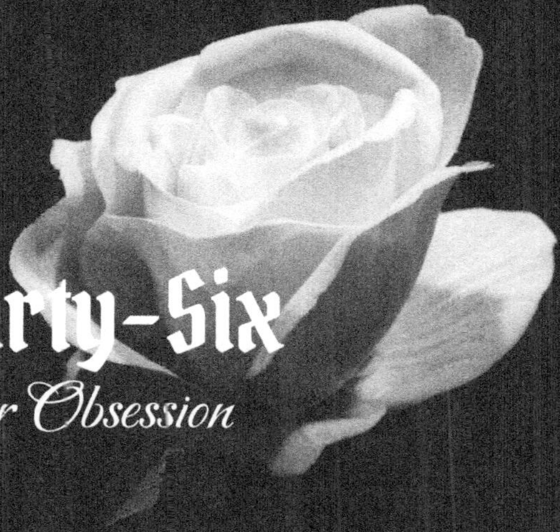

Thirty-Six

Their Obsession

Liv

I had made it back into bed. The memory of my phantoms had followed me into my dreams, and I knew I should keep them away, but deep down, I couldn't. Because for some fucked up reason, I didn't want to fight them anymore. Their hands on me, their kisses, and their huge dicks were all I fantasized about. They even haunted every corner of my dreams.

Their sweetness cursed me as I remembered them carrying me back to bed. Saint lifted my limp form into his arms and Sin tucked me in. Or maybe their caring gesture was all part of my dream?

I couldn't be sure as I shook my head in bed and heard my cell phone ringing off the hook. My groan filled the air, and I searched for the loud device on the nightstand. Hair blocked my view, and I pushed it aside while answering the vexing, shrill call, not caring who might be on the other end and wanting the sound to end.

"Hello?"

"Is this Ms. Valencia?"

"This is she," I answered, and I frowned as I sat up. "Who is this?"

"This is Dr. Paul Stevens calling. Is your fiancé Sebastian Chamberlain?"

"Yes."

"Earlier this morning, emergency crews rushed Mr. Chamberlain to the hospital, and he's currently in the emergency department because of his involvement in an attack."

"An attack?"

"A robbery, ma'am, and he sustained injuries."

A wave of shock—not worry about Sebastian—hit me as a hand flew up to my mouth, and the news threw me off. Asshole deserved the punishment, but I still had to appear to care.

"What type of injuries?" I asked.

"He suffered severe injury to his hands. Mr. Chamberlain also has a concussion from a blow to his head."

"Oh, my God! I'm on my way."

I smiled and cut the conversation short. I was a concerned bride-to-be who needed to hurry to her fiancé's side. The press would have a field day with this breaking news story, and I'd have to creep in through a back entrance.

I clapped my hands and jumped up with excitement from the bed. Poor Sebastian must be in excruciating pain. I couldn't wait to see him and witness his agony firsthand.

I hurried as fast as I could, but my ass hurt. The reminder of the baton shoved between the crevice of my hole stung. Literally. But I grew to love the anal fucking I had received and paid a blissful price.

"Fuckers," I mumbled as I cursed my ghosts and put on some high heels before walking out the door.

The hospital was a ten-minute taxi ride from home, and I searched on Google for the latest on my dear damaged fiancé. News articles came from all different media outlets. Word was out about Sebastian had been robbed in the old downtown with his wallet stolen and he had sustained non life-threatening injuries. But I bet this would bruise his ego for a lifetime.

I snorted while the cab driver peered at me in his rearview mirror with an arched eyebrow as if I was crazy. But I didn't give a shit. Sebastian was hurting, and I'd bask in joy at every moment.

"Please go around the back," I urged with my joy cut short, and I ignored his leering gander.

The cabbie swerved to pass a slow-moving car and ran a red light. A normal occurrence in the city. There was a crowd of vehicles in a traffic jam up ahead with news vans and video journalists. They held their microphones and video cameras, following them. Ready to get a glimpse of me, but I'd ensure they wouldn't because I didn't want to deal with the chaos today.

The taxicab ventured around the mayhem, and I spotted a way inside. "Let me out here."

Once inside the busy hospital hallways, I quickly found a nurse's desk. She kindly directed me to go down the hallway and make a left. Sebastian had a private room in the emergency wing and was receiving the finest treatment for a broken man who deserved much less.

Sebastian's room was the second one on the left and there was quite the crowd outside his door. Doctors in scrubs with charts in their hands were in deep conversation. I heard the words "acute fractures" and "mild traumatic brain injury," but those references made my heart beat with joy.

Patiently, I waited until the doorway was clear, and I held my breath for the sight I was about to witness. Slowly, I ambled forward as my head poked from the side of the door and my eyes found him. My dearly contused husband-to-be.

Sebastian was out cold. Fiberglass casts covered Sebastian's hands, and he wore a hospital gown. The look suited him. I crept in quietly, making sure not to wake him, and admired what the attack had done to him. Silently, I thanked whoever my angel had been. This time, luck had been on my side and evil hadn't won. Satan received a beat down.

Swiftly, matters shifted as my abdomen twinged with cramps and my lower back ached. I was due for my monthly cycle and the damn bitch had decided today was the day to show. A time to wreak havoc on me, surely with a heavy flow, opening up the blood gates of hell.

Fuck my life.

I had to find a restroom right away, and some distance from Sebastian would be nice. I'd come back after I got a tampon in me and some drugs for the pain. But I'd have to convince a nurse to give me some because I didn't have any.

Back down the hallway, I found an empty room. Private as much as Sebastian's, but unused as I made my way inside and closed the door behind me with a click. The bathroom was located further into the vast space, and I hurried toward it. A slight dampness was in my panties, and I knew the flow had already started.

Damn. The spare thong I kept in my purse would come of use.

I closed the restroom door, and my panties were mid-thigh when I heard a commotion. Voices came from the other side of the door. An argument ensued, but I recognized the voices.

Thirty-Seven

Their Obsession

Liv

"I look fucking ridiculous in this."

"Shut the fuck up, man. She'll fucking hear us," Saint hissed at him.

I almost giggled at their stupidity. But a slap caught my attention.

"Did you just fucking hit me?"

"Yep," Saint said with a pop of the *P*.

All right. This was enough. I tried to escape the mainstream media, not bring it straight to me. Those two idiots would draw unwanted attention because of their endless obsession with me.

I pulled up my panties, opened the door and huffed, "What are you two doing here?"

My arms folded across my chest as I glared at their dumbfounded faces and couldn't stop from laughing even if I tried. Sin and Saint wore blue scrubs. Scrub caps covered their hair and stethoscopes hung around their necks. But they still wore those stupid skull necklaces.

Saint smacked Sin on the head. "Too loud, man. I told you."

Sin's scrub cap flew off his head, leaving his hair a tousled mess, standing on edge. A grunt of frustration escaped him as he eyed Saint and his fists clenched. His temple pulsed from the sides of his forehead and shit was about to go down.

No way. Not on my watch.

"What the hell are you two idiots wearing?"

The sound of my voice drew Sin's attention back to me, and my distraction had worked. He ripped the stethoscope from his neck and threw it to the floor. Strands of black hair fell into his face as he slightly tilted his chin down and his dark eyes fell on me, but I swear I stopped breathing for all of sixty seconds.

Jesus, Sin could be intense.

"This was Saint's dumb idea to disguise ourselves, and I was a moron for going along with it."

"You look ridiculous." I giggled.

But truthfully, the best friends were incredibly delicious.

"It was a good plan until this asshole ruined it," Saint admitted with a scowl and took off his amusing scrub cap.

"It was doomed from the beginning," Sin grumbled as he glanced at Saint and a suspicious smirk grew. "But our other plan for destruction worked perfectly."

I curiously asked, "What plan?"

I uncrossed my arms and stepped closer toward them. A mistake? Maybe. But I wanted an answer.

"We had a prior commitment in the early morning hours," Sin said and ran his hand across my cheek. "Before you came all over Saint's face."

An electric current zinged from his touch, and I batted his hand away. Sin didn't stop. His fingers traced my lips and the voltage between us returned. This time I didn't fight; I was too sick of it. I was tired of the constant battle between us from the moment I met him. Talk about the wrong place at the wrong time. But in his deranged mind, he'd view the moment as the right fucking time, down to the very second.

"You still haven't answered my question." I glared up at Sin intensely. "What did you do?"

"We can't kill your fiancé," Saint answered as he came into view on the other side of Sin and pet my head.

"So we broke his hands," Sin added with pride and gave a laugh. "One by one we stomped on them, and the scumbag even pissed himself."

"Can you believe that?" Saint asked and their laughter overtook the room.

I couldn't. I wished I had witnessed the asshole wetting his pants, but again, another moment these fuckers had stolen from me. Or saved me from?

Fuck.

No. Their damn touch steered me in the wrong direction and veered me into a head on collision. Back on the road in the right lane, my mind tried to track, but my heart beat wildly at them doing this, and I knew straight away their plan was all for me.

"You did this for me?" I asked, needing verification.

"Yes. All for you. Sebastian hurt you. No one hurts what's ours." Sin glared and clenched his teeth.

"We had to ensure he couldn't do it again."

"And his hands cracked nicely," Sin said.

"Did you have to knock him out, though?" I asked with narrowed eyes and a tilt of my head.

"Yes," Saint growled.

"The unfortunate incident needed to look like a robbery."

Saint hissed, "And the asshole deserved more than a blow to his face."

"He should be dead." Sin's eyes swirled with darkness, and he pulled down my lower lip with his thumb. "We can still do it. Say the word and it's done."

I turned my head away from his touch. "No."

"I can play doctor and walk right in there. Some air could accidentally get into his IV line and poof..." Sin breathed into my face, with extra emphasis on the last word. "He's gone."

"Or I could take a pillow and suffocate him until his fucking eyes—"

"No. I need him alive," I interrupted with frustration as my belly cramped and my hands rubbed the painful ache.

Sin laid his hands on mine. "Something is wrong. What is it?"

"It's nothing," I said as I pushed away his hands. I didn't need his help.

Saint took my face in his hands, and his concerned eyes searched my face. His grip was rough and forced my lips to pucker, but the moment somehow was tender. My phantoms were rarely gentle and loved to bring me constant pain. But something about this was different, and maybe I was going insane.

I winced at the throb between my thighs and the shooting pain radiating down my legs. Medication wasn't an option when these fuckers wouldn't let me out of their sight.

"You *are* sore," Saint whispered as his warm breath fanned my face and his nose touched mine. "Tell us."

"I'm not," I argued and pulled my head back.

I couldn't breathe. Saint's sweet sentiment was too much. I needed space and room to think. He clouded all my better judgment and—

"Now," Sin growled as he put his hands over Saint's and made me aware of his internal need.

Stone-cold, dusty-coal eyes and an azure stare pierced right at me. No details were under looked as their gazes spiraled with worry and focused on me like laser beams. Red, sweltering heat blasted through me and flushed up my body as my hands pulled at theirs.

The world spun, and I was instantly dizzy. It had to be from my blood loss, a sure symptom from my condition they didn't need to know jack shit about. Their concern had no effect on me, and I could never give a damn about their feelings because they had none.

Or did I?

I needed to get away from them. Their stupid cedarwood scent was getting to me.

"Let me go," I voiced, struggling in their strong hold.

"You're in pain and we won't stand for it," Sin breathed as he clenched his teeth together and shook my face. "*We* are the only ones who will ever make you feel pain."

"It's none of your damn business," I snapped.

"Your discomfort is ours, and we'll do anything to make your hurt come to an end," Saint added with a crazy gleam in his eyes, and something about his frantic behavior made me cave.

"Okay, okay! I'll tell you, but let me go right this instant."

Immediately, their hands dropped, but they never backed away. Their fiery breaths were hot on my face and their eyes burned straight into my soul. Fire raged right at my essence's door and they blazed against it, trying to get inside.

"Tell us," they demanded in unison with urgency.

"I have my period."

Thirty-Eight
Their Obsession

Liv

An unfamiliar heat coursed from my toes to my already heated cheeks with embarrassment. Shame was clear in the air as my panties grew more damp and were uncomfortable to wear. They were garbage because these two dummies could only think of their dicks.

"I'm not an actual doctor, but we can help you," Sin said as he searched around the room at all the medical supplies and a gurney bed. "If you'll let us?"

Let them?

Hell no!

"I don't need your fucking help," I answered hastily. "Now, if you'll excuse me, I need to use the bathroom."

I took a step forward as they separated and made room for me to squeeze between them. Baffled by their change of heart, but I would not question them. I had a sore, bloody vagina to tend to.

"Okay. I tried being nice," Sin said as he grabbed me by the wrist and pulled me up against him, his breath in my ear. "But I'm not a nice guy."

Sin ran his tongue up my ear, and I shivered with mistrust. I cussed at him, but he didn't mind and threw me toward his best friend. My feet stumbled below me, causing me to trip on my heels, and Saint caught me before I hit the floor. He pulled me up against him, his breath heavy in my ear, and he nipped my earlobe. I was sickened with myself when my pussy ached with a sensation better than the never-ending throb of soreness.

"Asshole! Just let me use the—" Saint cut my rambled order off, tossing me toward the hospital bed further into the room.

My tits bounced as I huffed, and I watched the two dominant men take off their scrub shirts. They tossed them to the floor with grunts filling the air and stood there, blocking my escape. I had no way out except to run straight into their much too eager arms.

"We want to help ease your cramps, little obsession," Sin gushed as he licked his lips and bit the bottom one. "Stop your hurt with our pain and bring you pleasure."

"But I'm bleeding," I argued and lifted my dress. "See? We can't do anything when I'm on my period."

Slowly, blood trickled down my thigh because my panties couldn't absorb any more of my flow. My heavy menstrual flow always started right on time and the bitch cursed me.

"Wrong," Saint added.

"To hell with you!" I snapped as I dropped my dress and shot Saint the middle finger.

"Liv, Liv, Liv..." Sin tsked at me as he shook his head and continued walking toward me. "I thought I taught you a lesson with that finger."

"Well, your session must've sucked," I huffed and gave Sin a taste of my finger, too.

"This one won't," Saint said as he removed his stethoscope from around his neck and hung it from his ears. "Because your doctors are ready to see you now."

I couldn't help but notice the angel wing tattoos on his arms, with a wolf on one of his shoulders. The black ink had a design resembling a heavenly embrace, but Saint was too dark for God's golden gates. The old wound on his chest could attest to his evil behavior, but I pondered how he got such a nasty gash. A clear thunderbolt scar curved into his flesh, the same image his best friend had on his cheek. They not only shared matching necklaces, but their old wounds ran deep.

What were the fucking odds?

Saint reached me first with one long stride, and I gasped as his grip tightened around me. His strength was too much for me to fight against, but I still tried. I wiggled as he ran the circular part of the stethoscope down my chest and over my heart.

"Thump. Thump. Thump. Thump," Saint repeated as he listened to the muscle behind my ribcage and whispered in my ear. "This erratic little heartbeat will match each thrust we pound into your slick, red cunt."

"And this fluttering pulse..." Sin said as he held two fingers against my neck and peered down at me. "Will burst when you finally come with your crimson juices all over our cocks."

I couldn't help my wandering gaze as it ventured into the delicious world of Sin's inked body. Skulls mixed with fire and the true nature of his wicked conduct. Chains ventured along his arm sleeves and onto his chest with a snake wrapped around a skull and popping out of an eye socket.

"I'm on my monthly cycle! I'm not having sex with either of you—" my attitude ended there with Sin's hand wrapped tightly around my throat.

My airway constricted within his iron death grip as Saint stopped listening to my chest and lifted me off my two feet. My legs kicked outwards, but it was no use as Saint sat me roughly down onto the hospital bed and my body flopped. The bounce of me on the creaky mattress stopped because of Sin's tight hold around my neck.

"You're not going anywhere because you need us," Sin hissed against my cheek while Saint watched from behind him. "We won't let our girl suffer in agony."

Sin squeezed tightly as I clawed at his forearm, and my eyes bulged out of my head. Tears fell down my cheeks, and he licked the salty wetness away. Sheer panic ran through me as my fists beat against his arm in a frantic need to break free and breathe air into my lungs.

Suddenly, Sin eased up, and I choked out, "Asshole! You bring me pain from not listening to me and choking me half to death."

Sin let me go and stared me straight in the eyes. "Nonsense."

"Whatever..." I huffed as I rubbed my neckline and pushed at his face. "Now get out of my way."

"No," Sin said as he grabbed my arms and threw me further back onto the bed.

I yelped at the force as my backside hit the uncomfortable mattress again and Saint was on me in a matter of two seconds. He was on the bed with his hands binding my arms over my head, holding me down. I thrashed my legs with all my might, but I was no match for Sin as he grabbed them and spread me wide. My legs pressed into the bed with his knees on top of them and he hovered over me.

"We're going to cure this pain searing through you, darling," Saint breathed from above me as his hand found the zipper at the side of my dress and he pulled it open.

"That's right, Liv." Sin breathed heavily as his hand trailed inside of my panties, and he touched my slickness. "Do you know what cures cramps?"

I bit my lip and hid the whimper working up my throat as he rubbed the most sensitive part of me. Shudders ran through me, and I bit down harder, as his torturous touch didn't stop. He wanted to do me in, to hear me crumble, but I tried damn hard to reject my body's need.

I panted, "What?"

"Multiple orgasms."

Oh, fuck. I was in big trouble. The look on Sin's stubborn yet determined face spoke of everything he'd do to me as he pulled his hand from my cunt, and his fingertips were soaked red. He admired my crimson color and licked his fingers, which didn't surprise me coming from him. In his unhinged head he loved everything about me, even my bitch, Aunt Flo.

"I want a turn, man. I want to fucking taste her while she's on her rag," Saint pleaded from behind me.

"Be my guest," Sin said with red tinted lips, and he ripped my panties from me.

"Fuckers," I repeated as I thrashed while they switched places and Saint pulled my dress off my body.

I laid there naked with nothing on while Saint held my thighs open with his swollen forearms. The man could probably pop someone's head off with them! They were huge. But here was little old me, quivering beneath his strength with his breath against my bloody pussy.

A whimper escaped me as Saint licked up the entirety of my slit, and my head jerked back into the mattress. Sin groaned from above me while my eyes rolled. I loved his skilled caresses to my cunt more than I knew I should. My hips bucked, and I looked down at him just in time to see my menstruation on his tongue before he swallowed it down.

"Mm... So damn good," Saint breathed against my cunt.

The puffs from his mouth were warm, mixing with the rising temperature in me, and my feral need grew out of control. My breath was heavy, no longer able to resist. Especially once Saint attacked my pussy and ate me out while I was experiencing shark week.

Saint was the shark with his sharp fangs grazing against my clit and dragging them along my most responsive area. He pulled the flesh between his teeth until an untamed moan sounded from my open mouth. I couldn't stop the way my body reacted to him and I gave in. His head moved from side to side, and he never came up for air. He immersed himself in my red sea, avoiding getting caught in the harsh undertow and maintaining full control as if he couldn't get enough.

"Such a good girl, letting my best friend eat out your bloody pussy," Sin praised me as he watched everything unfold and held my wrists.

I jerked and thrusted into Saint's face, and my nails dug into Sin's hands. He held me while I rode the waves coursing through me, and the lust flowing erratically inside of me numbed the pain I once had. My release was close, and I was slicker than a fish with my red juices mixed with Saint's saliva trickling down my ass and onto the bed. The white sheets were wet underneath me, but I didn't care. All I paid attention to was this man with his mouth ruining me even more than I thought he ever could. He eliminated more barriers I had put up as my belly coiled tight—the spring was about to break loose.

"Saint!" I cried out into Sin's hand as he covered my mouth, and my orgasm let go.

More blood mixed with my pleasure on the stained mattress as Saint vigorously worked his tongue between my tightly clenched walls. I rode the waves of desire while the shark below me ate me up, and I had no time to worry about a mess. Only enough time to feel another bite mark as he freed his mouth from me and dug his teeth into my thigh.

"Fuck..." I moaned.

A wet crimson shine glistened around Saint's lips as he wiped his mouth with the back of his hand and grabbed my hips. Without warning, he flipped me over onto my stomach, and I yelped from the sudden movement. He only grunted and slapped my ass. I was too weak from the orgasm, barely able to flinch from the lash. Sin had already let go of me like he had read Saint's mind. The two assholes were more in tune with each other than I had realized. I tried to move my legs, but Saint pushed my knees up, and I heard a rustle from behind me.

"We're not done with you yet, darling," Saint said huskily, and his erection pulsated against my ass cheek.

I froze. Went as still as a cat with my eyes wide, and I got ready to attack. I couldn't take much more of this, wouldn't let them take another piece. There was still some fight left in me, and I had to do my worst. If I didn't, they'd have me right where they wanted. Undeniably theirs.

"You did such a good job giving into the need you cannot fight," Sin whispered into my ear as he stroked my hair and treated me as if I was a damn cat. "But we promised you multiple orgasms, and we intend to deliver."

Unexpectedly, I shot up like a cat out of hell with the back of my head banging into Sin's face, but his hand covered the blow. I attacked him with my upper body lashing out and my hands slashed in the air. I slapped Sin's face, but he deflected every single effort until something wrapped around my throat and choked me into submission.

Saint pulled the cable of his stethoscope into my neck and pulled me back against him, "That was very naughty, little obsession. Now be a good girl for Daddy, darling. Get down on all fours."

Thirty-Nine

Their Obsession

Liv

The struggle was gone. The will to gain back my control had ended. I was at the mercy of these two wild creatures with nowhere to go except give into them.

An aroused dick dug into my lower back while I observed Sin through teary eyes, and he reached down for his elastic waistband resting on his chiseled torso. Even with my air circulation very close to restriction, I still couldn't deny how goddamn sexy he was. Especially when he pulled down his scrub pants and revealed his cock I never could get over. His size was massive and unique, the same as the other delicious man behind me. My eyes followed the bob of his dick while it pulsated up and down with gravity, but Saint cut the show short when he let up on his strangulation technique.

"Asshole," I choked out as Saint gave me a slight push until I was on all fours on the bed.

"Oh, I love it when you talk dirty," Saint growled as he pulled the cable tighter and jerked my head back.

Sin's cock was within eyesight while Saint placed his dick at my red, soaked entrance. Blood trickled down my leg, and I felt dirtier than I ever had before. Some of the blood was fresh, while the rest was crusty from drying with the open air. Red stained panties had nothing on this, and I'd never view a period mishap the same way again.

"I bet you'd love it when—" My comeback fell short with a whimper as Saint pushed the tip of his cock inside of me.

"Fuck," Saint groaned from behind me as he inched in deeper and he stretched me wider. "Always so tight. Such a greedy little cunt."

I knew I could handle Saint's size because I had experienced it before, but the sting was no different as he stretched my tight walls. He pushed past my limit and hit the deepest part of me as a feral scream tore from my open mouth. He pulled the stethoscope tighter against my throat, making me arch my back. My eyes rolled into the back of my head while he plowed into me until black dots appeared in my line of vision. On the verge of blacking out while this beast, who was a tortured angel, wreaked havoc on me with more blood seeping into the crisp bedsheets. I was tainted, stained, and untamed as unimaginable bliss coursed through me, and I could sense nothing else. But I did the one thing I never dreamed I would, and I touched myself.

Pleased my clit while Saint drove into the very depths of my cunt, and I felt the coil tighten again. My hand was wet with the mix of my arousal and period blood, but I didn't give a shit. I let everything go, my eyes locked on Sin as he took my hand from between my thighs and guided me to touch him. Unable to dismiss my savage need to be one with both of them.

"Yes," Sin grunted repeatedly with each willing stroke I gave to him.

The sound of Sin's sinful euphoria was my undoing as I came again, and the sound of my second release ripped from me. The smack of our skin, mixed with my wild cry, made Saint ram into me faster, harder, until he hissed a loud curse, and he filled me full until his come dripped down my legs. My hand trembled with Sin's cock in my palm and mid-stroke he pulled away from me.

"My turn," Sin hissed as he grabbed my hips and lifted my knees off the bed. "Two down, one more orgasm to go."

I had no time to think, no time to react while Saint pulled himself out of me and let Sin take over. My pussy was an elastic band, stretched and ready for him as he slid in perfectly. He took hold of Saint's stethoscope and plunged into me at a speed fiercer than Saint's.

My tits bounced against his best friend's face as he lapped his tongue over each nipple and his teeth grazed the sensitive, erect buds. Another uncontrolled scream tore from me, but Saint's hand covered my mouth. He concealed my untamed passion while they shared me and claimed me as theirs.

After Saint finished his blissful torture with my breasts, he moved his expert mouth up my neck and his warm breath fanned over the previous marks they had each left. He licked the bruised skin in quick succession, and he left each one with a maddening kiss. More blemishes left at the hands of these two fucking men.

"Look at you, taking my best friend so fucking well as you bleed all over his cock," Saint whispered hoarsely in my ear and grabbed my earlobe between his teeth.

The muscle flicked repeatedly, and he dragged his teeth across the skin. Hot breath was against my ear as I heard nothing but him and his unsteady breathing. A sound I wouldn't soon forget.

Sin slowed his pace and grunted out with each thrust. "So. Fucking. Perfect."

But Saint's voice was my sole undoing. "Let go, darling. Show him no mercy and come all over his dick."

Ruthlessly, with no other thought, I willingly slammed my back end into Sin's cock over and over again. Thrusted to the same rhythm he had shown me, and he couldn't hold back. His release roared from him, and no one could stop him. My name was the only word coming from his lips.

The third climax they had promised to me came right along with Sin's. My walls clamped down and more come spilled from me. Gushed from my pussy and left the bed with an even bigger mess. One I should hold shame over, but I didn't as Sin dropped the stethoscope, and I fell back into his embrace. His warmth surrounded me as we collapsed onto the mattress with his dick still throbbing inside of me. Saint followed with his arms around me, facing me as we all breathed heavily in unison on the bed. The mess surrounding us stained us, and the act we had all taken part in tainted us. My phantoms might have started this sinful undertaking, but I had helped bring it to an end.

Thoughtlessly, I asked, "Where did you guys get these matching scars from?"

My fingertips trailed along Saint's old wound carved into his chest. The cut must've once hurt and must still sting to this day from the memory of how they each received one. I shouldn't give a damn, but their scars had piqued my interest.

Sin brushed my hair behind my ear and whispered, "We got them while being held captive in Iraq."

"We served in the United States military," Saint murmured as he looked down at me intensely, and my eyes locked on his. "But we became prisoners of war."

"After days of torture, I received a knife blade on my cheek because I was too outspoken and always put up a fight."

"And I got off easy, they told me," Saint whispered as his sky-blue eyes swirled with remembrance of a dark time and turned to hate. "Because I was the quiet one."

Sin added, "They wanted to brand an ugliness on our skin. Something to remember them by if we ever made it out alive. And we did, but not after they tortured us for sixty days straight because we wouldn't give them shit."

"My god..." I whispered and for some fucked up reason my heart broke in two for them, but I swallowed any emotion deep inside. "What happened? Were you both rescued, or did you both escape?"

"Rescued, but completely by mistake," Sin answered as I turned to gaze at him and he caressed my cheek. "We retired after being released from the hospital and agreed to open the nightclub together."

"And that's how you met Sebastian."

"Yes. Which led us straight to our greatest addiction," Sin breathed and kissed my cheek.

Saint touched my chin and tilted me to face him. "You."

Saint kissed the tip of my nose and unwound his arms from around me. He got off the bed and grabbed my purse from the floor. Sin slid his length out of me and joined his best friend as they searched through my purse.

"I didn't give you permission to—"

"Silence," Sin interrupted me with a command.

My mouth clamped shut as Saint pulled the extra thong from my purse and laid it on the clean part of the bed. But Sin held something else in his hand. Both, still fully erect, wandered back toward the bed, and I feared they desired another round. I was far too weak to move, to even try to refuse them if they wanted to. To endure their intoxicating greed, I would have to lie there and let it wash over my body. I prepared for impact as I closed my eyes while one of them spread my thighs and my shaky legs fell. I awaited destruction, their smell clouding all my judgment. I waited for their hands to devour me all over again.

"Please, I don't think I can do this. I—" All arguments disappeared after something slid inside of me and my eyes shot open to look up at my phantoms.

Sin and Saint inserted my tampon.

"What are you doing?"

"We're going to take good care of our girl," Saint answered and lifted me into his arms.

Sin peered down at me with an emotion I had never seen before, and he stole the breath right out of me. He took my hand in his and pressed my fingers against the thunderbolt on his cheek. The wound his captors gave to him for upholding his duty and being his gabby self.

"The torture we lived through taught us to wear our scars with pride. But we don't excuse anyone who hurts or tries to destroy what is ours because of the pain we endured," Sin explained with a need for me to understand. "We will be the judge of any suffering to those we love."

There was their confession. Sin and Saint loved me.

In their own fucked up way, these two unhinged men cared about me in a way no one else could. Cherished me as they walked toward the shower in the private room and Sin turned on the water. I didn't struggle with Saint as he wandered into the standup shower and water beads trickled down our bodies. Together, we stood in the shower as my blood and our sex washed away down the drain. They cleansed me and took care of me. They gave me all the affection I had ever dreamed of until their dedication hurt. These ghosts of mine wounded me straight through my heart and pried me open until I felt their love, too.

Forty

Her Phantom

Saint

Tonight, Liv was naked.

She had pulled her dress over her head and stripped off her thong. I had helped guide up the soft lace fabric over her beautiful thighs and snapped the elastic band over her shapely hips. She was a gorgeous vision after we took care of her in the wake of her many earth-shattering orgasms. A gentle gesture of affection was not our style, but our girl needed after-care and we'd provide.

She had responded effortlessly to each one and barely fought us this time. Her body had grown used to our force, earning her a higher gratification after all of her resistance. But I saw a crack in our obsession today, and we were close to owning all of her.

Her scumbag of a fiancé was still in the hospital, and with him not in the picture, she was free. Unchained to let loose and sleep stripped of him with nothing on. We did this. Sin and I. We took away any fear she had, even if it was for a little while. But the damn bastard deserved a gruesome death.

I watched Liv as she climbed into her bed without a care in the world and pulled the sheets over her body. She hid those fucking magnificent curves from me but had no idea I was tucked away in her closet. Hidden behind all her expensive clothes while she'd rummaged through, never finding me. I wanted to pounce on her, but I refrained since I knew she'd be sore after we took care of her. She required a break from my raging cock, and I had other intentions for her.

Our girl needed rest. She had earned a break. But not for long.

I smirked as I thought about all the things I wanted to do to her, all the inches of her body I wanted to revisit. I wanted to pound into that sweet pink pussy, slap her plump ass, and watch the waves roll. *Fuck.* My dick was as hard as a damn rock. Thank God those bed sheets covered her or my balls might bust.

Her eyes were closed, and her hair sprawled out across her white pillow as I emerged from my hiding place with a gift. She was such a knockout even while she slept. Little pebbles peaked underneath the sheet, and I was far too tempted to touch. To graze her, hearing her moan and watching her eyes snap open in surprise until they turned to terror. Her fear excited me every damn time.

I grunted, but Liv stirred with her lips parting for only a second and her soft breath emitting a small sound into the air—almost the sound of a soft purr. She was my little feline, and I was her owner, who'd pet my pussy anytime I wanted.

Instead, I touched her hair, stroked the soft locks on her pillow and laid a present meant just for her. A gift from her phantoms, the men who followed her everywhere she went, even in her dreams as she slept.

"Not too much longer now, little obsession," I whispered into the still air and creeped through her bedroom door, heading back out the way I came in.

Right through her front door.

Forty-One

Their Obsession

Liv

What in the actual fuck?

A basket was at the foot of my bed, wrapped with cellophane and two fake white roses. *Scratch that.* Two fake white roses with blood on them. But there was a card.

"While we aren't nearby, taking care of your pain, here are some alternatives to help you through. Sincerely, your phantoms," I read aloud.

But I quickly discovered that they had dipped the roses in the blood of my period.

Ew.

Gross!

What in the ever-loving fuck?

With caution, I grasped the flowers by their green stems and discarded them in the trash can. Two more roses to take out to the trash before Sebastian came home today. Another reason for me to be absolutely unsettled.

My fingers fumbled with the wrapper as it crinkled, and I readied myself for more gruesome surprises gone too far. Sin and Saint teetered like a ticking time bomb, and I never knew when they'd explode. They also had no limit, and this proved my point.

But what about me?

I let them fuck me in my blood. I got off on their devilish, naughty ways, for Christ's sake! Three times! Plus, I let them clean all the blood from me and cherish me with their sweet sides they loved to hide. But now the assholes do this?

Fuckers.

These men who lurked in the shadows had given me dark chocolates in the shape of hearts, even though it wasn't Valentine's Day. There were extra tampons in the care basket, along with pain relievers, to help manage any cramps. There were facial scrubs to clean up an unwanted acne outbreak, which was a damn curse no woman wanted when they bled for an entire week. A hot water bottle to soothe cramps and ginger tea to drink to help reduce my menstrual flow.

Again, they had gotten into my home while I had slept. I had ensured I locked everything. I had triple checked or else I'd go mad. Maybe I was on the verge of going batshit crazy because I had fallen for these two dumbasses. These two jerks who weren't big idiots after all and were extremely creative with everything they did.

This care package went to show their clever minds had a softer side I never imagined could live inside their delicious bodies. These men weren't just cold-hearted with skin and bones, but had real brains wired with actual feelings after I'd found out about their torturous past—a previous history they viewed as shaping them to be who they truly were, and I was their missing piece.

This had all started with blackmail and had turned into a screwed-up threesome. I was in an affair with two men who could very well own my heart. But I never wanted them to.

This situation should be unforgivable. I should hate their guts and maybe I still did. They had forced me into a mess I didn't know how to get out of, but I didn't know anymore if I had wandered into this willingly. My phantoms have captured every thought, all my pieces, and my heart was on the line. But once they captured my affection, I was a goner, and my soul wouldn't be too far behind.

I took the contents in the basket and opened my window, fully prepared to throw everything out onto the street. My eyes caught sight of the trees in the park swaying in the breeze. The greenery my ghosts chose to blend in behind and watch me from afar. Their eyes on me, lingering over my skin with goosebumps rising. They were there. I knew this, watching and waiting for me to make my next move.

I hesitated.

I couldn't drop the damn basket, my hand wouldn't let go. Sin and Saint had prepared this special surprise for me and my disregard for their out of the ordinary character would lead to a consequence. I felt this straight to my bones, but a small part of me wanted to keep the gift because the gesture was generously sweet.

"Fuck," I muttered as I slammed the window shut and dumped the contents on the bed.

I'd sort this shit out before Sebastian came home, and I'd dump the dumb basket into the garbage alongside the stupid flowers. As for this note? I'd rip the paper up into shreds like it never existed. And as for those assholes, they'd receive a piece of my mind.

I typed out a text message.

Me:

How did you get into my house?

Sin responded in a flash. He must live on his damn cell phone when I wasn't around to preoccupy his time. Ass.

Unknown:

Have your keys gone missing recently?

Wait a minute... They had! I had to get a new set of keys made. One for my condo and one for the mailbox. This all happened right after Sin entered the picture. *The jerk took my keys!*

Me:

You fucking stole my keys?

Unknown:

Yep.

"Real smooth," I mumbled as I typed in anger and was ready to throw my phone across the room.

Sin didn't care. He didn't even lie. He revealed the truth, as if taking someone's keys was a natural thing everyone did. Flat out psychotic.

Me:

I want them back!

Unknown:

I'll give your keys back.

Me:

Good.

Finally, there was the goodness in Sin he let creep to the surface. The same soft side who helped clean me up and put together pain relief supplies in a nice pretty basket with a red bow on top. This was the man I wanted to deal with, not the crazy side of him.

Unknown:

But first, I'll make sure I get extra copies made.

And the asshole was back.

Me:

I'll change the locks.

Aggravated, I sighed and knew he spoke the truth. Mr. Cruz's relentless pursuit of what he desired was driven by his obsession and unhinged state. I knew this for a fact.

Unknown:

Fine. We'll find another way in. Nothing will keep us from you.

Goddamn it. Sin would order Saint to kick my front door in, or he'd hurl himself at it until it caved in. I didn't need to clean up any more of their messes.

Me:

All right. Keep the damn keys. I don't need them.

Unknown:

Good. I'm glad we can agree. Now be a good girl and wave at me.

I heaved a heavy sigh and stomped toward the window. Each heavy footstep resembled a teenage girl angry at the world, and I waved out the window. I made sure I was visible enough but knew I didn't have to do much. Because Sin Cruz was somewhere out there mingling with the shadows and being the creepy fucker that he was.

Me:

There. Are you happy?

Unknown:

Extremely. Now go have some chocolate and make yourself some green tea. We want our girl rested and pain free.

Me:

Shithead.

Sin didn't even have to be present. He didn't even have to be anywhere near me. Because I heard his evil laughter like the sound lived inside of me.

Forty-Two

Her Phantom

Sin

A week had passed. Seven excruciating days since I was this close to my little obsession. I was so near I saw her chest move with each breath she took as I stood directly beside her while she dreamed of us with her scumbag fiancé sleeping right next to her.

I walked over toward Sebastian, who had bandages across his nose and the underside of his eyes was black. Bruised from the punch I had granted his sorry ass with before it was lights out. I wanted to do much worse and the prick got off lucky.

With clenched fists, I leaned forward, peering down at the man who brought pain to the woman I loved more than my life itself, and I was ready to end him. Eager to wrap my hand around his throat, his eyes popping awake and his mouth agape with not even a scream coming out. He'd be frightened, probably wet the damn bed, and he'd see his final moment. His last vision of the devil doing God's work with a fucking smile on his face. His last memory would be of me.

Not Liv. Not our girl. Our little obsession was the only person in this godforsaken life I'd burn the world for just to give her the universe.

A low growl seized the air but was too quiet to wake the dumbass who slept. A weak excuse of a man whose hands broke like a fragile twig. He had earned the cracked bones, but I still wanted to kick his face in. He was an ugly motherfucker and more hideous with his hands wrapped in molded casts.

Fuck him.

I treaded softly along the floor and was quite stealthy for a man with big feet. Being in the military had not only made me deadly, but shifty as fuck. I could sneak up on enemies with no problem and cut their throats with one slice to the jugular, with blood all over my hands and not a tear to shed over the murder I had committed for my country. The same killing I wanted to commit right now.

Loudly, Sebastian snored, and the idiot tossed onto his side. The awful noise kept going as I pulled a tin can from my pocket and slowly unzipped my trousers. Liv was in for a surprise. A gift I'd give her if she was a good girl. I'd leave it on her bedside table.

I opened the small jar with a squishy substance inside and placed the tin on the table beside the bed. Right by her phone, which was charging, and I pondered if I should snap a fucking picture of this. I'd love to see our girl's face when she turned on her cell phone to a picture of me on her home screen.

Fuck. The thought of the surprise made me wild as I held my cock in my hand and placed the putty around it. My beast of an erection was right over Liv, and if she were to open those fucking gorgeous eyes, she'd look right up at me.

My hand stroked my dick with the putty, making a slight squishing sound as I tugged back and forth. The rhythm was slow at first as my tense mouth partially parted, and my eyes caught sight of her cleavage. Her perky tits hid under her goddamn flannel pajamas, and I wanted to tear them right off her.

I jerked my dick harder, my nostrils flared, and my balls crushed up against me as the release grew. The dark flames inside of me burned out of control when she softly murmured something in her sleep. Jesus. I knew it. She was dreaming of me. Of us claiming her, consuming her, and fucking her until her brain spun. While her body quaked and she screamed out like a wild animal into the nightmare, ready to forsake her. But we were her terror because we owned her. She was ours, not some bad dream's.

Sebastian's annoying sound made me lose focus as I tried to enjoy our girl, and I wanted him to shut the fuck up. I wanted to reach over and rip his damn voice box out. One more goddamn time, and I'd hold Sebastian's Adam's apple in my grasp while I blew my load. Snore one more time you—

Liv's eyes stirred, fluttered once and twice until her vision grew accustomed to the darkness. I had missed her dark chocolate depths and the way her pupils searched my figure looming over her, but she only made me beat my cock ten times faster. All before her doe eyes widened in shock as I startled her awake.

A scream formed, but I covered her mouth with my hand and quietly mouthed, "Sh."

Our girl did just that. Liv shut up while my hand dragged up my shaft and pushed back down. The motion was smooth thanks to the putty which was cozy from the warmth I had already created. I was only getting started. She had seen nothing yet.

My naughty plan hadn't gone the way I had intended. I had wanted to jerk off over top of her pretty face and take a picture for a keepsake. My load would blow into the sticky putty, and I'd leave the tin can underneath the pillow as a present.

But Liv was awake. Ultimately, I preferred staring into her horrified, pretty eyes.

I held back a groan as Liv watched me, and her nostrils flared to life. Her breath was heavy against my hand as her fucking fiancé continued with his racket, but I didn't give a shit. I couldn't care less that he was in her bed with her when we should be the ones on either side of her. Saint and I curled up with our girl. Our hands touching her tits, kissing her skin, licking her pink cunt and making her scream. Not some fucker lying next to her who didn't give a shit about her. *Damnit.* Maybe I cared way too much.

But it didn't matter.

We were the ones who fucked her and made Liv come like a broken faucet. We were her phantoms who watched her every move, and I was sure Saint would tune into this. He'd see her put up a brief fight, and I hoped he could see the reflection of her fearful beauty in my eyes. Not scared of me. No. Terrified of what I'd do to her husband-to-be.

She wanted the bastard alive, and she had given no reason for us saving the asshole's pathetic life. *Make no mistake, Liv, we intended to break Sebastian's clock. He just didn't know it yet.* He lived on borrowed time and we were bound to crack him in half.

I towered over top of her, her head pressed back into the pillow and her hands clenched my arm. The grip from her touch loosened as she ran her hands up my arm and she caressed my forearm with her fingernails while her eyes undeniably turned from fear into red fiery lust. Her depths swirled with passion, and I got caught up in her.

My partially parted lips widened as I couldn't contain the beast inside of me, and I held the darkness at bay. The tide rocked with an untamed flow as I thrusted into the putty until I was fucking ready to explode. I wanted to fill the air with my grunts and be the alarm that woke everyone up in the neighborhood, but our girl alarmed me.

Liv covered my mouth with her hand, and I groaned into it, "Shit."

Squish after squish, I filled the motherfucking putty up with my come. The sound grew louder, causing Sebastian to flop on the bed, and the motion made Liv freeze. My wicked beauty had become untamed from below me.

Unlike her, I didn't care if the prick woke and saw me blowing my load over his fiancée. Hell, if this damn putty wasn't in the way, I would've come all over her face.

The fucker was lucky if you asked me. I kept his trophy wife clean, this time at least.

But Sebastian slept like a horse.

Liv's body relaxed as I twitched out the last of my seed with a swift jerk and kissed her palm. A shudder ran through her as she released me, and my dick throbbed again. I wanted her so fucking bad. I needed to rattle her intelligent brain, eat out her sweet tasting pussy, and devour those pouty lips until they bruised from my abuse.

But I'd take the alternative.

I bent down and placed a soft brush of my lips on hers. My tongue parted her mouth ever so gently, and I deepened the kiss. I wasn't harsh, but tender, and she'd feel me straight to the tips of her cute little toes. I captured her moan and ate the sound up. I wanted to gobble her whole and never let go, but I had to.

With our girl's sweet kiss on my greedy mouth, I placed the putty back inside the tin jar and craved more of her. I resisted all my better judgment and handed the tin to her. Surprisingly, she took the gift as I zipped up my jeans and walked backward to exit her bedroom. She only watched me as I waved and made my way out of the room. My quiet footfalls on the stairs as I went down and avoided the creaky step I had grown to recognize.

The addiction inside of me screamed to go back and grab her. We'd run away with Saint and never return, but she wasn't ready to be ours yet. The time was close, so near I could taste it. The same way Liv would relish in the flavor of my whiskey on her lips from our feverish kiss. A grapple of our lips she wouldn't soon forget.

"Until next time, little obsession," I whispered into the lonely dark and locked up her front door.

Forty-Three

Their Obsession

Liv

Why the hell did I still have this thing?

Days had gone by since Sin was here and masturbated into fucking silly putty. The squishy substance reminded me of a child's sensory toy, but all I remembered when I saw it was his aroused face. Him getting his rocks off while standing over me because he was such a loose cannon and needed to release his pent up sexual tension.

But I still kept the damn tin jar!

"Ah!" I yelled into my pillow out of frustration.

Once I finished my tantrum into the poor pillow, which didn't deserve my anger, I felt better. A heavy weight lifted off me, and I wasn't foggy anymore with my decision. I placed the tin jar of putty back inside the pillowcase and put it neatly back on the bed. The jar tucked away, hidden out of sight when I should take the stupid thing and toss it in the trash. But the dumb gesture made me think of Sin.

I couldn't get rid of the present when, deep down, I missed them.

I was screwed up, and I'd hold on to the freaking gift. For now. But I wasn't opening the fucking thing.

I was more clearheaded, but my mind was still a jumbled mess. My phantoms weren't the only problem I had, and my upcoming wedding weighed heavily on my mind. The big day was only weeks away, and the stress of all the appointments, phone calls, and viewings was too much to take. Flower arrangements, centerpieces, music, cake tasting, and the final touches to my wedding dress flowed through my overactive brain.

I needed a break.

Some fun was in order, and I wanted to get shit-faced—plastered out of my mind and forget all the troubles scurrying away inside of me, from my confused head down to my fucked-up heart.

I slipped on a sexy black dress with a low halter neckline that clung to my shoulders. The skimpy outfit hugged all my curves and had small cutouts in the fabric down the sleeves, across my cleavage, and down the sides of my body. I added a simple gold chain and light effortless makeup with black high heels. I had everything set to hit the club, and I knew straight away where I was going.

Sinful Saints nightclub.

I was an idiot. I could have picked any other club in the city, and I chose theirs. The ghosts who haunted me everywhere I went, and they were bound to know I had walked straight into their evil den. But Sin and Saint made me do crazy things. They made me have irrational thoughts, partaking in sinful behavior and I was scatterbrained.

A shit show.

I ordered a vodka shot from the nearest bartender, and the music flowed through my veins. My blood pumped with the beat as I swayed and threw back two more shots. I was a social drunk and didn't get out much, so the world quickly tilted sideways. Everything stretched out and back in, but the dance floor looked fun.

Along with my bright idea of coming here and getting plastered, but I saw an attractive man within the crowd of dancing people. He was in the thick of the vibrant streams of red, blue, and yellow strobe lights. The guy had a handsome face and a jacked physique.

He was just my type with not a single woman hanging off his arm, and I gathered he must be single. Pure eye candy I could indulge in, but I wanted to take things further because I needed the demons out of my head.

Suddenly, his gorgeous hazel eyes turned my way, and I realized I must've eye fucked him. *Oopsie-daisy.* I had caught the attention of a drool-worthy man. *What should I do?* Fuck it. I'd go over there and flirt with him!

Slowly, I strutted through the crowd, and it was like a laser beam attraction zinged between us. I bit the straw of my drink I had ordered last minute and took a few sips. I prayed my tiny nibbles against the plastic were sexy, and my heart beat wildly against my chest. The crowd opened up as if people knew we had connected and were destined to be, but only one problem nagged at me. Well, two, to be exact. My phantoms.

Oh, screw them!

"It's not polite to stare," he said over the music and took a sip of his beer.

"Oh, it's not, is it? Then why are you staring?" I asked sweetly and played with my straw.

He chuckled, and the sound was intoxicating. "Because your beautiful eyes were looking at me, and I couldn't turn away."

I grinned. "Why, thank you."

"Come dance with me," he commanded, and he left little room for argument as he took my drink from me.

"Hey!" I exclaimed, and I grabbed at my vodka on the rocks, but it was out of my reach. "I was drinking that!"

"I'll buy you another one," he whispered in my ear, his warm breath tickling me, "After you come dance with me."

I stared up at him and he peered down at me. The temperature turned up a notch and heat rose to my cheeks. Bodies bumped and ground around us as sweat coated my forehead. *Fuck, it was hot in here!* The booze or this extremely fine man had got to me, which one, I couldn't be sure. Until my cell phone chimed, and I looked down at the brightly lit screen, I knew the answer.

Unknown:

Stop flirting, Liv, or else.

I huffed as I took the stranger's hand, and we strolled into the crowd. His breath was hot on my neck as I typed, and I knew I had to get my two obsessed shadows off my mind.

Me:

Or else what?

Unknown:

We'll slice his eyes out.

Forty-Four

Their Obsession

Liv

I stopped dead on the dance floor; the guy bumped into my ass and his hands ran seductively down the sides of my body. A shudder ran through me at his touch, or maybe it was from the heat of their warning. Too late to know for sure, because his hands were all over me.

The man behind me grabbed my hips and breathed, "Oh, we're off to a good start."

I giggled and wished the boys could hear this attraction unfolding front and center, but their jealous stares would have to do the trick. Deep down, I had waited for this moment. They didn't possess me; I wasn't Sebastian's; I wasn't anything to any man. All men did was use me, abuse me, and force me, molding me into what they wanted. But tonight, I took back control with this eager creature kissing at my neck.

Another chime sounded.

Unknown:

Get his fucking lips off your neck.

Me:

No.

Unknown:

It's rude to carry on this way with another man under our roof.

Me:

I'm a paying customer.

Unknown:

Oh, you'll be paying with his life as your punishment for misbehaving.

Me:

I don't believe you. Now fuck off!

I ignored his threat and turned off my cell phone. The stupid device was only a way for me to stay connected to those two annoying idiots, and I was over them. I had moved onto this fine gentleman who pushed my rear end up against him, and I gyrated against him, then spun to face him. I didn't need to know his name, his profession, or anything about him. All I needed was to forget about those two fuckers who had stolen everything from me and given nothing back.

A wild scream erupted from my left. "You asshole!"

A chick stomped toward us like a wild banshee from the depths of hell. Her horns blazed as she leaped up and landed on his back with her legs wrapped around his torso. Bewildered by the chaos in front of me, I stumbled backward and almost fell flat on my ass. A kind stranger held me up as I regained my balance, and I watched a skinny woman beat her hands off his head. She was in a fit of rage as the man I had once thrown myself at tried to stop her.

Great. One night was all I wanted to forget everything. But I had chosen this?

This scenario unfolding was pretty obvious. The asshole had a girlfriend. I sure knew how to pick them.

A bouncer came to pry the batshit blondie from the prick's back and was successful after a full two minutes. She was small, but she was strong, and her furious eyes locked right on me within the bouncer's powerful hold.

Shit.

The cheating jerk actually got the balls to reach for me with his girlfriend breathing fire three feet away. His hand brushed my arm, but he clearly only thought about his cock. Dick.

I pulled away. "No thanks. You have a girlfriend."

"Yeah. Me! You little bitch!" she shrieked. She broke free from the bouncer and slapped me across the face.

"Ah!" I winced in pain as one of her red claws dug into my lower lip and scratched me.

She got ready to land another strike as my wide eyes locked on her hand, but her boyfriend intervened and grabbed her arm. "Easy, baby, easy... Come on, let's go outside and talk about this."

The cheating asshole was a smooth talker and clearly tried to patch up his adultery. He wanted to win her back. If he didn't, there'd be no piece of ass tonight.

She shouted, "I'm done talking because we're through! I'm..."

Her bitter words followed them straight out of view, and from the sound of it, he'd deal with blue balls for the rest of the evening. Asshole deserved it, but I didn't deserve a gash on my lip from the hellcat who pounced on me.

I stumbled toward the ladies' room. "Shit..." I bumped into the wall before I wandered into the bathroom.

My lip was vaguely sore until I peered in the mirror and saw the damage. Why does a cut hurt more once you see the wound?

I dabbed a damp paper towel at the blood. "Fuck."

The cut hurt like a bitch. The wild cat could scratch. I'd give her that.

Blood swirled down the drain and mixed with the whirl of dizziness from all the alcohol I had consumed.

I had wanted to get drunk, and I had achieved that goal. But my intoxicated judgment had cost me more.

My bladder was full, and I took advantage of the empty stall with my thong around my ankles before I even closed the door. The need to pee was fierce, and I lost track of the time as I turned my cell phone back on, realizing it was past midnight.

"Jesus," I hissed as my head continued to spin, and I struggled with my panties.

I should head home and crawl into bed without a sound. Yeah, right! Not in this inebriated state!

I shrugged my shoulders and remembered Sebastian was a sound sleeper. He could sleep through a hurricane and the house could come crashing down on him. He wouldn't even notice. Not until the bastard woke up in a pit of flames burning in hell.

I giggled at the thought and touched my hand to my forehead. I wished I could see straight, but I had no luck, not one ounce, as I headed to exit the restroom. I knew I'd have a hangover tomorrow.

My luck only got worse when the door swung open, and there was a bouncer. One of Sin and Saint's goons blocking my way without an escape in sight. The same guy who I dealt with last time at the club, and he gave me the fucking creeps.

I snapped, "What the hell do you want?"

He stepped forward and huffed, "These are for you."

An arrangement magically appeared from behind the big guy's back, wrapped in a decorative paper. Clearly, a bouquet was underneath as the white petals peeked through and he handed it to me. The gift was heavier than I expected, and it was an unwanted gesture.

"For me?" I asked and pushed them back into his chest. "I'm not taking anything from your bosses."

"Fine," he muttered and sat the present on the floor. "They said you'd refuse."

The awkward man stood up and straightened out his suit with a hard look on his face. I knew underneath the emotionless exterior was more instruction because chatterbox Sin couldn't ever shut up. He had probably barked the orders while his best friend put together the arrangement.

I crossed my arms. "They did, huh? What else did they say?"

"If you don't open your gift, there will be consequences," he answered without hesitation.

A tiny giggle erupted from me, and I tried to remain fearless, but inside I was shaking. "Of course they did."

"The choice is yours," he muttered as he turned his back to me and walked away.

Their bouncer wouldn't be far, this much I knew. He was their thug, hired help, who did whatever they wanted. This time, he was to deliver this arrangement and upon further inspection, there was red goo on the edge of the decorative paper.

My hands trembled as I kneeled down on the floor, the tile cold on my knees, and my fingers avoided the red streaks. Down in the pit of my stomach, my nerves wreaked havoc, and I wanted to run. I regretted my decision to enter Sinful Saints and wished I could turn back time, but it was too late for that. There'd be consequences. They had warned me, and I already suffered from this one.

My fingers grabbed the paper like there was something gross on it and I pulled it crinkled back. One side, then the other until there was nothing left to pull aside and the sight inside startled me. Instantly, I fell back onto my ass.

Eyes.

Hazel eyes with fake white bloody roses and I panicked.

"Oh, shit! No, no, no, no."

But there was a note smeared with blood.

We had fun with your punishment. Don't make us do it again. Smell the roses, be a good girl.

"Fuck this."

Forty-Five

Their Obsession

Liv

I scurried away from the morbid arrangement, and my legs couldn't go fast enough. Too quickly, I stumbled backward and fell, but my arms pushed my body up off the floor. My heels clicked as I ran, glancing back like they were behind me, coming out of the shadows, but all I saw were lifeless, bloodshot hazel eyes staring back at me.

The scent from the flowers lingered in my nose, the smell of Sin and Saint. The dreadful gift had cedarwood all over it, and I hated them. *Those fucking lunatics killed a man!*

Cut out his eyes because they warned me not to flirt with him. Made his heart stop beating for laying eyes on me because in their screwed-up minds, I only belonged to them. No other man could look at me, touch me or hurt me because Sin and Saint would end them.

With all the fear, anger, and hatred swirling inside of me, I found their bouncer straight ahead. I stomped up to him. He had his back turned to me, but I was dead set on finding the murderers who had killed for me in cold blood. I should run out of the nightclub, get a hotel, and hide away where they'd never find me, but I knew they would track me down.

There was no escaping my phantoms. Nowhere to hide because they'd go to the ends of the earth to find me. I had no choice but to face those fuckers head-on and beat them at their own psychotic game.

I tapped a finger on their bouncer's shoulder and huffed, "Take me to them. Now."

He only nodded with an irritated groan, like I was a pesky fly buzzing around his head and wouldn't screw off. His shoes tapped on the tile as he headed down another hallway and brought me toward his masters. Further into the nightclub, he took me back toward a place I recognized right away because I couldn't forget. The room where I met Saint for the first time, and he had devoured my pussy. Heat pooled between my thighs and the ache grew, but the journey wasn't pleasurable. The walk was awkward, unpleasant, and unnerving. But I needed to tell them to their faces, not to kill anyone else.

Would they listen?

I doubted it, but I had to shoot my shot. I didn't want someone else's blood on my hands even though Sin and Saint had been the ones to do the gruesome acts. The very thought of that poor man's life ending because of me made my stomach sick.

They must've followed him after his girlfriend blew him off somewhere outside of the club. Cornered him until he had nowhere to go while he begged for mercy and pleaded for his life. He was a cheating, egotistical asshole, but he didn't deserve to die. He shouldn't have had his eyes carved out of their sockets and put on display as punishment.

We got on an elevator, and the enclosure took us to the second floor. No longer anywhere near the nightclub as the doors opened, and the bouncer led me to a door. Bile collected in the back of my throat and threatened to come up, but I held the vomit back. Nerves knotted in the pit of my stomach, and my mind screamed at me to go back.

"They are waiting for you in their penthouse."

Of course, those assholes were.

Terror coursed through me as I walked through the door and into their home—a dark place like a Gothic dwelling. It was eerily similar to a haunted house. The walls had black paint, there were gargoyle statues, and my skin crawled as if there were cobwebs, but their cleaners would take care of the spiders.

These two not only were shadows, they lived in the shadows, too. Dark, frightening, and cold to the bone. A chill brushed against my skin, and I trembled in the thin air, but I was damn sure there was something there. Maybe an open vent was around me or a cracked window, but there was no evidence of either. I bet ghosts haunted this place.

This wouldn't surprise me one bit. Sin and Saint were ghosts, and they would live with them, too. Together with their creepy, fucked-up shit and creeping people out with their haunting ways.

Something furry rubbed against my leg. "Shit!"

Startled, a black cat meowed and made my heart leap up into my throat. The cat scared the crap out of me! But the cute little bugger purred as its head pressed into my ankle.

I bent down and picked up the kitty from the floor. The feline didn't appear to mind as it rubbed its head against my chest, and I pet the cuddly creature. The tame animal helped calm my nerves as I stood up and carried the cat with me.

"I see you've met Rocko."

"Jesus!" I yelled and spun around.

Sin stepped out of the shadows from where he hid, watching and waiting, while he peered at me inside his home. He took in the prey he had lured here with his gruesome bait. A trap set in motion for me as a punishment for my rude behavior under their roof. Fuck their rules. Screw them. I had had it with their sick and disturbing actions.

"Here, pussy, pussy," Sin called.

The cat wouldn't listen. He had a mind of his own. I liked Rocko, and I think we'd get along great.

"It's a cat. Not my cunt."

Sin growled, "Scram, you damn pest."

Loudly, he clapped his hands and Rocko hissed, but he leaped from my arms. The darkness ate up his black fur coat as he hurried off and mingled with the ghosts.

"Hey!" I exclaimed with an attitude. "I like him."

"And we like you, but we have other matters to attend to."

Saint came into view behind Sin. The pair belonged in the dark. They wore shades of black with ripped jeans and shirts showing off their tattoos. I was furious with them, but they were delicious. I couldn't deny their sexy good looks with Sin's hair falling over his forehead and Saint's intense blue eyes staring right at me. Their frustration with me was overbearing, but my anger faced them head-on.

"What the fuck is wrong with the pair of you?"

"Nothing," Saint answered.

"Like hell there isn't!" I exclaimed and took two steps toward them. "You killed that man in cold blood!"

Saint shrugged. "So?"

I can't believe this! They have no emotion. Not a care in the world.

"So, I should call the cops and have your asses thrown in jail," I threatened as I reached into my purse and took out my cell phone. "I bet they'd lock you up and throw away the damn—"

Sin launched forward and took my phone. "What the fuck? Give me that back!"

"No police."

I jumped repeatedly and tried to get my phone back from Sin's grasp, but all he did was laugh. His evil sound echoed throughout the room, and I hated him for making me feel so small.

"Look, Saint. She's our little bunny."

"A pretty bouncy one," Saint added.

Sin growled, "A sweet doe I want to chase, watching those perky tits bounce to and fro."

Sin grabbed the back of my neck as I yelped from his death grip, and a flash of light blinded me. The asshole snapped my picture! He had some nerve.

"I won't have you killing anyone else because of me," I warned through clenched teeth.

"And we won't have you misbehaving with anyone," Sin breathed as he heaved me toward his chest and spit hit my face with each word. "Do you understand me?"

"Make me, fucker," I snapped.

The tension between us could cut like a knife—slice through all the fear and chemistry and leave us with open wounds. Blood would pour from our gashes as we fought for control, and no one would make it out alive. We'd die together, but these two would love that. Our spirits stuck together in this goddamn haunted house. Forever.

To hell with that!

"We warned you. No one touches or looks at what is ours." Saint reminded me from behind me.

"His death is your punishment." Sin glared. "But he was a loser who only wanted to use you and get under your dress."

He jerked my head, yanking me to make me understand. Pain bloomed at the nape of my neck and tears bit at my eyes, but I pushed through the hurt. I forced myself to return his glare with not one ounce of fear because he didn't deserve it.

"So what?" I spat like a wild animal, completely enraged. "I wanted to use him too! To escape the pair of you!"

"Liv, Liv, Liv..." Sin tsked and breathed heavily against my cheek. "There's no escaping us. But now that you've received your punishment, you need a reminder of who you belong to."

"Fuck you."

Sin laughed. "All in good time, sweetheart."

He tossed me backward, and I stumbled into Saint's arms. He held me and licked up my cheek; the wetness left a feverish heat searing through me. But I jerked my head away from his tongue only for him to laugh at me, too.

"Disgusting."

Their evil laughter mixed into one as Saint said, "Run, little obsession, run."

"If we find you, we'll screw you," Sin promised through clenched teeth as his head bowed and he stared at me with insane certainty. "And we'll stick our dicks in every hole you have."

Forty-Six

Their Obsession

Liv

Saint released me, and I gasped as my ass hit the floor. Pain radiated up my tailbone, but my heels thrashed against the floor as I scurried backward until I hit the wall behind me. Startled, I stood up and raced down the hallway as their wicked laughter followed me.

The dimly lit corridor created shadows that leaped out at me everywhere I turned. Frightened, I hurried forward with only a brief glance backward. I saw nothing. But within this dark hallway, Sin and Saint were hot on my trail.

I passed rooms, furniture, and a kitchen. I heard hisses, but not from Rocko. More cats. The animals were everywhere as I stopped and searched around for anywhere to escape. My eyes landed on a patio door.

I darted for the back patio as I heard footsteps not far behind me, and my heart jumped up into my throat. I was certain I'd choke on the organ and those fuckers would find me. Adrenaline pumped as I got outside, and the cold surrounded me. There was a full moon shining from the dark sky above as my stilettos hit the stairs. I wobbled with each step until I hit the grass and fell flat on my stomach.

Panicked, I peered up to only see a dark figure on the balcony eyeing its prey from above. My legs pushed up, and I was off without another glance back, fearful of them reaching out to grab me and having me all over again.

My feet ached as I ran as fast as I could and darted through the park behind their penthouse. I had no idea where I was going, but all I wanted to do was get away from them—away from their consequences and the ownership they held over my head. I wanted to escape, and freedom was somewhere through these stupid trees.

I tripped over an exposed root in the ground and fell against a tree trunk. I panted, with strands of my hair moving in and out from my parted lips. Disoriented, I glanced left and right, unsure of the direction I had just been running. They could be anywhere by now, and I was a sitting doe with wide eyes, quivering from the damp, chilly night. *Damn this skimpy dress I had worn! To hell with my broken heel and all my dumb decisions leading me right to this moment!*

"Shit," I whispered when I heard a twig snap.

Dread pulsed through me as my hands worked with my heels, and I took them off. My bare feet were cold against the grassy soil as I hid behind the tree trunk and prayed they didn't find me. I wasn't one who believed in much, but I had to have faith in something. Because if they found me, I would be in trouble. Screwed.

I didn't make a peep, not even one sound, as I listened to the leaves sway in the breezy night and car engines rev off in the distance. The city streets were too far away, and I wasn't anywhere close to getting out of this park.

No wonder I never ventured here. This place was full of nature and bugs were everywhere. I could feel creepy crawlies on my feet and they crawled up my legs. It was an unwanted tingle as goosebumps peaked from the chill and perspiration beaded on my forehead. I tried hard to remain still, unmoving, as whatever insects wiggled on me, and I only breathed tiny puffs of air.

The coast appeared to be clear as I decided which direction to flee, and I shot out into the wilderness in a sprint. My legs moved fast, my pulse raced, and the air huffed from my lungs. I'd make it out of here in one piece with no dickheads sticking anything in my holes. Their threat was no match for—

In an instant, someone tackled me down. A body fell on top of me, and I wasn't sure who it was. A scream tore from me and howled into the night, but the vicious animal who had captured me didn't care. He covered my mouth and quieted his prey.

Somehow, I got out from underneath him, and his hand released me. I clawed at the earth and pulled my bodyweight until one of them grabbed me by my ankles. A fearful yelp escaped me as my hands sunk into the dirt, but I only dug a hole. A big deep trench I couldn't get out of as he trapped me and fingers wrapped around my throat. The powerful squeeze made it hard to breathe, and I gasped for air.

"Found you," Saint whispered into my ear.

"Asshole," I choked out with my cheek pressed into the earth. Black boots were inches from my face.

I watched as Sin bent down, rested an arm on his knee, and he brushed the hair out of my face. "Caught you."

"Go to hell," I spat out, and my nostrils flared.

Sin snapped his fingers, and Saint released me. The heavy weight from his body eased off, and I coughed into the grass. My hands rubbed my neck and tried to relieve the pain from the strangulation, but it was no use. I was in pain from my aching feet, the bug bites, my cold bones, and Saint's brutal force.

"Get on your feet, Liv," Sin ordered from above as he peered down at me like I was an insect he'd squash.

Scratch that.

Sin would control the perimeter of where I'd crawl. He'd spray insect killer all around me and trap me within his borders. He didn't want to kill me; he wanted to use me. Force me to do whatever he had in his dirty little head and claim me within his prison.

I listened to his command and stood up to face him. In the dark, I could still see the heat in his stony stare, and the temperature rose inside of me. My body shivered from the fight between hot and cold as my breathing picked up a notch. My kneecaps were dirty from the dewy grass and small twigs were in my hair. I was a mess, but they didn't care.

I snapped, "There. Happy now?"

"Not yet," Sin said as he pointed at my neck. "Remove your necklace."

I shook my head.

A loud slap filled the air, mixing with my whimper as Saint slapped my ass from behind and said, "Don't disobey him."

With staggered breaths, I obeyed and unclasped the gold chain. I held the bulky necklace in my hands, and my eyes never wavered from Sin.

"Give it to me," Sin demanded as he held out his hand, and I dropped the chain inside. "Good. Now get down on your knees to seek absolution for such an unforgiving mouth."

I did as Sin insisted because I had no other choice. There was no more running and nowhere to hide from them. I was out in the middle of nowhere, but my phantoms knew their way through this patch of woods. They lived here while they preyed on me, watched me, and now they'd have their way with me. But I couldn't deny, deep down, I wanted them too.

No matter the fight I put up, my refusal to quit, they still consumed me. It had only been a matter of time before I let them lure me right to this second, where I was down on my knees and Sin took out his cock. His massive girth throbbed, only a short distance away from my face, and my mouth watered at the delicious sight. I remembered what his dick felt like as my pussy grew wet, and I ached inside my heated belly. They had found me and would fulfill their promise, reminding me of who I belonged to.

Them.

They were savage beasts who owned me, as Saint took my necklace, and I sucked in a breath. Swiftly, he placed the chain against my throat right where it belonged, but he pulled it tight. My eyes bugged out of their sockets, and my hands thrashed out in front of me. Only for them to rest on Sin's bare thighs with his cock on the edge of my parted lips.

Forty-Seven

Their Obsession

Liv

"Don't fight it. He'll only pull tighter," Sin said through clenched teeth as he glared down at me and tears fell from my eyes. "That's it, relax. Be our good girl."

I could breathe, but barely. I watched Sin form a wickedly sinful grin as he bunched up my hair and let Saint grasp the tousled mess at the back of my head. Saint kneeled behind me with his pants already discarded and tossed to my right. They were eager, horny, and ready to have their girl.

Slowly, Sin inched his dick inside my wet hole. Saliva coated the sides of my mouth, and I had fond memories of the last time he filled the wide hole in my face. Fast forward to this present starry night, and the scenario wouldn't work out the same. Because I gulped down his enormous cock before he tried to stop me.

"Jesus, Liv. You're fucking eager to please, my little—"

The change of habit caught Sin by surprise, with his mouth agape and his hiss filling the night. I watched with teary mascara running down my face as he closed his eyes, and his fingers dug into my shoulders.

I dove in again and tried to go deeper, but his size was too much. Saint saw me struggling and pushed me forward with a growl. The sound made me so damn horny as my throat relaxed around Sin, and Saint bobbed my head repeatedly. The wet noises from me deep throating Sin's cock sounded out into the night, and our moans echoed off the trees.

My eyes remained open through my watery vision, and I watched Sin interlock his hands behind his head, fully letting me unleash my worst onto his untamed, massive girth. The damn bastard looked like he was sprawled out, relaxing on the beach!

The necklace pulled tighter from Saint's excitement, and my nails bit into Sin's muscular thighs. I blinked several times as Saint let me breathe, but only slightly with my mouth still wrapped around his best friend's throbbing length. Precum oozed into my mouth and the salty taste had me licking it up with my tongue swirling around him and nipping his mushroom head. Saint let me play with his friend before Sin pulled his raging cock away from my wet hole. My mouth craved for more as my eyes beamed up at him full of red-hot lust.

Unmoving, I stayed where I was, delirious with the passion roaring through me, and the pair of them changed up positions. Sin kneeled behind me, but his hand pulled up my dress. His fingers dug into the plump skin on my ass, and he squeezed me until I yelped from the pain. A low growl vibrated against my ear, and he grazed his nails up to my hip, my ass pressed up against his erect dick.

"Stretch your hole wide for him, sweetheart," Sin hissed into my ear and pulled the chain tight.

His strength made me open up as I gasped for air, but half of me did as I was told. I didn't fight Sin, and I gave in while Saint lodged his dick down my throat, buried himself deep until I gagged, and he pulled back out. He was far more impatient than Sin and wanted to show me his dominance. The need to be in control as he hunched over me and thrusted his hips, fucking my face hardcore. Saint held my cheeks in the palms of his hands as his thumbs swiped at my messy tears, but he didn't let up. He hit the back of my throat over and over again until I was sure I couldn't take anymore of him, but he proved me wrong.

Sin groaned all the praise I needed as I took his best friend's ferocious desire and let Saint do his worst. He made my head bob to each pound he graced me with, and the sounds coming from me were unlike anything I had ever heard before.

This was more than a face fuck, it was a deep throat of insanity. An asylum wouldn't even take us. Nothing could keep these men from me. Saint showed me I was owned, and Sin told me I was theirs. They fucked me beyond recognition.

"Goddamn, darling," Saint snarled as he let up, his voice hoarse. "You did such a good job taking my dick like a pro."

He popped his cock from my mouth, saliva stuck to the tip of him attached to my drooling mouth. I licked my lips when Sin loosened my necklace, only to surprise me when he clasped it back in place. The skin hurt, and I was sure there was a red line, but Sin soothed the ache with fingers tracing the marks he had made.

"Take off your dress," Sin whispered in my ear.

"Slowly," Saint added as he backed away from me, and my eyes lay starved on his cock.

I didn't speak, not a word was uttered, while Sin backed off and gave me space. He gave me enough room to grab the bottom of my skintight black dress and pull it up. I obeyed their requests and painstakingly lifted the dress past my thighs, ass, up my navel, and over my breasts. Until there was only my head left covered by the fabric, and I heard their grunts of satisfaction. I was fully aware they were stroking themselves as they watched me give them a show and display my naked body to them.

I pulled the dress over my head and tossed the thin piece of fabric to the ground. I inhaled a sharp breath at the delicious sight, as both men jerked on their cocks, giving me their own personal wicked grins. One snarled with a lip up, while the other's grin spread right across his mouth. The slickness between my thighs called for them, but I held back and hung onto the last thread of decency I had left.

"We're going to pound you until you're raw," Sin promised as his eyes landed on my bouncing tits with each aroused breath I took. "Until you can't walk and you can only rely on us."

"And when you feel the sting we inflicted, you'll remember that you belong to us," Saint added as his hungry gaze never wavered from my pussy. "Take that fucking thong off."

I shimmied the panties down past my thighs until it dropped to the ground, and I stepped out of it one foot at a time. "Now what?"

A few breaths passed between us until Sin said, "Run."

Without thinking, I spun around and ran like the wind. My tits bouncing, my ass jiggling, and my heart pounding. My feet were numb as adrenaline surged through me. I was naked, awakened, and so fucking turned on. I was a wild animal running freely in the wilderness while two people hunted and targeted me. They followed on my heels as they played with their prey before they had their way with me.

I shrieked when a hand slapped my behind, toying with me before the other captured me. His arm wrapped around my waist and lifted me off the ground. Only to push me forward into the base of a tree. The bark scratched against my skin as they pawed at me. Their hands were on my ass, running down my back and over my stomach as Sin flipped me over onto my back.

"Ah, fuck!" I cried out as Saint pulled at my legs, and my back scraped down the side of the tree trunk as he guided me to the ground.

Saint spread my legs wide when I hit the soil and Sin got between my thighs. His large hands groped my chest as a feral moan escaped my mouth each time he pinched my nipples. He cursed at the noises I made and squeezed my tits, only to let go and grab both of my ankles.

"Spread wider for us, sweetheart," Sin encouraged as he stretched my legs backward and the top of his head tapped the tree trunk. "Time for daddy domination."

I was bent like a pretzel with my feet on either side of my face. Exposed, with my slick, hot cunt biting at the chilled open air. I cried out from the uncomfortable position Sin held me in, but he only silenced me with his tongue diving between my lips. I gave into his heated need and lashed out against his lapping muscle. Only to moan into him as Saint kneeled behind and pushed his dick into my pussy, stretching me until I was full of him. There was no warning, only a rough thrust in. He pulled back out with his dick wet from my arousal. Sin broke the kiss and crouched over me while Saint stood behind him with his hands on his best friend's back.

"What the fuck—" I couldn't finish my sentence as both men forcefully thrust their dicks into me, causing me to make an animalistic sound.

Saint in my ass and Sin in my pussy. My backside dug into the dirty ground as they both pumped into me and didn't let up. They fucked me harder and rougher than I had ever felt before, while all I could do was lie there and take the forceful thrusts.

"Here's a picture of us," Sin whispered as they slowed their pace, and he licked at my cheek.

The flash from my phone's camera lit up our entangled bodies.

"You are both the devils incarnated," I snapped as my body shuddered with heat.

"We're devils?" Sin questioned as his breath fanned across my face and he picked up speed. "But you're clenched around our cocks, little obsession. What does that make you?"

An evil entity bound to burn.

I cried out as their inhumane thrusts returned, feeling totally out of this world. My asshole and cunt were filled full while their cocks surely felt each other, only a thin barrier of flesh between them. Their dicks were massive and sure to leave some tears, but I didn't care.

I whimpered on repeat, "Oh, fuck."

I was alive underneath them as my hand willingly traveled down, and I touched myself. Caressed my clit while our moans, grunts and groans filled the park. We'd wake the animals as the early morning sunrise was only around the corner. The sounds of our wild sex were an alarm clock for all to hear.

"Mine," Sin grunted with a thrust into my pussy.

The tip hit my G-spot and left my mouth agape.

"Mine," Saint groaned as he pounded my tight asshole.

Their massive lengths coiling the tension in my cunt until the spring let go.

A feral cry released from me and wave after wave of pleasure shuddered through me. My climax stirred something in them as they went full-force and fucked me into oblivion. My vision shattered; my brain rattled as pound after pound they each chanted I was theirs.

Until Sin filled my cunt full of his come and groaned, "Ours."

"Forever," Saint hissed, with his seed seeping out of my ass while he drilled into me.

They had filled me up, stuffed me completely, until I was overflowing with their feverish need. They had pounded me until I hurt all over, but it left me elated. I was theirs heart, mind, body, and soul.

"Have we proved our point?" Sin asked with a shaky breath.

"Yes."

Sin let go of my legs as both men pulled out of me, and they collapsed on either side of me. Saint on my right and Sin on my left. Sedated, we all laid there lost in the unexpected passion they had delivered, and I knew I'd never be the same.

Forty-Eight

Their Obsession

Liv

Weeks flew by without warning and my phantom's addiction to me grew stronger. They had their way with me whenever they wanted, and each time, I gave more of myself to them. I lied to myself and blamed their blackmail, but I knew deep down it was more than that.

After they hunted me through the park and proved they owned me, I knew I was in too deep. Saint had carried me through the forest with their come dripping down my thighs. I had let them drive me home, but Sin stopped the car down the street. Their lips each bruised me with their affection and reminded me of our passion. But I saw in their heated glares that they didn't want to return me to the devil. Because Sebastian was far more sinister than them.

I knew this was true, but I was in over my head. It was too late to turn back and call off an arrangement that would save my family. Status was more important than my fucked-up affections for two men who had forced me to give a shit about them—two assholes who fixated on me and followed me everywhere. *Jesus.* Our situation had turned into a mess.

Was this love?

Because if it was, the affection I had held no boundaries. It was beautiful, raw, and it fucked me up. Love was like a wilted flower coming back to life after being cared for with water and basking in the sunlight. Only, their love had periodic moments of bliss before the wind created chaos and the petals drooped. The blossom would require fertilization to keep flourishing into the lovely bloom the flower was meant to be. Until one day the delicate flower couldn't breathe.

And this was me.

In over my damn head, unable to catch my breath. Worn thin by the constant back-and-forth emotions fogging my every thought. There was no proper answer in sight.

I now look at Sebastian's displeased face as he peered down at his cell phone and back up at me. Oh, no. Something was wrong.

His face was unsatisfied while he could barely hold his phone because of the casts on his hands. It had been weeks since the damage was done, but his healing was coming along nicely. This was unfortunate news for me. I wished my phantoms would break his hands for good, sawing them off might even be a better plan.

God, I was turning out to be exactly like them.

"What the fuck are these?" Sebastian asked as his words spit into my face, and I had the powerful urge to wipe the wet specks off.

"Flowers," I answered as I glanced down at the beautiful orchids I had chosen for the wedding and back at his enraged face.

"Lose the smart mouth, bitch!" he yelled in my face.

Frozen, I stood there and took Sebastian's wrath. I had no other choice. I listened to how much he hated them. Each curse word bruised my soul, and I wanted to hit him—to take my clenched fists and make him hurt. Not my phantoms. Me.

Sebastian Chamberlain was a mean, egotistical, abusive jerk. There was never a pleasant moment between us, and I was over the fake relationship before it even began. I didn't know how I'd last married to such a cruel man. My soul died a little more with each hurtful word, every embarrassment, and every strike. The only thing breathing life into me were my ghosts. The shadows I had never wanted, but needed, more than ever. I clung to their darkness through my vicious fiancé's fury over flowers until his cell phone started ringing.

"Fuck! What now?" Sebastian exclaimed through clenched teeth and answered on the third shrill ring.

I loathed him with everything in me as my being seethed with madness, dreaming of all the ways to end this torment I'd lived through for months. *I wanted out.* My mind was prepared to leave and run away from everything I knew into the unknown. That would be better than dying a slow, painful death inside.

"You need me at the nightclub tomorrow?" Sebastian questioned in a businesslike manner, a complete one-eighty from him unloading on me a few seconds ago.

I listened as I kept myself busy and pretended to rearrange items on the table. Everything was fucking spotless already and nothing needed tending to. Sebastian's stupid rules. I was over them.

"Okay, I'll be there."

The phone call ended. I only caught half of the conversation and wasn't good at piecing shit together. Sebastian's brows narrowed together, and I could swear he appeared nervous. The change in his demeanor sparked my interest, and I wanted to know what had him on edge.

"What was the call about?"

"None of your damn business!" he snapped and rubbed a hand over his forehead. "Lose those ugly flowers."

Sebastian stomped away with his shoes tapping against the floor and a gloomy cloud followed him overhead. The atmosphere drastically altered, all because of whoever was on the other end of the phone call. Normally, Sebastian would've carried on with his rampage, leaving me cowering on the inside. But something or someone had gotten to him.

The thought disappeared with a single chime.

Forty-Nine

Her Phantom

Saint

I hated hearing his voice. I wanted to reach through sound waves and rip out his larynx. Hold his tender delicate windpipe as the squeaky sound lessened and blood coated my hand. Sebastian sounded like a pumped-up balloon full of helium and he annoyed the shit out of me. I preferred talking to the motherfucker over text to avoid listening to that train wreck, but he was upsetting our girl. His behavior was barbaric and inexcusable. He went off on her over fucking flowers, for Christ's sake!

Sin was about to fly off the handle and drive over there to hurl his ass out of the condo. He was definitely ready to kill him right there in the street with him bowed over the hood of our car, and he'd probably chop his head off execution style. Sin wouldn't care about the crowd or the damn media blitz on the breaking news story. My best friend would make front page news and wouldn't even blink an eye. He'd go to jail all for Liv.

I had stopped Sin, grabbed my phone, and made the call. I had invited Sebastian to our club to discuss important business when, actually, our precise discussion would be about Liv—his mistreatment of our property. Mr. Chamberlain was in for a big surprise.

Sin growled from over my shoulder as he peered down at the scene as we watched Sebastian give his rude command to Liv. Normally, I'd give her silent praise for her bratty mouth, but she didn't intercept. I was thankful. Her stubborn attitude got her into too much trouble. We knew full well of the extent, and she was smart to keep her damn mouth shut. That was our good girl.

I typed out a text to Liv and hit send after the confrontation ended. A message to meet us at the club by no later than nine because there was something we wanted her to see. We had a big surprise and wanted to celebrate with her and reward her.

A wicked smirk lit up my face at her fast response.

Liv:

I'll be there with my party dress on.

Me:

No. Wear your birthday suit.

Liv:

Naked?

Me:

Yep. Naked underneath a coat because someone will gladly take it off.

I watched her pace back and forth on the floor. The ground swayed so much I was dizzy, but the thought of her all frazzled kept me grounded.

Liv:

Hell no!

God. I liked it when she fought back. My flaccid cock turned into a raging boner. *Fuck.* I'd love to get my dick wet right about now.

Me:

Do it. Or else you won't like the consequence we give you.

A nice raw ass slap. I'd go to town on those cheeks until she begged me to stop. I'd stick my dick between the crevice of her asshole, lube my cock up and ram her until she screamed each time I hit her beloved G-spot. Hell, maybe she'd squirt all over Sin and he could enjoy the liquid pouring all over him.

Liv:

Fine.

Me:

Don't be late, little obsession.

Goddamn. I needed to jerk off.

Fifty

Their Obsession

Liv

I got to Sinful Saints early wearing nothing but a Dolce and Gabbana pure white cady coat. The material was smooth against my bare skin and only two buttons kept it closed. I felt promiscuous, sexy, and a bad girl bound to get caught. Adrenaline rushed through me. My pussy was slick, and I honestly prayed those two evil bastards would make me come. I was aroused even before I walked into their damn nightclub!

God, I had turned into an easy bitch, but my phantoms had me all riled up.

They caused the wicked temptress I had become. A sinful woman who craved their dicks in me, shoving them wherever they pleased because they brought me undeniable pleasure, wild moments of passion I couldn't get enough of.

Being with Sin and Saint was a high I had yet to come down from. An addiction they had introduced me to, and I couldn't get enough of. They were a drug I should quit, but the withdrawal from those two made me want another damn hit.

"A vodka on the rocks, Ms. Valencia?" A bartender asked.

The dude knew me by name.

Shit.

"Yes. Um... How do you know my name?"

"I do work for Mr. Cruz and Mr. Sullivan, ma'am."

"Right. Sorry, dumb question."

"No, not stupid at all," he assured me and handed me my drink. "It's on the house."

I nodded my thanks and took a sip from the straw as I peered around at my surroundings. My eyes searched for either Sin or Saint but came up empty. Those fuckers knew I was here and played with me while I yearned for them and lusted after them like they were *my* prey—the roles were reversed. I lurked as a pussy would in heat and hunted for the men who had grown on me.

The club was busy, as was usual for a Saturday night, and the music was perfect. Electrifying, inviting, and unstoppable. It was a sure mix to get anyone intoxicated in less than twenty minutes with the drinks flowing and being passed from person to person. There was alcohol spilled on the floor, growing sticky against the bottom of my heels, and I avoided a spill all over my crisp coat.

They never instructed the overcoat to be white and targeted for a giant stain. What the fuck was I thinking? Show up naked in a long overcoat.

Clearly, I wasn't. My throbbing cunt between my legs could attest to that. My juices flowed like Niagara Falls and there should be a wet floor sign because someone could have a terrible fall. They'd fall face first into my arousal, but my phantoms would kill anyone brave enough to even try to get a taste.

I should've worn a damn thong at least. The soaked panty cupping my cunt would have been better than the slickness of my folds rubbing between my thighs. The dull, pleasurable ache in my belly was never-ending as I explored the electric atmosphere and spotted a familiar face.

Saint.

I headed toward him but stopped short, with my heart thumping erratically against my chest, and I thought I might throw up. Bile collected in my throat and threatened to reach the surface. I'd earn the wet floor sign before the end of the night at this rate.

Suddenly, someone grazed my hips and whispered in my ear, "Come with me."

Sin.

His erection pressed into the small of my back, and a wicked shiver ran up my spine. The electric current zinged between us and he took my hand in his. My palms were sweaty, but he didn't seem to mind as he led me away from my nightmare and took me to safety. It was a security I never imagined I'd find with such a dangerous man, but I did. Despite being unhinged, Sin Cruz was a force that nobody dared to mess with when it came to me.

"Where are we going?" I asked, confused.

"You will see," Sin answered.

Curiosity overtook me as Sin led me away from the energetic crowd and down a hallway full of mirrors all around. He peered up and down the hallway, ensuring no one but us was around. His hand touched a particular spot and pushed against it, only for it to pop open with a tiny gasp escaping me.

A secret entrance.

How fucking cool!

I questioned with a raised eyebrow, "What other tricks do you jerks have hidden up your sleeves?"

Sin grabbed the front of my coat and pulled me close. "You're about to find out."

Sin let go of the opening and traced a finger up the coat. The tip of his nail grazed across my bare skin at the base of my neck and trailed along to the tip of the V shape, plunging into my cleavage. He groaned as his eyes darted to where his finger had gone, and he peeked inside, fully aware I had listened to instructions and was naked underneath my coat.

He cursed and pulled his hand away when I yearned for his dangerous touch. My breath heaving from the intensity shared between us as he pulled me into the hidden, enclosed space and the invisible door closed behind me. I found myself trapped with a man who made my heart race with excitement when it should beat with fear. I should yell, kick, or fight, but he intrigued me. Sin stirred up feelings I had never had in my entire life and made me want to explore more.

The enclosure appeared to replicate a hallway and was dark inside, but there was a good reason for the blackness. I could see everything on the outside. Secret two-way mirrors designed for Sin and Saint to watch everywhere within their club. These mirrors were all around except for the bathroom, but I had figured they had some creepy obsession with glass. These fuckers not only stalked me, they creeped on everyone who stepped foot inside of their nightclub.

"This is fucked up," I mumbled.

"Is it though?" Sin asked and pulled me in further to where I once had been. "I think it's genius. We can see everything going on in our club. Every scheme, anyone trying to screw with us, we know every little thing there is to know about a person as soon as they walk through our front door."

My eyes landed on Saint, seated at a round table, and Sebastian sat down across from him. I had never expected Sebastian to set foot in Sinful Saints, but I shouldn't be surprised. He was doing business, and I was only shocked from fear he'd find me. But my phantoms had a plan of their own.

"What are you two up to?"

"Let's tune in and find out," Sin answered as he opened up an app on his cell phone and voices came through.

"Enough bullshit, Sebastian," Saint said.

"Bullshit?" Sebastian questioned as I watched him shrug his shoulders, and he made a perplexed face. "There's none of that, my friend."

"Oh, cut the crap."

A Bluetooth transmitter! Who the hell were these guys?

Spys?

"I know you've been mismanaging our other property," Saint added.

"What the fuck?" I whisper shouted at Sin and covered the cell phone with my hand. "We can't listen in on their conversation."

"Yes, we can," Sin answered with a devilish grin and took my hand in his. "Because Sebastian is hurting our property."

My pussy throbbed.

"Is this about yesterday? About how Sebastian hated the flowers? You saw that?"

"We have a way of seeing everything," Sin said as he sat his cell phone on a ledge against the glass and stood behind me. "As you can see with your own eyes."

"How?" I breathed as my lips parted with his hands trailing down my neck and he traced the necklace they gave me.

"I'll never tell," Sin whispered as he traveled further and his tongue licked at my earring.

"I have done no such thing," Sebastian said.

He sounded outraged, and I watched the scene play out as Sin's fingers landed on the buttons of my coat. He tugged one at a time, pulling until the front of the material opened and his hands dove inside. His touch was cool against my hot, feverish skin and a slight hiss escaped my agape mouth. Saint peeked in our direction, and I knew he could hear everything. These fuckers were not only insane, but their dangerous ways made them incredibly smart.

Big-brained men with massive dicks.

"Yes. You have, Sebastian," Saint added as he glared at him and sat back in his seat with his arms crossed over his chest. "We've seen for ourselves. You haven't been taking good care of what is *ours*."

"The woman who *owns* our affection," Sin breathed from behind me as he cupped my tits and brushed the pads of his thumbs over my nipples.

My breathing hitched, and I sucked my lower lip into my mouth. I tried to conceal my moan of pleasure with my lip tucked between my teeth, but I couldn't. Sin was so tender the sound tore from me, and I could see Saint tense up at the table. His broad shoulders were tight with sexual tension, and I swore I heard him groan.

"Okay, I will admit I have been preoccupied with preparations for my marriage to the woman of my dreams," Sebastian said.

Bullshit!

Liar. Liar. His pants were on fire. But if he wasn't careful, my phantoms would hang him by his tongue from a telephone wire.

Saint tilted his head down and asked, "Have you?"

"Yes, I have."

I could tell it took all of Saint's willpower not to lunge across the table at Sebastian. To punch his fist right through his chest like a savage creature and rip out his cold, fraudulent heart from behind his ribcage. He'd hold his beating organ until the muscle stopped pumping and shove it into his mouth full of lies so the jerk wouldn't tell an untruth ever again.

"That lying sack of shit doesn't deserve you," Sin hissed into my ear as his hands grazed down my belly and landed over my pussy.

"Sin I—" I lost my words as a feral moan ripped from me when he slapped my cunt.

"Look at you all slick with come before we've even had our hands all over you," Sin breathed as he nipped my earlobe and held up his hand to my face. "Taste it. Lick the arousal you've willingly given to us."

All my rational thoughts screamed at me not to, but my lips wrapped around his two fingers. My tongue swirled around his fingertips with Sin making a sexy sound from behind me. The bittersweetness of my juices came to life on my tastebuds, and the flavor made me moan. My eyes were closed as I slid my lips to the end of his fingers and a loud popping sound filled the electrified air.

"Good girl."

Fifty-One

Their Obsession

Liv

Before I could open my eyes, Sin was back at my pussy. One finger was inside while his thumb circled my clit. My lips parted with a soft purr as he placed a second finger inside of me and my hips rocked to his rhythm. Back and forth, I moved while I circled my ass against his crotch.

"Oh, fuck!" I panted repeatedly as he pumped three fingers inside of me. His breath was hot on my cheek.

"Open your eyes, little obsession," Sin ordered as he bit at my lower lip and groped my tit. "Look at the man who took too much from you."

I opened my eyes as my belly coiled and was bound to explode. The sound of my juices squishing with each pump of Sin's fingers from the suction between my tight walls excited me. I was fucking slick and tremendously turned on, ready to climax.

Sin took his fingers out of me and slapped my pussy. "Oh!"

"Do you see him?" Sin asked, and his three fingers dove back inside of me.

"Yes, yes!" I cried out.

"Good." He groaned and plunged into me with a vigorous speed. "Now. Grab every piece he's taken from you and take it all back."

My release wavered and teetered on the edge. I heard Sin's heavy breaths resembling the wind as he tried to push me over the edge, but I couldn't. I was fearful of what I'd become after I gained everything back.

"I can't. I don't think I—"

"Yes, you can. You will come like a good girl all over my hand," Sin roared as he pinched my erect bud and pushed his fingers in to the hilt.

My eyes widened, and my hips thrusted out of control while a loud scream of pleasure tore from my throat. The sound was like an animal calling out into the wild, staking its claim and owning its rightful place. I was on top of the world as everything shattered and fell back into place.

"So. Fucking. Perfect," Sin growled each word with a peck on my lips.

And Saint continued with a fake smile on his face. "I guess congratulations are in order."

My body shuddered with the aftershocks of my orgasm as Saint poured champagne for two and passed Sebastian a glass. He clanked his flute against his and raised it in a toast. "To new beginnings."

"Here. Here," Sebastian cheered and took a sip. "So, are we good?"

"Absolutely," Saint answered with a nod.

Suddenly, Sin grabbed the shoulder pads of my coat and ripped it from my body. I gasped as he spun me around to face him and ran his hands down my naked form. My breathing was heavy with hair trapped between my lips and the strands puffed in and out. The two-way glass was cool against my backside with my ass cheeks pressed up against it.

"Little does that scumbag know we had paperwork drawn up yesterday and our business dealings with Mr. Chamberlain are through," Sin admitted as his lips trailed up my skin and his face stopped right between my cleavage. "His disrespect toward you has shown he isn't someone we want to tie ourselves to. Especially when we belong with you."

Sin's charcoal eyes lit up with a brilliance I had never seen, and the clarity in his stare made me quiver with need. He was certain and sure of all of us belonging together while I still wobbled on the edge of uncertainty. Because of all the shame, brutal force, pain, and torturous pleasure. Time and time again, but my heart still beat for them after everything they had put me through. I loved them and felt them etched deep within my bones. My ghosts' essence had captured my soul and would haunt me forever.

But I wasn't ready to tell them. I wasn't prepared to speak the truth.

"Has a thorn pricked your tongue?"

"No," was the only word I could formulate.

Sin took a nipple between his teeth and brutally grazed the bud until he sucked it into his mouth. I gasped because I couldn't talk, and I was afraid I'd blurt out my devotion to them. Instead, I let Sin do his worst like he always had, and I fell deeper into the darkness.

I heard Saint speak, "Help yourself to these fine women I purchased for you."

"Oh, my friend, you're far too good to me." Sebastian chuckled as I envisioned him pulling the hookers close and staring at their boobs. "Why don't you join me?"

Pig.

"No. I have far more important matters to attend to."

"Suit yourself," Sebastian said as the line crackled and disconnected.

Sin went to town on my tits. My back arched as I gave him full access, and he groaned at my eagerness for him to fully indulge. He bit into my skin, and I hissed as my hands flew into his hair. I pulled at the strands until he bit me again and bruised me with another mark. He attacked my plump flesh, reminding me once again of how much he loved to claim me. To mark me as theirs.

"Jesus. Fuck," I moaned as I bit my lip until I drew blood and tasted the bitterness on my tongue.

"Having all the fun without me?"

My lustful eyes landed on Saint in his silver suit as he unbuttoned it and tossed the jacket aside. I was delirious, lost in Sin as he marked me again and lapped his tongue over the wound he had inflicted. His fingertips kneading my nipples and making my pussy drip even more than before.

Sin tore his mouth from my bust. "No, man. I'm just warming her up."

"Good. I'm all pumped up and ready to rail our girl," Saint expressed as his cock sprang out from behind his pants and they fell to his ankles. "Especially after dealing with that fucking prick."

Sin flicked his tongue at my nipple and laughed. "Well, his sorry dick is about to get chlamydia."

"What?" I gasped with disbelief.

"We bought Sebastian a dirty farewell gift." Saint laughed right along with Sin.

They got my fiancé escorts and knew one of them had an STD. These fuckers were the real deal, and no one messed with them. Not even Sebastian Chamberlain. He'd have an itch to scratch, a swollen member, and a great deal of pain. I couldn't fucking wait.

Sin locked his eyes on my bewildered ones. "And we're going to enjoy his fiancée."

"Bring her pussy to me," Saint ordered.

Instantly, Sin grabbed the back of my neck, and a squeak of surprise escaped me. He yanked my body off the glass with my ass pointed in Saint's direction and he slapped me. I whimpered from the force. My plump cheeks jiggled, and he grunted as he repeated the lashing.

"We bring you pain," Sin breathed as his hot breath fanned over my face and he held me still. "And then we bask in your pleasure."

"Yes," I whimpered and was met with another blow.

Saint smacked me until I was sure my behind was beet red. The tender flesh was raw with the blemish stinging, and his hands squeezed over the pain he had made. A feral moan released from me as he spread my ass cheeks apart and dipped his enormous dick inside of me. His huge mushroom-head tip inched deeper inside. My pussy stretched to accommodate his size, and I always thought he wouldn't fit, but he always did.

"Yes, that's it. Our good little slut with her tight little pussy clenching my best friend's gigantic cock,"

Sin groaned while he placed his dick between my wet thighs, and I clenched them together.

Both men grunted as they thrusted against me. One man was inside of my pussy while the other enjoyed my slick juices that had trickled down between my legs. Saint pounded faster as he found my sweet spot and made me cry out his name. Each motion bounced me toward Sin and his groans of passion were wild in my ear. My ass smacked off Saint's muscular thighs, and he railed into my pussy with his one hand squeezing my hip. The other hand slapped me over and over like I was an untamed horse he needed to train. But in this case, his lashings made me come.

"Oh, Saint!" I cried out as my cunt clenched down around his cock, and I dug my nails into Sin's shoulders.

Saint couldn't hold back and let go with his release gushing into me. We rode the waves until Saint pulled out of me, his come dripping from my pussy, and he picked me up by the waist. Startled, I clung to Sin's shoulders as I peered down and saw him position his cock right above my entrance.

"Your turn," Saint growled as he placed me down on Sin's massive dick, and his best friend dove right in.

"Oh, god!" I whimpered with an open mouth and wide eyes.

"Jesus Christ," Sin hissed between my boobs and worked his hips. "You feel so damn good, Liv."

Saint had already worked my pussy, and it foamed from the mouth with come. All Sin had to do was bounce me up and down with my tits jostling into his face. He loved me in this position as my backside hit the glass and he fucked me up against it. Pound after pound, he brought me closer toward another orgasm with my legs wrapped around his waist and Saint watched on from behind him.

"You're our slut and no one else's," Saint breathed with heated eyes as he grazed his fingertips up the back of my thighs, and he dug his nails into the flesh of my ass. "Tell us."

Saint bruised me with his death grip and Sin made rippling waves cross my skin as he railed me into oblivion. The pair would be the end of me, and I had nowhere to fall except into their arms.

"Yes! Yes! I'm your little slut!" My scream was untamed as my eyes rolled and I saw bright stars. "I'm yours and no one... Oh, fuck!"

My world exploded.

My cunt clawed and dug into Sin like a bitch in a ferocious heat. My hips moved, but barely did anything against Sin's frantic thrusts. He was in control as he gave one final plunge and buried his big length into me. He cursed with my name on his lips, and his come mixed with ours. My phantoms' seed oozed out of me and down the sides of Sin's dick as he throbbed inside of me and released every drop.

"Fuck," Sin breathed as he collapsed against me, and his body weight pushed me up against the glass.

Raggedly, I breathed into his dark hair and wrapped my arms around his neck. Sin laid his cheek against my breast as he listened to my fast-paced heartbeat, and Saint came over to kiss me. His lips brushed me sweetly at first, then turned into a bruising, passionate kiss. He stole my breath and let me go. Only for Sin to breathe air into my lungs again with his mouth on mine, concealing my moans.

Slowly, Sin moved inside of me and pulled me from the two-way mirror. His kiss moved down my neck as I watched his best friend lube up his dick, and he gripped my buttocks until his hard length pushed between the crevice of my asshole.

These fuckers would have me again. And the worst part, I'd let them.

Fifty-Two

Their Obsession

Liv

Sebastian had been a bigger asshole than usual lately. He displayed aggravation and irrational behavior like he was on his period. I had kept my distance as much as possible since we remained under the same roof, but I couldn't help giggling at him every time I saw him scratching his crotch. Jerk. He'd slept with those hookers, and my phantoms weren't lying. They had ensured he had a severe case of chlamydia.

Sin and Saint had also cut ties with Sebastian and Sinful Saints was no longer doing business with him. They had found out they no longer needed an investor and could run their businesses on their own. No wonder my husband-to-be was throwing temper tantrums.

"I'm going out!" Sebastian had hollered over an hour ago.

I had questioned where he was off to, but he informed me it was none of my fucking business. A typical conversation between us, with him giving me attitude and expecting me to listen and be a doting bride-to-be and tend to my womanly household duties. Sexist prick.

Little does he know, I knew exactly where he was off to. Sebastian was gone for a doctor's visit to find out why he was in discomfort. I'd love to see his face when he found out he had an STD.

My cruel fiancé deserved everything he had coming to him. All the stress, his finances were dwindling, and he'd have to recoup the lost income, but do everything while he was in pain. With hardly any use of his broken hands.

I laughed out loud as the doorbell rang. I knew I was overdue for a delivery. My heels clicked across the tile until I came to a stop at the front door. But my amusement turned into worry when there was no delivery man on my front step.

"Hey, baby."

The guy from the business party!

What the fuck was he doing here?

"Um... I think you have the wrong address," I said quickly and pushed the door closed.

He caught the door with his hand. "No, I don't."

"Yes, you do." I glared with clenched teeth and jerked at the door.

But it was no use.

The stranger, who I had let eat out my pussy, was too strong for me and pushed his way inside. I gasped and breathed heavily as I stumbled backward. His gigantic form towered over me as he walked toward me, and I panicked.

"It wasn't nice, giving me a fake phone number," he seethed and shook his head. "You leaving me hanging disappointed me."

I really did. His cock had probably stayed flaccid since because I was that good. A fake number was the oldest trick in the book, and I had done it a handful of times. But I've never had any man come looking for me like this fucking creep. Time to play along and hope this psychopath left.

"I did?" I gushed a fake-ass apology. "I'm sorry. I was wondering why—"

"Bullshit," he snapped with anger and reached out to touch my face. "But no matter. It's all in the past now."

"How did you find me?" I asked.

"You were easy to track down. Sebastian led me straight to you."

Fuck. I really should convince Sebastian to hire some security guards. Maybe even put up security cameras. Better yet, I needed to stop assuming who was at my front door and look first before I answered.

"So you tracked me down. Creepy."

"I'd like to think it's romantic," he said as his fish oil breath fanned across my face, and I almost gagged on the smell.

Gross! This guy reeked! What the hell had I seen in him?

He needed a damn mint. Hell, even spearmint gum. He also needed to learn some manners and not force his way into someone's house.

"Well, you can take everything unromantic about this situation and leave the same way you came in," I snapped back as I pointed to the wide-open door behind him and the back of my thighs hit a table.

"Nope," he refused with a pop of the *P* and grabbed my shoulders. "You owe me for all the trouble I went through to find you."

"You mean by stalking me?" I glared angrily. "Get your fucking hands off me!"

He pressed his body up against mine, and I couldn't escape. His hot breath was on my cheek as he ran his hands down my body, and he pushed a leg between my thighs. He spread me open as I tried with all the strength I had to push him away, but he only laughed. Forcefully, he dipped his head underneath my chin and kissed my collarbone.

After he bruised me with his lips, he hissed in my ear, "No. I'm in the mood for getting my dick wet."

He licked his fingers and lifted my skirt. Only to push my skimpy panties aside and rub my clit. The circular motion made me dizzy. Arousal stirred, and normally I'd change my mind. But two damn ghosts haunted me.

"Stop it," I urged with tears biting at my eyes. "Please."

I wasn't in the mood, not when he had forced himself on me. My body might respond, but my mind and heart were somewhere else. Nothing belonged to this jerk.

He wouldn't listen, and he made the mistake of moving backward while he tried to kiss me. There was enough room between us to lift my knee right into his crotch. The quick attack made him remove his filthy hands from me and cup his aching nut sack.

"Fuck!" He winced.

I let him have it and my hands slapped at his face like a wildcat. The sound of my abuse smacked off his nose, cheeks, head, and anywhere I could strike him. Startled, he fumbled backward and back outside.

"Jesus, fuck!" he shouted as the door slammed in his face, and I locked it behind me.

"Go away, asshole!" I yelled.

Frightened, I pressed my backside against the door, worried he might get back inside. My breath heaved while my heart raced against my chest and he pounded against the door. The tears fell as I wiped them away and held onto the doorknob for dear life.

"You bitch!" he yelled at me and threw his body against the door. "I'll get you for this!"

The door rattled against its hinges, and I warned, "Get lost before I call the police!"

Suddenly, I heard a commotion, and the thumping stopped. My door no longer moved, and I put my ear against the door, listening while I held my breath. No sounds or movement came from the other side, and I stood still for what felt like an eternity.

My heartbeat calmed, my hands were no longer clammy, and beads of sweat dried on my forehead. I was still on high alert, but I exhaled a lengthy sigh and slid to the floor against the door. Thankfully, the coast was clear, and he must've heeded my threat, hightailing it out of here with his stupid dick between his legs.

"Asshole."

Once I was safe, I moved away from the door. My eyes never left the wooden structure until I heard a chime from my cell phone. I peered down at the device while the screen lit up.

Unknown:

He'll pay a hefty price for laying his fingers on what is ours.

I tossed and turned in bed. My sleep was shitty because the temperature had dropped with the holiday season fast approaching, and my feet kept finding their way out from underneath the comforter. My nerves were in high gear, not only from the non-consensual encounter, but from my upcoming wedding. I was only days away from me speaking the words "I do" and spending wedded bliss with a man I despised.

I was totally freaking out.

Some would call this cold feet, but I called this wanting to run to save my life. To secure my sanity and avoid being treated like a piece of garbage for the rest of my life. Sure, we could get married and soon after, I could file for a divorce, but Sebastian was too possessive of me. He wouldn't let me go that easily, and I had to save my family. He'd make me pay for the rest of my life.

"Shit!" My cell phone rang and broke me from my thoughts.

I put the device on speaker. "Happy birthday, sweetheart!"

"Oh, Mom... How sweet of you to remind me," I mumbled.

My slumber was also terrible because I was an entire year older. I despised celebrating the day of my birth and entering this shit hole called life. Born into nothing but chaos with brief moments of elation.

"Of course I'd remember! Besides, you are our only child."

This I knew all too well. All the pressure and expectations fell on me because there was *only* me, and I hated everything about being an only child.

I didn't get to share my frustrations with anyone else. I had nowhere to turn when I needed help. I was the one who had to save everything, and this was how I got into this goddamn mess. Out of obligation.

"Thanks, Mom." I sighed and heard a knock on the front door.

I got up from the sofa, and my heart raced with memories of yesterday. My mom somehow calmed me while she kept yapping away about how I was the cutest baby she had ever laid eyes on. She also informed me I was a baby who had bouts of explosive diarrhea and she hoped the gene didn't live on. I didn't think so because children weren't in the foreseeable future for me.

I peeked out the window facing my front door and there was a tiny white box on my step, not a single person in sight. The unexpected visit from the bastard taught me a lot. I wouldn't answer the door without looking again. At least, not for a while.

I said, "Mom, you shouldn't have."

My hand was already on the doorknob when she asked, "Shouldn't have what?"

"You can drop the act now, Mom. I know what you did." I pointed at the box with a smile on my face. "You called me right when you knew my birthday present would arrive."

"Sweetheart. I don't know what you're talking about?"

"Wait. Really? Mom, come on. There's a white box right on my..." My assumption ended with the sight of red cursive written on a note.

One moment passed, maybe two, as I stood there with my mouth agape as my mom rambled on. When I saw the words "little obsession" written in fancy red liquid, time slowed down.

"Sweetheart? Are you still there?" she asked.

"Yes, Mom, I am, but I'll have to call you back."

"Okay, but remember we're meeting in two days to go over everything for the big day and—"

"I know. I'll be there, but I have to go," I mumbled as I ended the call with shaking hands and knew exactly who this parcel was from.

My phantoms.

I looked left then right, but only saw cars, trees, and strangers. No tattooed men in business suits with sexy hair and gorgeous eyes. Sin and Saint were nowhere in sight, but I knew they were close. They always were.

I kneeled down and picked up the white box. The note made my heart do a flip.

Happy birthday, little obsession. We sliced this up just for you.

I was either going into cardiac arrest, or those fuckers left me feeling all gushy inside—tingly with mushy emotions, making me want more. Well, fuck them!

I stormed into the house only to slam the door behind me, and I hoped they had seen my wrath. Those idiots did some crazy shit and then they do nice things. They bought me fake roses, brought me coffee, comforted me when I had my period... Well, they also forced me to have multiple orgasms to help with pain relief, but this was all beside the point. They were—

A big slice of red velvet cake greeted me when I opened the box with human fingers sticking up.

Ten, to be exact.

Real human fingers.

"Holy shit!"

I dropped the cake onto the floor while icing splattered in the box, and some fingers fell. The ends were coated with dried up blood and my stomach heaved. A hand covered my mouth, and I felt the bile build up. I was ready to hurl all over the gruesome present my phantoms had left me, but I held the puke at bay.

Through all the vivid thoughts running through my head, my eyes caught a ring on one finger. A particular silver band I recognized from the man who'd had his hands all over me. The predatory pig hadn't left of his freewill, he was forced, and his fucking fingers were cut off!

My cell phone chimed, making me jump right out of my skin and the screen lit up.

Unknown:

Did you like your birthday present?

Me:

You can't be serious! Is this some kind of sick joke?

Unknown:

Oh, those fingers are the real deal, sweetheart.

I wanted to throw my phone, smash it onto the floor right with the cake. But I refrained, kept my cool, and gave them hell.

Me:

What the fuck is wrong with the two of you? You can't just go kill a man and cut off another guy's fingers!

Unknown:

Why not?

Me:

Because it's insane!

But I was too. Trapped in the madness of their affection for me. Blinded by their addiction to me. No matter what these two did, they did everything for me.

Unknown:

Is it?

Me:

What?

Unknown:

Crazy. Or is that man, who treated himself to what is ours and tried to steal what we've claimed, downright vile? He would've corrupted your soul.

Me:

Yes, what he did was disgusting and he should go to jail. Not have his fingers cut off because of it!

Unknown:

Well, he won't be touching you again, now will he?

Very good point. But in a completely fucked up way.

Me:

Yeah. You and your lap dog made sure of that.

Unknown:

Oh, you wound our hearts.

Good.

Another text message came through.

Unknown:

But we're more vicious predators, Liv. I'm more of the alpha in a wolf pack and Saint's the beta. But you are the prey.

I wanted them gone. Out of my heart and absent from my mind. They had lost all hold on sanity, and I caused their destruction.

I yelled at my phone and typed out each word, "Just leave me alone!"

Unknown:

No can do. Our addiction to you is our salvation, and there's no turning back now.

Fifty-Three

Their Obsession

Liv

Soft music played, and the restaurant smelled like candles. My parents sat across from me while my mom rambled on, and she fussed with her short, crimped brown hair. Her brown eyes stared at me with a brilliance full of excitement for my wedding. But I couldn't care less about the dreadful event.

Gloria Valencia had everything from her posh clothing to her perfectly manicured nails. She had all the extravagant materials life could give her and lavish trips across the world. Frank Valencia, my father, gave her all he could give or whatever he had left. A huge addiction consumed him, and my mother paid no attention to it. She only lived for the expensive lifestyle while he kept quiet about their dwindling bank accounts. We both knew she'd lose her mind if she ever found out the truth and the pressure was on me to ensure it never came to that.

But I was hesitant.

Marriage to Sebastian would be a death sentence while I awaited a lethal injection on death row, behind bars, a prisoner in my own home. He'd ensure I didn't get a last meal and send me off to die with bruises and black eyes. One day, he'd kill me over something small and end my miserable life.

I didn't want that—to be lifeless, broken, and alone. I wanted to give a damn and feel alive, not dead inside. Captured by the darkness, I had grown used to until two men had forced their way into my life.

My phantoms had woven their blackness around me and owned every part of me. Piece by piece, they sliced me open until I only bled for them, and I fell deeper into their abyss. A place where we created our screwed-up story, and they awakened a beautiful beast I never thought they could.

My love for them.

A devotion extremely powerful I couldn't break it. No matter how hard I tried to turn off the light they had switched on inside of me. The beacon only grew more radiant each day, and their obsession with me had stayed. They gave me something to hold on to and a way to break free from this life sentence: be with them and not stay chained to Sebastian.

"Did you hear me, sweetheart?" my mom asked with narrowed eyes. "About the flowers?"

Oh, those stupid flowers. Another issue Sebastian could blame me for. Another reason not to go through with this wedding.

"Yes. They will be late. I know."

"Well, dear, this is a big problem we can't afford," my dad huffed with his dark eyes searching my face.

"Okay. I'll hire a new company." I shrugged.

Honestly?

I didn't give a shit. They would die in less than a week. Fake flowers were the best. The same kind my shadows loved to give to me.

"But there's no time. The wedding—"

"I know. The wedding is this week."

My dad asked, "Is something wrong?"

"Yes, sweetheart, what's going on? You seem awfully distracted."

Yeah. *I fucking was!*

I had my parents breathing down my neck when all I wanted to do was get up and run as far as I could. Pack up the little belongings I had and leave the man I hated behind me, never to see him again, but I couldn't.

Not with my mom's worried eyes on me and my dad's stern face. We both knew I had to do this or else our situation would worsen. I'd live with the truth of our mistake, my dad would suffer, and my mom would hate his guts for the rest of their lives.

"I don't know, I—" my doubt was cut short when I caught sight of two men I should've known were close by.

Sin and Saint. But they were coming straight toward me.

Crap.

"I'm not so sure we need flowers," I carried on.

Bewildered, my dad said, "Don't be ridiculous, dear. You need flowers. It's your wedding day, for Christ's sake!"

I turned my attention back to my father and sighed. "Dad, I don't care for real flowers. They don't even live very long."

"But fake flowers do," Sin cut in and stole the show. "They live on forever, even after we die."

"And who the hell are you?" my dad asked, baffled by the intrusion.

Saint opened his mouth to speak, but I silenced him with a glare. He clamped his lips together and pressed them tight. He could fuck with me, but not with my parents.

I answered for them, "Mom, Dad, this is Mr. Sin Cruz and his business partner, Mr. Saint Sullivan. Sebastian was their investor."

"Was?" my father questioned.

Shit. My big mouth.

"Um, yes—"

"We simply don't require Mr. Chamberlain's expertise anymore," Sin interrupted with a sexy and convincing smile.

My father glared at them like they were insects who needed to be squashed on the spot, and he was right. Sin and Saint were massive pests, but a shoe stomping them wouldn't bring them to an end. Killer bug spray might do the trick.

"Well, it's a pleasure to meet you both." My mom beamed with kindness but cut the conversation short. "But if you'll—"

I cut in, "Excuse me for a minute while I have a word with these gentlemen in private."

"But sweetheart, I—"

Before she could utter another word, I left the table and my perplexed parents. My father shook his head and my mom sat there, stunned, with her mouth agape. I silently mouthed at them, "I'll be right back."

Both men followed behind me with their laser beam eyes directly on my backside. Without question, Sin had his dark lustful gaze locked on my ass while Saint's roamed up and down my body. I sizzled from the top of my head down to the tips of my toes as we rounded a corner until we were out of sight.

"What on earth are you two doing here?" I huffed.

"We happened to be in the neighborhood," Sin teased and brushed my bare shoulder.

I shuddered at his touch but pulled away. "Yeah, right."

"Fine. We followed you," Sin admitted as he rolled his eyes and flashed a devilish smirk. "But we enjoyed every second."

"And we got to meet our future mother-in-law and father-in-law," Saint said as he caressed my cheek and his blue eyes gleamed with excitement. "I think they liked us."

"What?"

"Shocking, we know. Especially considering the timing with the wedding you will not show up to..." Sin rambled on while I stood there dumbfounded by his confidence. "All the lying and falling in love with us behind Sebastian's back."

I pushed Saint's hand away and lied, "I'm not in love with either of you."

"Yes, you are..." Sin growled as he stepped closer and intensely peered down at me. "You love us and so will your parents once you become our wife."

Saint was inches away from me, his hot breath on my cheek. Sin sweetly grazed my other cheek until his hand trailed down and cupped my collarbone. Without warning, he tightly squeezed, compressing my airway as it burned for freedom and caused my eyes to bulge.

They owned me, claimed me months ago, and loved me unconditionally. I just needed to admit I loved them, too.

"Please—" I squeaked, unable to utter another word.

"Tell us," Saint encouraged me and licked my cheek.

"Admit your heart burns for us. Don't deny it, Liv," Sin threatened through clenched teeth. "Or you'll live with the regret forever."

"I love—" unable to go on with no breath left.

"*Sin*," Saint hissed.

Sin eased his hold around my throat when I couldn't get the words out. He gave his best friend an order to let me go so I could finish what they had started. An addiction turned into painful passion and had spiralled out of control.

I choked, gasping for breath as a said, "To hate you both."

Saint argued, "No, you don't."

"Yes, I do. This obsession with me needs to end."

Sin was fed up, and I feared he'd strangle me right on the spot, but he didn't. Instead, he grabbed my hand and took the big diamond engagement ring off. He tossed the golden band over his shoulder until it bounced off the wall behind him and it fell to the floor.

"Liar," Sin growled through clenched teeth and made me stare at my naked ring finger. "This will be where we place our wedding ring, not motherfucking Sebastian."

My heart ached as I uttered the hurtful words, "I'm marrying him and not either of you."

"Sebastian doesn't own this pretty little finger. We do and we'll fucking prove it." Sin glared, refusing to quit.

Instantly, Sin opened his mouth and swallowed my ring finger whole. His lips wrapped around the knuckle of the tiny digit while his teeth bit into my skin right where the engagement band had sat. I yelped from the pain, but Saint concealed the sound with his mouth. The devil had branded my ring finger, but I had let him inside and he claimed me as his. A mark of ownership to ensure we never part.

"Saint..." Sin breathed heavily when he released my finger and glanced at his best friend. "Your turn."

Saint freed my lips, and I pleaded, "No, no, please, I—"

"So pretty when you beg," Saint interrupted before he took my finger in his mouth and bit down on the tender flesh.

A cry of pain tore up my throat as his teeth embedded on the other side of Sin's bite mark, but lips devoured my sore ache. A sizzle of heat rose through me, and the coil twisted tightly in my belly. Pleasure mixed with pain as Sin kissed me and Saint sealed the deal. My phantoms marked me forever.

"There will be no more denying, no more arguments." Sin breathed against my mouth and his lips brushed mine. "We are yours for the rest of your life."

My heart pounded in my ears, pain radiated from the open sores. Saint released my finger with a pop and blood tinted his lips. I watched him lick the red color away, and a possessive smile took over his face.

"Ours."

"Fuckers! You bit me!" I glared as I pushed them away and licked at my wounds.

They only laughed. The familiar evil sound coated my soul and embedded my heart. I tasted blood as I scrambled for Sebastian's ring and reached for it on the floor. Only for Sin to press his shoe down onto my hand until it hurt.

"Stop it, Sin!" I shouted, tears blurring my eyes.

My voice echoed down the hallway and was sure to catch onlookers' attention. It was only a matter of minutes before someone came to stare, but I didn't care. I was hurt. They had harmed me, and I had disappointed them, too.

"Look at me," Sin snarled.

I looked up at him and cried, "Leave me alone!"

Sin kneeled down and Saint glanced over his shoulder. The heartbreaking image would never leave my mind. My phantoms peered at me with desperation in their eyes, but they were certain I'd be theirs for an entire lifetime. This moment would etch into my memory long after I became Mr. Chamberlain's wife.

"We won't ever let you go, Liv," Saint assured me.

"No man will put a ring on what is eternally ours. We've scarred you for life. Not even death will part us because we'll haunt our wife into the afterlife."

Sin lifted his shoe, and I pulled my hand away. Slowly, I stood while I vibrated all over, but I couldn't turn away. I had to make them stop. I must break them.

"I'm marrying Sebastian," I said and stood tall. "Not either of you. Sebastian. He's my future."

"No, you aren't," Saint snarled with a twitch in his upper lip.

"You aren't, Liv," Sin growled with possession. "The only princess cut diamond ring on your finger will be ours. Not his. *Ours.*"

I had got to them—cut them open and bruised them deep. Their wounds would never heal without me, and I hurt everywhere when I left them behind. My heart tore apart as I turned my back on them and walked away.

I headed back to the table where my parents sat while the men I loved went back to being my shadows. Where they watched and waited for me to make my next move. Their eyes were on me when I let Sebastian's engagement ring fall into my purse, but I kept my hand in my dress pocket. My freshly scarred marks of ownership would remain our secret from the rest of the world.

Fifty-Four

Their Obsession

Liv

I was livid. Over the top out of my mind and ready to throw a punch at my target: Sebastian's smug-ass face.

"What the fuck are these?" I asked and waved papers in front of him.

I had found a legal document Sebastian had drawn up, and he had already signed on the dotted line. A prenuptial agreement to protect his beloved estate from me and keep all his assets to himself. The greedy fucker didn't want me to see a penny of his money in case of an impending divorce—a split I had contemplated in my head several times, and I still wasn't sure I'd have the balls to go through with it. But he made the answer simple. I wouldn't have to marry his sorry ass.

"A marriage contract to keep your gold digger hands off my money," Sebastian answered.

I found the prenup after I made my morning brew. Sebastian had been clever and left the paperwork out where I'd see it on the morning before our wedding. When I realized the stunt he had pulled, it shook me up and added to my already rattled nerves. I drank my coffee in two minutes and didn't even feel the burn on the way down because I was boiling with red, furious rage.

My nostrils flared as I stared into the eyes of the man who had kept me chained to him and beat me down whenever he pleased. This arranged engagement had all been for nothing, and I wouldn't stick around one minute longer. I was taking my control back and to hell with Sebastian Chamberlain!

I slapped the binding agreement on the countertop beside him and glared into his emotionless eyes. Sebastian didn't budge, he didn't blink. He was an empty, bottomless pit and a good-for-nothing dick.

"I'm out of here," I breathed as I turned my back to him and walked away.

"If you leave this house, you are as good as dead."

My footsteps froze. I stood there as beads of perspiration collected on the back of my neck along with boob sweat. Sebastian had a way of instilling fear in me. I tried so desperately for him not to see. But he held no control over me anymore because this agreement was through.

"So?" I said as I got ballsy and spun around on my heels to face him. "It's not like you haven't already killed my soul after everything you've done to me."

Sebastian pulled his cell phone out of his pocket and calmly said, "All I have to do is make one phone call. One press of a button, and you'll be on borrowed time."

This asshole was threatening me. Again. Screw him.

"Fuck you." I glared as the sweat beads grew and coated my forehead.

"You wouldn't even see the end coming, Liv," Sebastian taunted as he circled around me like a vulture hunting a mouse and luring me into evil. "Your death could happen on the subway, hailing down a taxi, or simply out for a walk in the street."

"I'd rather be on the run for the rest of my life than spend a lifetime in hell with you."

"I'd still find you," he hissed into my ear. "But if you feel your pathetic life doesn't amount to anything, then maybe your parent's lives will?"

I saw red. I could claw this scumbag's eyes out and not even hold an ounce of remorse. My being shuddered with hatred and my nostril flared resembling a fire-breathing dragon. Sebastian had crossed a line, but my blood ran cold because I knew he was dangerous. He was a rich, ruthless, calculated man who knew no limits because he was an egotistical fuck.

"If you so much as touch a hair on their head, I'll—"

"You'll what? Kill me?" He laughed cruelly and held the papers with a pen in my face. "Sign the prenup, Liv."

I pushed the paperwork away.

"No. I don't believe—" my refusal ended with a hard headbutt to my face, and I fell to the floor.

Pain radiated through my nose, cheekbones, and lips. Everything went black as stars danced, and I couldn't think straight. My face felt bruised after the impact and my world spun. The tiles on the kitchen floor were uneven as I held my face and pulled back with slick red blood on my hands. Bloody with hot tears, I swore I'd never cry because the bastard didn't deserve a fraction of my emotion.

"I have friends in high places who'd do the dirty work for me, and no one would find out the truth. Your parents would be taken out next before your corpse even gets cold. Sign the damn papers or you, along with your family, are dead."

Sebastian was dead serious. I could hear the certainty in his voice, and when I peered up into his heartless eyes, I knew he had gone mad. I had lived with Satan for far too long, and I should've known I wouldn't ever be able to leave. He made sure of it.

I fought against the pain and staggered from side to side as I stood. The bastard only watched me struggle as I tried to balance on unsteady feet and moved out of the way because he didn't want to get blood on his new shirt. Fucking asshole.

This lethal man I had let into my life knew everything about my unsuspecting parents. He knew where they lived, their schedules, favorite restaurants, and the destinations they loved to travel. I had placed a target on both of their backs, and I'd be the one to pull the trigger.

All my power was gone. My dignity robbed, my soul ripped open, and any ounce of freedom vanished as quickly as it came back. Sebastian had taken everything from me, but I couldn't let him steal anymore.

Uncontrollably, tears fell, and I asked, "Why are you doing this to me?"

"It's too late to turn back time, and I'm stuck with you." He shrugged, showing me how meaningless I was to him. "I'd appear weak after a failed engagement under my belt, and I can't have that. Despite my disdain for everything about you, you still belong to me. I *own* you, Liv."

I wanted to run. To pick up my broken pieces and never look back. I wanted to leave all of this behind me.

My weakened legs couldn't hold me up any longer, and I stumbled into the kitchen counter. I reached for the pen with a shaky hand and signed my life away where my signature was needed. Forced to comply with the man I was soon set to marry, breathing down my neck.

Dread fell over me when the paperwork was through. I knew by the hateful gleam in Sebastian's eyes and the way his ugly face twitched that I was in for a beating. Not even half-healed, broken hands could hold him back after all the hell I had put him through.

I should've cowered, raised my hands, or yelled at him to stop. Instead, I stared him dead in the eyes, and let him headbutt me all over again until I thought I'd go braindead. My lip split, bruises formed on my cheeks, and I felt immense pain. With the blemishes on my face, only makeup could hide them for the wedding.

No big deal. I could get through this. I'd get through a thousand more touch-ups if it meant saving my parents' lives. But the vibrations of pain coursing through my body assured me I might not have much more time left.

A human could only take so much. An essence only lit for so long until their flame burned out. *My clock was ticking.*

Sebastian left me alone on the floor, battered, bleeding, and broken. I was to spend the night alone in my bridal suite, a sanctuary my parents had paid for. It was tradition for the future bride and groom not to see one another before their wedding, so they could spend the night longing to be together.

While this was far from the truth, I was thankful for the distance, especially after he had bashed in my face and I wished for more. All I had was hope and faith that I'd make it another day, that I need only one extra breath until I made it out of this alive.

Desperately, I did something I had never done. I kneeled down to whoever the fuck was up in heaven, and I prayed to the Almighty. I begged for forgiveness for all my past sins and to be millions of miles away from the devil who would kill me.

Fifty-Five

Her Phantom

Saint

Screams came from the room, and I peered up as more blood gushed from his wounds. I was thrilled. A new finger sliced off and red dripped from where his thumbs had been. Along with punches to his ugly face, I made the motherfucker far nastier than he had been before. But his appearance wouldn't matter much when we sent him where he should've been months ago.

In hell.

The scumbag would hold two seats for us, but we'd still beat his ass to a pulp even in the fiery depths of the devil's den. Satan couldn't even hold us back from getting our hands on him. We'd kill him too.

Sin had wanted a turn, and it took all of my willpower to walk out of the room. I had done severe damage but cleaned his blood from my hands. The pig stunk, and I required extra soap to get the caked-on crimson off my skin. His time was up, and he'd rot for everything he had done.

Fucker even got blood on my shoe.

Goddamn it.

I wiped the black leather clean and tossed the dirty rag in the garbage, but I almost choked on my heart. The wind in my airway got caught up as my eyes saw the most breathtaking sight I had ever seen in my entire life. Liv.

There on my phone's screen was our girl, radiant, glowing, and as beautiful as ever in her wedding dress. She looked at her reflection in a large mirror with her white faded ombré manicured nails against her silky beaded gown. Her makeup was pristine and didn't show a speck of the harm the fucker had inflicted.

I growled when images flew through my mind at what he had done to her. She shouldn't have to cover up, our girl was naturally flawless, and makeup only added to the beauty that was underneath. Liv Valencia was a fucking goddess who brought me to my knees.

Immediately, I saw her sharp intake of breath, the part of her pretty pink lips and the way they trembled in terror. My fists clenched at my sides, and I wanted to go back into the room and pummel the bastard for instilling fear in those gorgeous milk chocolate eyes. The blood in my veins boiled because he had threatened to kill her. He had wanted to end her life and take her away from us, along with her parents. All because he was a possessive motherfucker. But we were too, and Liv wasn't his. He didn't own her. We did.

Sebastian had hurt her for the last time, and we'd do our worst. All silent promises to keep him alive were off, and we vowed to end her suffering. We upheld our devotion like a wedding band, one we'd place on her finger soon for everyone to see. She was truly eternally ours from the scar we had marked her with, and a precious princess cut ring would be something pretty to place over top.

She'd haunt us, and we'd haunt her. *Forever.* Not even death would part us. Liv was our naughty little obsession, and she'd always own our dark souls.

Instantly, the hairs stood up on the back of my neck when I saw a shadow creep up from behind her. Surely, this large figure was her father coming in to see his daughter before he walked her down the aisle. But this person, *this man,* was too big to be her dad.

A chilled shiver ran up my spine, and I knew it wasn't from the damn ghosts who haunted the hallways. Sweat coated my forehead as I held the phone closer and tried to see who this man could be. But I stopped cold and I was dead inside when Liv's eyes widened with fright.

Whoever this motherfucker was wore a black hood and concealed his face from the light. This asshole was an expert, but he was up to no damn good.

Fifty-Six

Her Phantom

Sin

Sebastian had hurt Liv. Again.

I was through letting the bastard breathe another day and so was my best friend. All the willpower I had kept inside from fucking up this asshole was gone, and I let the wild beast out. We didn't wait and captured his sorry ass right from his front step. The place where he had felt safe until we held a knife to the small of his back and led him to our car. Only to bring him to our home and into the place we called hell.

We didn't even conceal our faces because we wanted Sebastian to stare into the eyes of the monsters he had created. He had damaged what was ours and broken her to pieces—battered shreds of glass we had picked up and fixed until he smashed them all over again. But we'd be there for our girl in this life and after, piecing her back together.

We held Sebastian in the same room where Saint first met Liv. We tortured him and the motherfucker would miss his damn wedding. What a shame.

The piece of scum deserved everything coming to him, and I seethed on the inside as I wiped my necklace clean of his blood with a rag. The white fabric was stained red and was no longer crisp. I threw the piece of cloth into a pile with the others and admired the masterpiece I had created with my best friend. Sebastian Chamberlain would fit in great when we returned him back to hell.

"Fucking asshole!" Sebastian spat as his boogers dripped onto his lips and his beaten face was tomato red. "You're finished, you hear me? Finished!"

I hated the sound of his squeaky voice, unsure how anyone had ever found the noise appealing. My ears grew tired of the annoyance long ago, and I couldn't wait for him to stop talking. I don't even think the scumbag had hit puberty yet.

"No, Mr. Chamberlain. I believe you're the one that's finished. All because you couldn't stop hurting our girl."

"Liv?"

"Yes," I hissed.

"I fucking knew it!" Sebastian exclaimed as he wiggled in his confinement, tied to the arms of a chair, and he grinned up at me. "Your precious girl is as good as dead."

I growled. Sebastian knew he had hit a nerve, and the bastard twisted his hand until he tried to pull out my heart. He pressed on and tugged at the muscle more.

"I'll take everything from you. Your damn business, your freedom, all your wealth, and your girl. After I land your asses behind bars, I'll sue you, but the best part? I'll spend every damn dime on getting Liv killed with her severed head specially delivered straight to you and your fucking best friend behind bars. You fucking lunatics!"

He thrashed in his chair while he desperately tried to yank at the ropes we had tied him up with. The prick was persistent, I'd give him that, but he was an idiot. He was a mouthy little motherfucker who didn't know how to shut up. He spewed threats again at Liv, right to my face. But I was sure Saint had heard every word, and he was ready to kill him as much as I was.

I snarled at him with my upper lip raised, and I pulled the black wire tight in my grasp with the fishing line digging into my flesh. Ending his life consumed me so much that I didn't even flinch. But first, Mr. Chamberlain's punishment must resume.

"No, please! I didn't mean it! I—" His plea ended after I wrapped the line around his last remaining pinky finger and made a clean, perfect cut.

Our signature move was inflicting pain and getting answers.

The skull necklaces we wore were far more than an accessory. Blood stained them with years of hurt and hours of damage. The same injuries had met the fate of the bastard who had inappropriately laid his fingers on our girl, and we gifted them to her on her birthday.

Never would he touch her again.

Sebastian howled with his body shuddering in a great deal of pain as I pressed on the wound of his missing fingers and blood dripped down. Red spilled onto the severed little limbs, laying in a pile on the ground. I lived for the sight of the carnage we had made and gave myself praise as I jammed into another injury.

The shit bag smelled like fresh flesh, and I couldn't wait for the scent of his rotting corpse to fill the air. I'd lay in the stench of his decaying body all day and not care to move. Because I'd know Sebastian Chamberlain no longer walked the earth to harm our girl. Instead, the demons would punish him and kill him over and over again. They'd deliver a far greater pain and torture his evil soul.

"Fuck! Scratch that. I'll kill the bitch with my own damn hands." Sebastian breathed heavily and his head fell to the side as he glared at me.

The asshole had some nerve. Fucker begged for his life when I inflicted pain, but liked to talk smack when he had the chance. He was a goddamn rollercoaster I didn't want to be on, and I'd soon loosen his restraints. Only to happily watch his body break in half on the way down and his brain splatter all over the concrete.

Sebastian wouldn't stop. I was seething. My pulse throbbed in my neck and was ready to explode. This idiot was giving me a headache. No more waiting. I was fucking done.

I couldn't wait anymore.

Saint would have to watch me slice this fucker's jugular and end him on the spot. He could be pissed at me for the rest of his life, but this nuisance would be over.

I wiped off my necklace and got rid of the crimson color dripping from it. As I hung the fishing wire back around my neck, the scent of his vital fluids teased my nose. I ignored all rational thought because Sebastian didn't deserve any. He needed to die.

"Ha! Now you are going to fucking kill me?" Sebastian talked trash with an inflated ego.

I clenched the handle of a knife. "I should've done it in the alleyway when you cowardly pissed your pants, and we broke your fucking hands."

Realization shone through one eye's slit while the other eye had swelled shut from our punches to his face. Sebastian laughed like he had reached the point of insanity, and I grabbed his hair. My hand yanked back until he winced from the greasy strands leaving his scalp and I held the blade up to his throat.

"Any last words?" I asked through clenched teeth.

"Fuck you, you sorry—" The door to the soundproof room opened and Saint barged in.

"Stop!" my best friend shouted as he held up a hand and pried the knife from me.

I glared with rage down at Sebastian's neck and a slight nick of blood trickled from it. Far from the slice I wanted to inflict straight across his throat and watch life leave the crack of his swollen eye while his body twitched. He'd gargle on his last words and never speak again.

"What the fuck, Saint?" I snarled with anger and roughly released Sebastian's head. "I was about to slit his throat."

"This fucker can't die yet." Saint breathed heavily like he had ran in a marathon, but he ran like a fucking girl.

"What do you mean, he can't die?" I questioned and grabbed for the knife, but Saint was too quick for me.

"Sebastian. Cannot. Die," Saint spat out each syllable like he hated every damn word.

"Look, man... I know you want to be in on this too, but I had to take matters into my own hands. He was talking fucking smack back there and—"

Saint grabbed the collar of my shirt, and I heard the stitching break. I was about to give him shit, but he peered at me dead in the eyes with a look I had never seen from Saint before. *Fear.*

"Listen to me, Sin. We *need* this bastard alive, no matter how much we want him dead."

Somewhere in the pit of my disturbed soul, I knew something was very wrong and breathed, "Tell me everything."

Fifty-Seven

Her Phantom

Saint

I rewatched the horrifying event from my screen over Sin's shoulder and my world collapsed all over again. The fright on Liv's face would haunt me for the rest of my days. Sin's shoulders tensed and he felt the same emotion I had when I watched the incident only moments ago. Painstaking fear. The terror that ripped open an unsuspecting soul.

Liv said, "I believe you have the wrong room."

"No, I don't."

Despite Liv's incredible strength, she succumbed to emotional brokenness after the damage caused by Sebastian. She was physically drained, and all she wanted to do was get everything over with. Our poor Liv was in so much pain.

Uncontrollably, she trembled, but asked, "Did Sebastian send you to kill me?"

"No. But the prick stole money from my boss."

His boss?

Sebastian was into some shady shit from the sound of it. He invested in a large number of companies, not only ours. He had gotten greedy and messed with the wrong people. I always knew the asshole dealt with dirty money, and he corrupted his multiple bank accounts. *But who did he take cold hard cash from?*

"Well, Sebastian is here and—"

"I know," he interrupted, and I wanted to reach through the screen to strangle his sorry ass. "But my boss sent me to collect what is his."

"I don't understand..." Liv stammered in confusion. "This has nothing to do with me."

He pointed his index finger right at her, revealing a gold ring. "Oh, but yes, it does. It starts with you, Liv."

Our girl got her fight back, and she gave him hell. I was fucking proud as she turned on her heels and lunged at him. Liv was dead set on clawing his eyes out, but he overpowered her and grabbed her wrists. There was a struggle, and he had placed her hands behind her back.

"Let me go, asshole! Help—" Her scream for rescue made my heart break, and he must've covered her mouth with his hand.

Bite him, darling! Hurt him!

"Fuck." He winced in pain.

That's our girl.

"No, please, no—" she pleaded, but he placed a cloth over her face.

Chloroform.

"Stupid," he seethed, and the camera shook until her necklace fell to the floor. "You won't bite me again. It's lights out, bitch."

I heard Liv's scream fade, and I knew she'd smell an ether-like scent. The fumes would fill her nostrils and a sweet taste would coat the inside of her mouth. She'd blink once, twice, and then the fight would leave our girl.

Lost in a torture we had never known, we watched this thug lift Liv's limp body into his arms. The necklace's hidden camera angle caught everything from the carpet as he left the way he had come in and carried her out the door.

Deep suffering tore through me when her father ran into the room, and I knew he had heard her cry out for help, but it was too damn late. Within minutes, our world had changed, and we let out angry wails infused with sheer agony.

Fifty-Eight

Her Phantom

Sin

Someone *stole* our obsession.

Our girl was gone.

To be continued...

Join and Follow the Author

Come join Breanne's Blazing Beauties readers group on Facebook! It's a place where you can talk about Breanne Bergie's books, get exclusive book teasers of upcoming releases, and more! Don't miss out and send a request to join today!

Breanne's Blazing Beauties Readers Group

Follow me at:

Facebook:

http://facebook.com/MrsBreWrites

Instagram:

https://www.instagram.com/mrs.bre_writes/

Twitter:

https://twitter.com/MrsBre_Writes

Website:

https://mrsbrewrites.wixsite.com/mysite

More from Breanne Bergie

TRUE SERIES

True Bliss

Truly Undercover

True Devotion

DARING HEARTS SERIES

Love in Quarantine

Love in Tragedy

Love in Flames

MISTER SERIES

Mister Bennett (Stand-alone)

Mister Lawson (Stand-alone)

Mister Dixon (Stand-alone)

Mister Stark (Stand-alone)

Mister Lane (Stand-alone)

Mister Marshal (Stand-alone)

Mister Steel (Stand-alone)

Mister Reed (Stand-alone)

Mister Stitch (Stand-alone)

Mister Lyric (Stand-alone)

Mister Riggs (Stand-alone)

STAND-ALONES

Frostfully Yours

VAMP SOUL ACADEMY SERIES

Wednesday Pierce - Book 1

Wednesday Pierce - Book 2

Printed in Great Britain
by Amazon

48588625R00228